Truffled
Feathers

Also by Nancy Fairbanks
in Large Print:

Chocolate Quake
Death à l'Orange

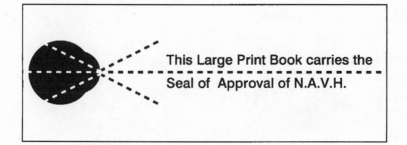

This Large Print Book carries the
Seal of Approval of N.A.V.H.

Truffled Feathers

Nancy Fairbanks

WHEELER
PUBLISHING

Published in 2004 by arrangement with The Berkley Publishing Group, a division of Penguin Group (USA) Inc.

Wheeler Large Print Cozy Mystery.

The text of this Large Print edition is unabridged. Other aspects of the book may vary from the original edition.

Set in 16 pt. Plantin by Minnie B. Raven.

Printed in the United States on permanent paper.

Library of Congress Cataloging-in-Publication Data

Fairbanks, Nancy, 1934–
    Truffled feathers / Nancy Fairbanks.
      p. cm.
    ISBN 1-58724-761-5 (lg. print : sc : alk. paper)
    1. Blue, Carolyn (Fictitious character) — Fiction.
2. College teachers' spouses — Fiction.   3. Pharmaceutical industry — Fiction.   4. Women food writers — Fiction.
5. New York (N.Y.) — Fiction.   6. Large type books.
I. Title.
PS3606.A36T78 2004
   813'.6—dc22   2004043072

For Bill, My Dear Husband and
Fellow Traveler

As the Founder/CEO of NAVH, the only national health agency solely devoted to those who, although not totally blind, have an eye disease which could lead to serious visual impairment, I am pleased to recognize Thorndike Press★ as one of the leading publishers in the large print field.

Founded in 1954 in San Francisco to prepare large print textbooks for partially seeing children, NAVH became the pioneer and standard setting agency in the preparation of large type.

Today, those publishers who meet our standards carry the prestigious "Seal of Approval" indicating high quality large print. We are delighted that Thorndike Press is one of the publishers whose titles meet these standards. We are also pleased to recognize the significant contribution Thorndike Press is making in this important and growing field.

Lorraine H. Marchi, L.H.D.
Founder/CEO
NAVH

★ Thorndike Press encompasses the following imprints: Thorndike, Wheeler, Walker and Large Print Press.

Grateful acknowledgment is made to author Sharon O'Connor for permission to reprint copyrighted recipes from *Dining and the Opera in Manhattan*, Menus and Music Productions, Emeryville, California, 1994.

Prologue
Champagne on the Plane

Champagne, bubbly and delicious in a flute or tempting in a cocktail glass as a Bellini, a Kir Royale, or a Champagne Cocktail, is a favorite both here and abroad. However, this wasn't always so. In New York City in the 1790s, it was very *unpopular,* quite possibly because it was heated before serving. How unpalatable does that sound? Wouldn't the heat have dispersed the very bubbles we are so fond of?

> Carolyn Blue,
> "Have Fork, Will Travel,"
> *Tampa Sun Times*

Carolyn

Forebodings, premonitions: Some people claim to have these before appalling events, but I have never had a premonition in my life, at least not one that bore fruit. I don't even believe in dreams anymore. And my husband, Jason, derides all such things. He is

9

too much a man of science, and I am too much given to the sane and ordinary. Perhaps this is a good thing. Otherwise, the two of us could not have basked so innocently in the pleasures of traveling to New York in first class on American Airlines that Monday. We might not have fully appreciated the comfy blue leather seats, the extra legroom, the early boarding, or the obsequious service of food and alcohol. Needless to say, we are unaccustomed to traveling in such a luxurious and expensive fashion. Few academics are. Not that I am an academic. I am an academic's wife and, having received an advance for a book to be called *Eating Out in the Big Easy*, a "self-employed person."

This is my first venture into the ranks of wage-earning women; for years I stayed home raising my children and giving charming dinner parties for my husband's colleagues, but now my children have gone off to college, and I avoid the kitchen if at all possible. I find it more fun to write about food than to prepare it.

"Champagne?" asked a perky stewardess. "Or orange juice?"

Jason looked up from his copy of the *Journal of Environmental Toxicology*, which, needless to say, was not provided by American Airlines, and smiled at the young lady. "We'll have both." Before I could protest, the smiling stewardess had provided the makings for mimosas, two screw-top bottles of champagne and two glasses of orange juice.

"I wasn't going to have a drink," I said to Jason. No use telling the stewardess; she was already wending her way down the aisle, tempting other passengers into the midday consumption of alcohol.

"I suppose you were hoping for something tastier with your champagne," Jason responded. "Kir? Peach schnapps?"

"It's not that." I could feel the pressure of my waistband. After a recent trip to New Orleans, I had discovered that the pursuit of material for my book had provided not only reams of notes but also an unwelcome inch or so on my waist. I, the lady who prided herself on an active metabolism, had gained weight! I can only explain the dismaying outcome of my new profession by blaming my age. I am over forty, alas. "I've been thinking of going on a diet," I admitted to my husband.

"You can't be serious!" he exclaimed.

"Toasted nuts?" Another American Airlines temptress appeared beside my husband, who had taken the aisle seat so that, without jabbing me in the ribs, he could draw little chemical pictures in a notebook when the impulse overcame him. The stewardess didn't wait for us to accept. She simply deposited small white containers of mixed nuts beside our mimosas.

11

I sighed. Champagne I might have been able to resist, but nuts? Never. I love nuts. "Don't say a word," I murmured sternly to my grinning husband as I selected a cashew and pondered how nice a combination it would make with a mixture of champagne and orange juice. Oh well, it was all grist for the mill of the busy culinary author; I could type up notes on eating toasted nuts, *hot* toasted nuts, at 36,000 feet.

"You are absolutely the last woman in the world who needs to watch her weight," Jason assured me as he reopened his journal, preparatory to reading fascinating things about his favorite subject, toxins.

"You're not wearing my slacks," I replied and bit into a smooth, salty Brazil nut before sipping my orange juice down far enough to add champagne.

"I don't think your slacks would become me," Jason said dryly. Then he was gone, lost in the realms of serious science, leaving me to my interrupted thoughts and my snack. I poured champagne into my depleted juice glass after opening my computer on the tray table. Imagine a computer that fits into one's handbag! Jason had found it on the Internet. I created a file for New York notes and entered my thoughts on champagne and toasty nuts. Then I saved and opened the second chapter of the New Orleans book. Immediately my spirits plummeted.

My visit to New Orleans had been very traumatic, so traumatic that I couldn't think about it without having to repress tears. But I could hardly write chapter 2 without considering its subject, so what was I to do? It had occurred to me that I could use this trip to collect material for a second book, *Eating Ethnic in the Big Apple*. But if I couldn't write the first book, the publisher would hardly want to hear my ideas for a second. And I was to meet my editor for the first time. Would he be sympathetic to my problems with the New Orleans book, for which I'd already accepted an advance? Doubtless he expected something other than weepy excuses in return for the publisher's money.

Then there was my agent. I'd never met her, either, and she already had 15 percent of the advance. Even if I returned my portion, she wouldn't want to give her share back. And by not producing the book, I'd be ruining my budding career as a cuisine writer. Three articles in the local newspaper, some picked up by other papers, do not a career make. What a pickle I was in!

"Something wrong with the computer?" Jason asked.

"No, it's working beautifully." To prove it, I typed in my opinion of the joys of making roux, base of gumbo, and other New Orleans delights. Fledgling food writer or not, I've never made a decent roux in my life. I don't like to make roux. I don't even like to cook.

"I like other people's cooking."

I stared at what I had just typed. Although it was quite factual, it did not belong in chapter 2 of my book. And why did I want a career, anyway? I didn't need the money. Not really. Our children have scholarships. We'd actually made money on the sale of our previous home because real estate in El Paso is so much cheaper than it was in our former location. We have no mortgage! And we were going to New York because a big chemical company was interested in hiring Jason as a consultant.

Although Jason had no intention of giving up his teaching position at the university, he wasn't averse to earning a decadent amount of money by answering questions for Hodge, Brune & Byerson (Cleaning the Environment Through Chemistry). Especially since the consulting involved toxins. Jason loves toxins. I glanced over at him. I'd venture to say that the little drawings he was busily sketching into his notebook would, if in their natural state, kill everyone on the airplane, or at least mutate their DNA or cause their cells to reproduce wildly. Unchecked cell reproduction equals cancer, in case you're not familiar with the concept.

At any rate, we don't need my small advance on royalties or any royalties I might earn in the future. I could have refused. I

14

could still give the money back and be covered by Jason's new source of income, providing he and the company came to terms. But what would my husband think of me throwing up my new career? Jason has never encouraged me to get a job, but on the other hand, he is a thrifty man. And his mother! The eminent professor of women's studies at the University of Chicago! Well, I can just imagine what she'd say. She'd certainly consider me an even bigger source of embarrassment than she had in the past. I can hear her complaining to some fellow feminist, "I thought my daughter-in-law had finally developed enough gumption to join the workforce, but . . ."

I guess I'll have to write the book. But not this very minute. I closed my computer and reached into my carry-on for a wonderful cookbook Jason had given me for my birthday: *Dining and the Opera in Manhattan* by Sharon O'Connor. It has a CD enclosed featuring opera arias, some by singers of bygone days with voices so beautiful they make me wish I had been old enough to hear them in person. And the recipes! They are so tempting that I actually cooked my husband an anniversary dinner from the cookbook. If I do say so myself, the results were superb, and Jason was beside himself with delight. I fear that I gave my husband unrealistic hopes for the future. Ah well!

I opened the book and thumbed through, daydreaming of visiting some of the restaurants from whose chefs the recipes derived. With any luck, our industrial hosts might take us to one or two, providing me with useful culinary notes at no expense to the family budget.

These culinary daydreams cheered me up considerably. Gourmet food, wonderful museums, maybe an opera, certainly a play (we already had theater tickets) — I foresaw an exciting week in the nation's most sophisticated city. What I didn't foresee was the web of conspiracy and violence toward which we were flying. First class.

Carolyn's Anniversary Dinner

Le Cirque's Sea Scallop Fantasy in Black Tie
Fantaisie de St.-Jacques en Habit Noir

- Trim the muscle on the sides of *16 sea scallops (1 oz. ea.)* if necessary; reserve the muscle. Rinse the sea scallops and pat dry with paper towels. Cut each scallop crosswise into four 1/4-in.-thick slices.
- Preheat oven to 300°F. With a truffle slicer or potato peeler, cut *2 or 3 fresh or canned truffles (1 oz. ea.)* into about 50 paper-thin slices no larger in diam-

---

16

eter than the scallops. (If using canned truffles, drain and reserve juice). Place 1 truffle slice between each slice of scallop and reassemble the scallop; for each one there will be 4 slices of scallop and 3 of truffle. Chop scraps of leftover truffles.

- In a small saucepan, cook *¹/₄ cup white vermouth, preferably Noilly-Prat,* and any reserved muscles over medium heat until dry. Reduce heat to low, add any reserved truffle juice and *1 tbs. heavy whipping cream,* and whisk in *8 tbs. butter,* 1 tablespoon at a time; the sauce will thicken and emulsify. Add *salt and freshly ground pepper to taste* and place pan over barely tepid water to keep sauce warm.
- Melt *2 tbs. butter.* Place *1 bunch spinach leaves (8 oz.), stemmed,* in a bowl, and toss with 1 tbs. melted butter. Arrange spinach leaves on serving plate and place in preheated oven for 2 to 3 minutes or until they are slightly wilted; set aside.
- Sprinkle scallops with salt and pepper. In a large, nonstick pan, heat remaining tbs. melted butter over medium heat, and sauté scallops on one side for 3 minutes. Turn over, lower heat, and sauté for another 3 minutes.
- If you like, cut each scallop in half hori-

zontally so you can see the layers of black and white. Arrange scallops on top of spinach leaves. Add minced truffles to butter sauce and coat each scallop with sauce. Sprinkle with *2 tbs. minced fresh chervil* and serve.

SERVES 4

Lutece's Caramelized Rack of Lamb
Carre d'Agneau Caramelise

- Have your butcher prepare *2 racks of lamb (8 chops each)* by removing most of the fat and the chine (backbone). Have the rib bones French cut (so that they extend from the meat by $3/4$ inch). Ask the butcher to give you the chine and rib ends along with the racks.
- Preheat oven to 375°F. In a small bowl, stir together *2 tbs. honey, 2 scant tbs. Dijon mustard, 2 tsp. dried thyme, crumbled,* and *juice of I lemon;* set aside. Brush lamb with *2 tbs. peanut oil* and sprinkle with *salt and freshly ground black pepper to taste.* Place racks in a roasting pan and surround with reserved bones. Roast in preheated oven 4 minutes, then turn and baste the meat. Roast another 4 minutes, then turn, baste the meat, and roast another 4 minutes. Add *2 small onions,*

cut into 1/3-in.-thick wedges, 2 carrots, peeled and cut into 1/3-in. pieces, and 2 unpeeled garlic cloves to roasting pan, and roast for 5 minutes. Turn and baste meat, stir vegetables and bones, and roast another 5 minutes. Place lamb on platter and let sit in warm place for 5 to 6 minutes; leave bones and vegetables in roasting pan.

- Meanwhile, preheat broiler. Pour all fat from roasting pan. Add *1 1/2 cups dry white wine or water* to bones and vegetables. Place pan over high heat and boil liquid for a few minutes, stirring the bones and vegetables with a wooden spoon. When liquid has been reduced by half, strain it through a sieve into a sauceboat. Press the vegetables through the sieve with the back of a spoon, but do not attempt to push all the solids through the sieve.
- With the lamb racks meat side up, brush the top of the racks with the honey mixture. Place the meat under the broiler for about 3 minutes, or until the top of racks are nicely caramelized. Cut each rack into 8 chops and arrange 4 on each of 4 plates. Pour liquid from roasting pan over, garnish with *watercress sprigs,* and serve with *green beans and potatoes.*

SERVES 4

Lutece's Pears with Calvados
Poires au Calvados

- Preheat oven to 350°F. Lightly butter a dish or ovenproof casserole just large enough to hold the pears.
- Peel and core *4 ripe pears.* Halve them lengthwise and cut each half into 4 wedges. In a sauté pan or skillet, melt *2 tbs. unsalted butter* over medium heat and add the pears. Sprinkle them with *$1/4$ cup sugar* and sauté the pears until they are lightly caramelized. Add *2 tbs. Calvados,* let it warm, ignite with a match, and shake pan until flames subside. Place pears and Calvados mixture in the prepared dish.
- In a medium bowl, whisk together *2 eggs* and *$1/4$ cup sugar* until eggs are frothy and pale in color. Add *pinch of ground cinnamon, salt to taste,* and *1 tbs. all-purpose flour.* Slowly stir in *$3/4$ cup heavy whipping cream* and *2 tbs. Calvados.* Pour this mixture over pears. Bake in preheated oven for 35 minutes or until top is lightly golden brown. Serve warm.

SERVES 4

20

1

Low-Fat Canapés
and Bad News in a Limo

Carolyn

Having been helped into our resurrected-for-the-trip wool coats by the stewardess, we left the airplane, computer cases dangling from our shoulders, and hurried down the freezing umbilical cord that connected our plane to the gate. "Looks like Max isn't here to meet us," Jason said after studying the crowd inside.

He sounded disappointed, although I wasn't surprised. After all, Max Heydemann, the man who wanted to recruit Jason, was the director of research and development. He and my husband had evidently taken an instant liking to one another. Even so, a man with Dr. Heydemann's responsibilities was unlikely to drive out to a distant airport in the middle of the business day.

"So. Cab or bus?" Jason asked.

I knew Jason was hoping that I'd choose the bus, which was much less expensive and possibly much safer than a cab. I'd heard

21

frightening tales about New York taxi drivers. On the other hand, if we had to drag our bags aboard a bus, Jason would realize how much I had crammed into my suitcase.

Fortunately, I spotted rescue from marital discord in the person of a very slender man in a long, black overcoat. He wore a snappy chauffeur's cap and had dark skin with a narrow mustache that looked as if it had been drawn on his upper lip with an eyebrow pencil. While beaming at the disembarking passengers, he held against his chest a sign that was neatly lettered with the words "Welcome, Dr. and Mrs. Jason Blue."

"I believe they've sent someone," I said, nodding toward the driver.

We introduced ourselves, and he folded his sign carefully, as if he might have use for it at some future time. "I am being Radovan Ramakrishna," he said.

Radovan? Wasn't that the given name of a Serb general? Now, Ramakrishna sounded right. With his thin features and dark skin —

". . . driving you to New York City in the limousine of the company which you are visiting, please. Are you having valises to retain from the baggage-go-rounds?"

We agreed that a visit to the "baggage-go-rounds" would be necessary and followed our chauffeur, now festooned with our computer bags, through the corridors of the bustling airport. I personally kept a very close eye on him in case he proved to be a computer thief rather than a limo driver. A professor of urban minority poetry had had her computer stolen in the Newark Airport, and I did not plan to follow in her footsteps. However, my paranoia almost caused me serious injury. I was so fixated on my own computer, hanging from the driver's shoulder, that when he stopped abruptly, I walked right into Jason's computer case (which Mr. Ramakrishna held in one hand), thereby sustaining a painful rap on my knee.

"A thousand pardons, madam," cried Mr. Ramakrishna, looking stricken as I rubbed my knee and blinked back tears. "Are you injured? Do you require a practitioner of medicine — traditional, holistic, alternative, herbal — I know an excellent doctor of herbal —"

"She's fine," said my husband, patting me on the shoulder. "Aren't you, Carolyn?"

"I am begging to differ, sir, for one can see that your good lady has suffered —"

"— the consequences of pedestrian tailgating," Jason finished for him. My husband took my arm and assured me that my knee would feel better once I started using it, which was true. I was hardly limping at all when we got to the baggage claim area. Once there, Mr. Ramakrishna not only refused to give up our computer cases but also insisted on taking our baggage claim checks and dragging luggage off the moving belt at our direction. In his zeal, he also dragged three other bags off by mistake. In one such case, a woman in a purple fur and mauve faille shoes with chic, clunky heels snatched her bag away from Mr. Ramakrishna, threatening to call a police officer and demand a luggage-theft arrest. Our driver took this altercation with equanimity, although he murmured to us, once she had stalked away, that she was obviously suffering from the excess aggressiveness engendered by eating meat. Then he maneuvered our wheeled suitcases outside and left to retrieve his limousine while we thin-blooded desert dwellers shivered in a cold wind.

Once Mr. Ramakrishna returned and tried to heave my huge suitcase into the limousine trunk, I was again attacked by guilt. Jason had to assist in the transfer from sidewalk to vehicle, and our poor driver was panting when the feat was finally accomplished. However, this did not prevent him from ushering us into the plush interior of the passenger compartment and pointing out the refreshment bar. It was stocked, as he proudly informed us, with "a most refreshing and healthful Indian tea," a "delicious" mango and yogurt drink, and a tempting array of vegetarian canapés, all of which had been provided by his cousin's restaurant and catering service in the East Village. Then he handed us a business card for the restaurant, admonishing us to tell his cousin that Punji had sent us and we were to have the honored-client, 15 percent discount.

Was Mr. Ramakrishna Punji? I wondered, feeling a bit dazed by the time he had climbed into the driver's seat and sped abruptly into traffic.

Jason poured himself a cup of tea and sampled a tidbit that looked like a fragment of nan smeared with an unidentifiable orange-red paste. When Jason nodded approvingly and tried another of the offerings, I reached out for one myself. Mr. Ramakrishna, head poked through his open window, which was turning the limousine exceedingly chilly, screamed "Bloody eater of sacred cows!" and swerved wildly to avoid a hotel van that had cut him off. Jason's tea slopped onto the canapé tray and scalded my hand, which I withdrew hastily. The only topical ointment available was the cold mango-yogurt drink, which I applied.

Having glanced into his rearview mirror, Mr. Ramakrishna nodded approvingly. "Very good for the skin," he enthused. "Not only most delicious on the tongue, but used by temple dancers to achieve skin of satin."

"Peachy," I mumbled. My hand was still stinging.

"Mango," he corrected. "Please be noting the aggressive nature of non-Hindu drivers and be assured that I, Punji, am at your service to protect you from all manner of bloody accidents. Also to recommend fine places for vegetarian consumption so that you, too, can become calm and healthy without blood-carrying vessels compacted with death-dealing and disgusting meat products."

Jason leaned into the corner, out of rearview mirror range, and rolled his eyes. I clapped my hand over my mouth to keep from giggling. "Vegetarianism has a long history in the United States," I said conversationally. "For instance, a vegetarian society met in New York City in the 1890s." I had been reading food history in preparation for our trip.

"Hindus are being vegetarians for many thousands of years," Punji replied, unimpressed by vegetarianism in our country.

"I believe the banquet included, among other things, bread with curry sauce."

"Curry sauce is being very tasty if properly concocted," said Mr. Ramakrishna, "but Western bread has texture to be avoided."

"Ah." Chastened, I munched on a healthful canapé, as Mr. Ramakrishna tore onto a busy highway, causing a wave of outraged honking, to which he responded by sticking his head out the window and shouting, "May the curse of vipers fall on your pig-breath heads!"

I sighed and wished that we had taken a

cab. Or a bus. Or any vehicle not driven by this produce lover, who thought his diet precluded aggressive behavior.

Jason leaned forward and said, "When we get into the city, I'd like to be taken straight to Hodge, Brune & Byerson."

"You're going to leave me alone with him?" I whispered anxiously.

To my dismay, Mr. Ramakrishna proved to have very acute hearing. "Do not fear, Mrs. Jason Blue. I am not a danger to American ladies. I am a most respectable man of good but poor family in my native country. Most certainly no harm shall come to you in my vehicle." Then he cut across two lanes and scooted in between a large truck and a small Volkswagen painted Easter-egg lavender with white daisies on the door panel. The driver of the eighteen-wheeler blew his air horn while the driver of the daisymobile brandished his middle finger at Mr. Ramakrishna, who leaned out his open window and shook his fist, shouting, "Lizard-eyed eaters of smelly sheep!"

I wrapped my cashmere neck scarf over my ears, which were freezing in the rush of frigid, automotive-scented air. My husband calmly requested that the window be closed. I myself was not at all calm; in fact, I was considering a leap from the limousine. Had it not been exceeding the speed limit and surrounded by other vehicles, I might have tried.

However, I imagined landing on the hood of a speeding car, in which case I would suffer a death of a thousand cuts as I was hurled through the front window into the lap of the driver. *Death of a thousand cuts?* I was beginning to sound like Mr. Ramakrishna.

Once the window was closed, Jason continued, "Before you take me to Hodge, Brune & Byerson, you can drop my wife off at the Park Central Hotel."

"My instructions, sir, are to deliver you both to your hotel, from which you will be picked up by Dr. and Mrs. Sean Xavier Ryan at 6:30 P.M. for a festive evening of dinner and opera, a noisy, Western performance with many loud singers."

"How lovely!" I exclaimed. "*Mefistofele* is playing tonight. We've never seen it, Jason."

Jason completely ignored the desirability of our proposed entertainment and frowned. "I promised the director of research and development that I would come straight to his office to confer on an urgent matter."

I hadn't heard anything about an urgent matter and turned to look inquiringly at Jason, who shrugged and said, rather evasively I thought, "It's about chemistry."

"There's a surprise," I murmured, wondering what was going on beyond the consultancy interview that was Jason's reason for this trip.

"Would the gentleman who is to meet you

be Dr. Maximillian Frederick Heydemann?" asked our driver.

"Yes, and he's expecting —"

"I am most sorry to inform you, Dr. Jason Blue, that the unfortunate Dr. Maximillian Frederick Heydemann is no longer among the living."

Jason looked stunned. "You must be mistaken. I talked to him yesterday."

I hadn't known that.

"Yes, he met his tragic end over a large sandwich piled high with a very fatty and odoriferous meat called pastrami. No doubt, the meat killed your friend Dr. Heydemann, as meat is being most frequently guilty of doing. You would be wise to insist that your hosts take you to a safe and healthy vegetarian restaurant this evening. By doing so, you will avoid early and calamitous death, both you, Dr. Jason Blue, and your good lady, Mrs. Jason Blue. My cousin's restaurant serves not only a healthy and delicious vegetarian menu, but also the vegetables are organically grown. No pesticides or unhealthy chemical fertilizers are used in the production of my cousin's vegetables."

"I've read some very interesting research," said my husband, "showing that a person eating vegetables and fruits ingests many more natural pesticides produced as a defense mechanism by the plant itself than any pesticides sprayed on by man. In the mean-

29

time, because effective pesticides are out-lawed, malaria is flourishing and killing millions of people."

"Jason," I whispered, "I don't think Mr. Ramakrishna is interested in —"

"Malaria?" sharp-eared Mr. Ramakrishna interjected. "Many people in my native land are dying from malaria. Nonetheless, Mrs. Jason Blue, they have otherwise healthy bodies and nonaggressive characters because of their vegetarian diets."

"When did Dr. Heydemann's death occur?" asked Jason.

"Over his meal of pastrami," replied the driver. "This very day, I am hearing, he went, as was his custom, to a meat-eating es-tablishment and ordered an inordinately large sandwich. Then, while consuming this un-healthy meal, Dr. Maximillian Frederick Heydemann fell over into the plate of the person beside him. It is a most horrifying tale, is it not? The person whose meal was contaminated by his meat-eating neighbor embraced the unfortunate Dr. Heydemann from the rear and punched him in the stomach. Then, it is said, he attempted to kiss Dr. Heydemann, perhaps to atone for having attacked him, but it was too late. Your friend was dead, as was soon discovered by men in a siren-bearing vehicle with stretchers and electric shockers. A most sad and bizarre tale, which I am sorry to tell you."

Jason was silent for the rest of the wild ride into the city. Mr. Ramakrishna, perhaps as a mark of respect for the dead, perhaps because his window was closed, no longer belabored other drivers for getting in his way. However, when provoked, he did murmur things like "Pig-breath worshipper of Allah" and "Devourer of rancid intestines."

I was left to consider his bizarre story. Did it represent a misinterpretation of events? Or were the strange happenings described to us symptomatic of widespread psychoses induced by the stress of life in large, overpopulated urban areas? I remember, as an undergraduate, reading an article about the deteriorating behavior of rats when too many are confined in too small a space. Whatever had happened, my husband's friend and mentor at Hodge, Brune & Byerson was dead.

Not an auspicious beginning to our visit. Nor did the situation improve.

2

All-You-Can-Eat Sushi and Shocking News

In case you haven't run into it, sushi is a sticky rice ball spiced with a line of wasabi (red-hot green paste) and wrapped with thinly sliced raw fish and sometimes seaweed. For the uninitiated, that sounds disgusting, but it isn't; it's delicious, and often quite expensive. Therefore, an all-you-can-eat sushi bar is a source of wonder and delight to those of us who live in the country's interior, away from sources of fresh fish.

With sushi, fresh is very important. After all, old fish smells bad, and the idea of eating old, raw fish is insupportable, which makes New York City a good place for sushi, because there's no dearth of supply; the Fulton Fish Market sells 90 million pounds of fish a year. The all-you-can-eat sushi chef can rush down to the market early in the morning and order, on a handshake, whatever he needs for the day.

But what if the fish doesn't show up? A chef at Versailles named Vatel is said to

32

have thrown himself on his sword over an order of fish that failed to arrive for a banquet. Having lost face because he had no fish for his sushi customers, one might anticipate that a Japanese chef would commit ritual suicide with the family samurai sword. Right there in the restaurant. So steel yourself for possible violence, but don't miss the all-you-can-eat sushi in New York.

Carolyn Blue,
"Have Fork, Will Travel,"
Butte Miner's News

Carolyn

"Who is Dr. Sean Xavier Ryan?" I asked as I put the finishing touches on my coiffure. Since we would be going to the opera, I had created a French roll instead of staying with my customary, tied-back-with-a-scarf hairstyle. And I was wearing an evening dress, something I rarely get to do at home. Straight-line black silk with an embroidered jacket. Black is always a safe choice in New York and for two months a year in El Paso. The other ten run from pretty summery to hellishly hot, and only the young care to wear black when it's hot, so I have a full-length green silk for the other ten months. El

33

Paso has only two opera performances a year.

I turned to inspect my husband, who looked very distinguished in his dark wool suit with his dark, silver-touched hair and close-clipped beard. Jason had been ready for ten minutes and was reading a journal article, from which he looked up when I inquired about our hosts for the evening.

"Ryan's an inorganicker. Particularly interested in heavy metals. Good chemist." He sighed, gathering from my overly patient expression that I expected something more personal. "Well, young. Actually, the fact that we're being entertained tonight by one of the junior researchers may be telling. If they were serious about making me an offer, they'd send along someone higher on the food chain."

Jason didn't seem particularly concerned, which was surprising, since he found this company so interesting. Hodge, Brune is less than twenty years old but very successful with its emphasis on environmental chemistry. They were looking at lots of intriguing toxins, according to Jason. On the other hand, my husband is, after all, an academic. He likes to do his own thing without being pushed to consider the potential for profit in his research.

"Well, whatever happens, we're being provided with first-class airline tickets and a hotel room, although it is rather small and plain." I looked around me and compared the room to the limousine. "Not to mention dinner and a night at the opera. Maybe they'll take us to one of these famous restaurants." I pointed to *Dining and the Opera in Manhattan*, which rested on the nightstand.

"I don't see Ryan as the fancy-restaurant-grand-opera type. I imagine Max got the opera tickets. He and his wife went regularly. Now, suddenly, he's dead." Jason shook his head, obviously baffled. "I'd put him in his early fifties, and he seemed to be in excellent health."

I stuck a few jet beads into my hair and studied the effect of black against blonde hair. Hair ornaments are such fun. "What do you think of this?" I inserted a fan of black and gray pearls attached at the ends of almost invisible wires. They projected several inches above the back of my head.

"You look like a flamenco dancer but without the ruffles," Jason replied.

Needless to say, I removed the pearl fan. However, I did leave the beads in. "You're feeling bad about Max Heydemann, aren't you?" I asked sympathetically.

"I liked and admired him," Jason replied. "And I'm not sure that I'm interested in Hodge, Brune now that he's gone, even if they do make an offer."

"Whatever you decide." I smiled and

35

dropped a kiss on the top of Jason's head. He has such thick, springy hair.

When the telephone rang, Jason answered, then rose and collected our coats. "Don't you find the lobby here peculiar?" he asked as we headed for the elevators. I myself rather liked the lobby: very Art Nouveau with purple or green swoopy-backed velvet sofas and armless chairs with fringe, black and white diamond-tiled floors, and a lushly flowered beige and purple area rug.

Once there, we came upon a lively family argument. "Look, Patsy," Dr. Ryan said belligerently, "if I have to spend the evening at the fucking opera, I'm God damn well going to eat someplace I like." He was a short, wiry young man with a long Irish face and muted carrot hair.

I remember an excellent carrot mousse of that color at a French restaurant in Chicago. The occasion was the celebration of our tenth anniversary, which occurred during a visit to Jason's mother. I chose the restaurant; my mother-in-law complained about the new fetish for gourmet food among yuppies, which saddled working women with extra time in the kitchen. That was in the days before gen-Xers came along expecting to pick up their gourmet food at the local supermarket on the way home from the office.

Mrs. Ryan retorted, "The company's paying, Sean, so could we, for once, go someplace to eat that prides itself on quality rather than quantity?" She was a petite brunette, unfashionably curved, rosy-cheeked, and irritated. "And stop complaining about the opera. If you had a smidgen of sensitivity in your mean Irish soul, you'd be glad for me. I may never get to see another opera unless I divorce you. Maybe I *will* divorce you."

"Nonsense. What would you do with the kids?"

"Give you custody, move to New York, make a fortune at an ad agency —"

"— and languish all your days missing your sexy husband."

I could see that Jason was trying to think of a tactful way to break into this scene of marital discord, which was being played out between a man with feet planted pugnaciously on a flowery carpet and his wife, who had plopped herself down on a purple chair that towered about three feet over her head. To rescue Jason, I approached the wife. "It's so wonderful to meet a fellow opera lover," I said and extended my hand. "I'm Carolyn Blue. You must be Mrs. Ryan."

She bounced off the chair as if she were a cheerleader being tossed to the top of a pyramid. "Now see what you've done," she hissed at her husband, then smiling hospitably at me, "I'm Patsy Ryan. Welcome to New York. We're so pleased to be chosen to entertain you tonight."

37

Ryan shook hands with Jason, not a whit embarrassed to be caught complaining about opera within earshot of two opera lovers. "Don't pay any attention to my wife. She knows damn well we'd never have been here if it weren't that Max died this afternoon."

"We heard," said Jason grimly.

"Yeah. Well, can you believe that? Fucking New York! It's worse than Philly."

"Oh, surely not," said his wife sarcastically. "But it *is* awful about Max."

"Good a scientist as they come," said Ryan. "Better."

"I was certainly impressed," said Jason.

"Well, he was with you, too. Said you'd be invaluable if you'd come aboard. Some of the assholes in the group feel threatened by academics. Think professors read too many journals. So how do you feel about sushi?" He was hustling us toward the entrance and a cold, driving rain. We had seen snow over the Middle West. In fact, we made it out of O'Hare just before flights began to be canceled. Once in the New York area, there were patches of snow in New Jersey, but New York seemed to be clear. I hoped that it would continue that way.

"Sean!" wailed his wife at the mention of sushi. He ignored her.

"Love it," said Jason. "So does Carolyn." He introduced me to the irrepressible and foul-mouthed Dr. Ryan. Had I been his mother, I'd have washed his mouth out with soap years ago. But of course, he probably doesn't talk that way in front of his mother. My children don't.

"Great!" said Ryan and hailed a cab, ignoring the doorman and ushering Jason, Patsy, and me into the backseat so quickly that we didn't have time to put up umbrellas. Ryan took the seat beside the driver. Since Patsy looked mutinous, I suppose I could have intervened, but fair is fair. She was getting the opera. He was getting the sushi. Maybe they'd take that into consideration and stop squabbling. Not that they didn't seem to relish it.

"We're going to this great all-you-can-eat sushi place up near the Met," Ryan announced.

"I've never heard of all-you-can-eat sushi," said Jason. "It's a novel idea."

"Damn right. Everywhere else you pay through the nose for each piece or order some plate, the Hirohito Special or whatever, and half the stuff on it you don't like anyway. At this place only the *uni* costs extra, but hell, Hodge, Brune is paying, so we can eat all the *uni* we want. You like *uni?*"

Jason loves *uni,* which I call, to myself, swamp paste. We were going to reek of fish by the time we got to the opera, and there was always the danger of green wasabi splotches on clothing. On the other hand, I

39

do love sushi, and an all-you-can-eat sushi restaurant should make an excellent subject in my embryonic second book. If I got to write it. Well, I wouldn't think about that. "Have you ever seen *Mefistofele*, Mrs. Ryan?" I asked.

"Oh please, call me Patsy. No, I haven't, but the cast is supposed to be wonderful. I used to work at an ad agency on Park Avenue, and we'd walk up to the Met and buy standing-room tickets after work."

"You're a writer?" I asked, assuming she'd been a copywriter at the agency.

"Artist. Freelance now. Imagine trying to keep up a home-studio career with little kids underfoot. Not that they're not adorable."

"How many children do you have, Patsy?" Jason and Sean Ryan were talking chemistry, of course.

She didn't get to answer because we arrived and had to dash through the rain into a long, narrow establishment with rosy lavender tables and black leather booths on two sides of the long sushi bar. Behind the bar, six sushi chefs, some of whom looked like Japanese bandits, patted, molded, and wrapped their lovely delicacies with deft grace and arranged them artistically on plates and wooden boards with piles of crispy, pink, pickled ginger. My mouth watered at the sights and smells as my eyes took in the clientele.

The place was mobbed with a crowd notable for its cultural diversity. Next to us a gray-haired, middle-aged Hispanic man with the expansive gestures and voice projection of an actor talked to a beautiful young woman. In the back was a table of broad-faced, brown-skinned natives of some Pacific island. A Caucasian couple in front of us at the sushi bar kissed and exchanged soulful glances while popping sushi into each other's mouths. Had you told me when I was a girl that I'd be eating raw fish, much less enjoying it, I would have gagged. Now I ordered enthusiastically: *ebi* (shrimp), *hamachi* (yellowtail), *sake* (salmon), *maguro* (tuna), and *unagi* (eel), not to mention an avocado-eel roll and a California roll, a bowl of miso soup, and a pitcher of hot sake. Jason and Sean Ryan were even more adventurous in their choices. They ordered things that I knew to taste fishy, plus *uni,* which tastes swampy. Patsy, looking pained and admitting that she could never remember what was what, said she'd have the same thing I was having.

"Why don't you have the same thing *I'm* having?" her husband asked combatively.

"Because you'll eat *anything,*" she replied.

Our miso was served, rich and hot, perfect on a nasty winter night during what should have been spring. In El Paso, summer was blowing hot breath down the backs of our necks, and air conditioners were being turned on.

"It's cloudy," said Patsy, staring down at her soup. "It looks positively toxic, and the spoon is unusable. What kind of spoon shape is that?"

Before Jason could launch into discussion on possible toxins in miso soup (I'm sure he could find some; he says anything can kill you if you eat enough of it), I said, "It's perfectly acceptable to drink it from the bowl," and I demonstrated by doing so. The soup was followed by wooden boards with the sushi pieces, the wasabi, and the ginger, plus shallow porcelain dishes on which to rest the chopsticks and in which to mix the soy sauce with dabs of wasabi for dipping — very carefully. Too much wasabi will send an electric shock right up one's sinus passages.

"For heaven's sake," exclaimed Patsy. "How am I supposed to eat those?"

"Like this, babe." Sean, wielding his chopsticks with dexterity, dipped a rice ball with a pile of pasty orange *uni* on top into his soy sauce and popped it into his mouth. Jason did the same.

"If I try to eat with chopsticks, I'll end up with rice and fishy bits in my lap," Patsy wailed.

"I can't believe I married a woman who can't use chopsticks. Everyone knows how to —"

"Just pick it up with your fingers," I murmured and demonstrated with a piece of eel sushi, held daintily between thumb and forefinger. I dipped it in the soy sauce with just a brush past the wasabi, and ate it, as if I ate messy things with my fingers every day. I do love eel. It has the most wonderful rich, sweet sauce on it and crunchy little seeds. Patsy followed my example, even to the choice of eel. Then we both tried, inconspicuously, to get the sticky rice off our skin. I was regretting my own magnanimity in suggesting fingers to save her from chopstick humiliation.

"It is tasty," she admitted.

"You just ate eel," said her husband, looking smug. I suppose he didn't dare make fun of the finger wielding, since I had suggested it.

"I did not," his wife protested.

"Try the tuna next," I suggested, pointing to it. "You'll wonder why you ever liked your tuna canned."

"When is Max's funeral to be?" Jason asked. "I'd like to attend."

"Beats me." Sean was devouring *hamachi*, piece after piece, and answered with his mouth full. "I don't suppose Charlotte can make any plans until the police release his body."

"The police?" Jason and I spoke in shocked chorus.

"Sure. Since he was murdered, there has to be an autopsy."

My husband and I exchanged stunned glances. "Our driver didn't say Max was murdered," said Jason. "He seemed to think Max had died over a plate of pastrami."

"He did, but the pastrami didn't kill him. He was stabbed. They don't know what with, last I heard."

"It was probably some crazy street person," said Patsy. "I've seen very disreputable men hanging around the front of that deli."

"They're delivery boys," said Sean.

"No matter what the mayor says," she continued, "this is a dangerous city. Crazy people talking to themselves on the subway, the homeless attacking innocent pedestrians with bricks. Thank God we've moved to Connecticut where the children can grow up in a safe, sane environment."

"Oh, right!" said Sean. "Now they're out in the backyard eating dirt and getting lead poisoning."

"They're not eating dirt," his wife protested.

"There's a parkway two lots over, been there forever," Sean said to Jason. "Hundreds of thousands of cars speeding by every day for God knows how many years."

"It's walled off," snapped Patsy.

Jason was nodding over a bite of raw shrimp. "Unleaded gasoline."

"Bet your ass," said Sean. "More green space you got in an urban area, the more lead settled into the ground before lead-free gasoline. That's why New York has less lead poisoning than Philly. Philly has more green space."

"Well, I'm not paving over the backyard." Patsy had poked her unused chopstick into the wasabi. Before I could stop her, she raised the chopstick to her mouth and sampled the hot mustard paste, then emitted an agonized shriek. The roar of conversation stilled, and the rail-thin, black-garbed manager with his shaved head came rushing over.

Sean grinned at him. "White ghost female eat wasabi."

The manager glared at both of them and bustled away. He handled everything from greeting guests to reprimanding waiters, waitresses, and sushi chefs and running the cash register.

Jason ignored them all. "Max was murdered?"

"Looks like it. Fucking New York." Sean waved the waitress over to order more sushi.

Murdered? How terrible! And frightening! I hardly noticed the rest of the meal, or the hullabaloo when Sean, paying the bill in the crowded aisle by the cash register, turned and swept an order of sushi, board and all, onto the floor with his briefcase. After that we ran — not my favorite activity — in

45

pouring rain to Lincoln Center, where the fountains were shrouded by tents, but the huge arched windows fronting the Matisse lobby paintings beckoned to us. At the sight of those sparkling lights, the excitement of opera at the greatest house in the world overcame my gloom.

3

Mefistofele at the Met

Jason

I could see that my wife was appalled. How ironic that the company should send, as a substitute host, Sean Ryan, whose speech is, admittedly, somewhat "contemporary," although he is as promising a young scientist as I've met in recent years.

So there we sat, through an excellent sushi dinner and an opera performance that Ryan hated, while my wife winced every time he opened his mouth. Caro takes special offense at the use of the word *fuck*. It's fortunate that she doesn't have to spend much time among today's college students. I remember with amusement the occasion when our son Chris complained to me that his mother had reprimanded him for his language, which he, as a college student, felt was no longer a matter under her control.

Happily, my son is a logical person with a sense of humor. I responded, "Then you won't object if your mother, having come under your linguistic influence, says to you at Christmas break, 'Chris, get in there and clean up your fucking room.' " My son looked shocked, then laughed, and has never since offended his mother with unacceptable language. I doubt that strategy would influence Sean Ryan.

At any rate, in the Ryans' company Boito's *Mefistofele* is not a performance that I am likely to forget. Caro was enraptured with the Chilean soprano, whom neither of us had ever heard, and the bass and tenor were equally good. However, it was the staging and the audience, at least our small portion of the audience, which were so memorable.

Patsy Ryan, a woman who makes me appreciate my own wife even more than usual, took it upon herself to arrange our seat placement, ladies in the middle, Caro beside Ryan, me beside Patsy. Obviously, Ryan's wife did not want to sit next to him while he made audible comments such as: "Look at this sucker" (in reference to the back-of-seat subtitle screen, with which he experimented during the first ten minutes of the performance before he fell asleep) and "Why do they think heaven looks like a God damned opera house?"

Leaning forward to glare at him, his wife hissed back, "What do *you* think it looks like, Sean? A chemistry lab?"

Then in a peculiar scene onstage, during which Faust was seducing Margarhita in a pseudo–apple orchard on a tilted grass platform, which was turned by an old woman with a hand crank, Ryan said to Carolyn, "I'll be damned. They're playing boccie." Carolyn replied, "Those are apples, not boccie balls. The apples are probably another facet of a symbolic Adam and Eve theme. Now please do hush up, Dr. Ryan."

An ancient gentleman behind her became quite animated during intermission in response to her remark on Adam and Eve and offered a long dissertation on the influence of various Christian sects on the Faust story. His companion, a handsome woman of middle age, who never took off her fur coat during the performance, interrupted him to say that it was just the same old story: libidinous men blaming illicit sex on women and making them pay the price. "Look at poor Margarhita!" she exclaimed. "She refused to run off with Faust and was hung."

"Her soul was saved," snapped the old gentleman.

"So was Faust's," said Carolyn acerbically, "and all he had to do was think up some pie-in-the-sky, benevolent monarchy scheme, to be presided over by himself."

"Exactly," agreed the lady in mink.

"I read the other day," Carolyn added, "that Jenny Lind refused to sing in operas because the heroines were so often impure."

"Lind would never amass a following today with that attitude," sniffed the befurred lady.

"Unless it was with the Christian right."

"Maybe not, but around 1850, she was so popular in New York that people of all persuasions fell off the pier in their eagerness to greet her ship."

My dear wife, always the purveyor of some curious historical tidbit.

"I need to go to the ladies'," complained Patsy.

"Tough, babe," said Ryan, who had just returned from fortifying himself with a stiff drink. "They're hauling up the chandeliers."

One of the interesting innovations of the new Met at Lincoln Center is the elaborate and retractable chandeliers. I wonder how many people still think of it as the "new Met." My mother took me to what she calls "the real Met" when I was a boy, an unimpressive, yellow brick hulk close to a gaggle of pornography shops, from whose fascinating windows I was dragged away. That particular building replaced the Academy of Music, which did not have enough boxes to satisfy the demand in 1883 from new millionaires like the Rockefellers and Vanderbilts. Carolyn had apprised me of this information before the performance began; it was evidently part of her New York research. To Ryan this most recent seat of New York opera would undoubtedly be remembered as the "damn Met" after the night's experience.

At the next intermission, Carolyn allowed

herself to be talked into accompanying Patsy Ryan to the ladies', and both returned incensed, partly because Ryan greeted them by saying, "That must have been the world's longest piss," but mostly because, in the face of formidable lines of women waiting for the facilities, there were evidently only four stalls available. I offered my sympathy, knowing from recent experience that "potty parity" is a sore topic with women.

Ryan's final and most amusing faux pas occurred during the Helen of Troy sequence when Faust offers Helen one red rose, they pledge their love, and then plan a bucolic future together. One has to wonder about Faust. Why would a scholar want to spend his life lounging in a meadow among sheep and agricultural types — even in the company of Helen of Troy? During the scene, Ryan, having been awakened by the snores of the elderly gentleman behind us, turned to Carolyn, and said, "That's not me doing the fucking snoring."

"Not this time," murmured Carolyn through gritted teeth.

I might have been more amused by the interplay had I not been so uneasy. Among her many conversational gambits, Patsy Ryan bemoaned Max Heydemann's "pastrami habit." "If he hadn't insisted on going off once a week to eat pastrami in that deli, he'd never have been murdered. Max was a creature of habit," Patsy assured me. "Every Monday at twelve-thirty he went out for pastrami. You couldn't get a meeting with him around lunchtime on pastrami day, isn't that right, Sean?"

Ryan shrugged. "He went there to think."

"How could anyone think in a place that crowded and noisy?" she demanded.

"He claimed he had his best scientific ideas with his mouth full of pastrami."

I hadn't known that about Max.

"He wouldn't even schedule a trip if it interfered with pastrami day," said Patsy. "He never took a vacation longer than six days. Charlotte told me so." Patsy sounded indignant on Charlotte's behalf. "I don't know how she stood it."

I could see my wife digesting this information. Perhaps she was wondering how angry a wife might be (angry enough to commit murder?) if all her vacations were limited to six days by her husband's love of pastrami and science. I could understand Max's devotion. Even we scientists are given to superstitions in the matter of idea generation. I know a photochemist who does his deep thinking in a particular pair of socks, which he does not allow his wife to launder. I myself find pistachio nuts conducive to scientific inspiration, although I've always meant to investigate the compounds in them for psychoactivity. Perhaps Max knew something about pastrami ingredients the rest of us don't. He was fond of saying, "It's all chemistry," as an explanation for just about anything that happened. As for his wife Charlotte, I've met her several times, and she never expressed any irritation with her husband about pastrami or anything else. They seemed quite devoted. I would need to mention that to Carolyn before her curiosity led her to investigate Charlotte Heydemann.

Whatever had happened to Max, I was sure that it was not a random street or, in this case, deli killing, and the news that Max's Monday visits to the deli of his choice were predictable did not change my mind. Of course, I hadn't mentioned my last conversation with Max to Carolyn. My poor wife was still recovering from traumatic events in New Orleans, about which she had spared me the details, although a policeman there did tell me about her many close calls. But Max had telephoned before we left El Paso. He said that a serious problem had developed at Hodge, Brune & Byerson about which he hoped to use my contacts and expertise, a problem that he did not want to discuss on the telephone. Now Max was dead, and I was left wondering what this problem had been and what relation it had to his murder.

No, this was not something I would mention to Carolyn. I had no wish to place my wife in danger, and I fear if she knew there was a mystery afoot, she might naively put herself in harm's way out of curiosity or indignation. Carolyn likes to think of herself as a sedate, retiring faculty wife, but in truth, time is bringing out a forceful side to her personality. Still, I did not want my wife mixed up in whatever was going on at Hodge, Brune. She has her own problems, namely the meetings with her editor and agent. That should keep her busy this week, that and culinary research and cultural activities. Carolyn loves museums almost as much as she does classical music and interesting historical data. How many women can name all the medieval kings and queens of England? In order?

4

Breakfast at a Crime Scene

Although smoked salmon is appreciated all over the country, more is consumed in New York City than anywhere in the world — possibly ten thousand tons. If piled up, how many stories of salmon would that be? New Yorkers eat lox, the salty, brine-cured and smoked variety of Eastern European ancestry, with their bagels and cream cheese or, on a canapé, the more expensive, lightly cured Nova caught in Canada and processed in Brooklyn. The rest of us are probably buying our smoked salmon frozen.

A delicious and easy-to-make canapé for a cocktail party or predinner nibble requires only a loaf of dark Russian rye, smoked salmon, a half and half mixture of mayonnaise and Dijon or horseradish mustard, chopped red onion, and capers. Cut the bread into finger-food sized pieces, top with salmon, dab with mayonnaise/mustard, sprinkle with capers and onion, and serve on trays with wine or cocktails.

Carolyn Blue,
"Have Fork, Will Travel,"
Macon Dixie Messenger

Carolyn

Imagine liking to run so much that you'd do it in a strange city when the temperature is below freezing. Yet that's just what my husband must have done. With any luck, the exercise lifted his spirits, which had seemed low last night when we returned to the hotel. Runners do something called "hitting the wall." I take that to mean they eventually get so tired that they become giddy. The giddiness is called "runner's high." I've experienced giddiness from flights of fancy, but I can't imagine any outcome from running other than exhaustion and injury and any reason to run other than flight.

I glanced at my watch as I combed my hair back and tied it with a scarf. Jason was breakfasting with people from Hodge, Brune, and I had been warned last night to expect lunch and a museum visit with someone named Sophia Vasandrovich, the wife of a senior scientist. In the meantime, I could consider my waistline and skip breakfast or . . . really, I shouldn't . . . give in to curiosity and trot down the street to the deli where Max Heydemann died. Patsy had mentioned that it was close to our hotel.

Hunger and curiosity won. I called my agent, whose name is Loretta Blum, confirmed our ten-thirty appointment at her office, declined with regret her invitation to lunch, bundled up, and set off with Loretta's New York accent echoing in my ears. "Just be sure you're free on Friday. We're eating with your editor, the big-time gourmet."

The deli, which was only a block away, didn't look that prepossessing, even if it did serve fabled pastrami, and I certainly wouldn't be having pastrami for breakfast. I almost turned away, but as I glanced down the long corridor beyond the front counters, I saw a plate of bagels, lox, and scrambled eggs. Lovely, almost translucent salmon beckoned to me from atop a rich, whipped mound of cream cheese. The sunny yellow of the scrambled eggs, still emitting steam, was too much to ignore. I let the door close behind me and entered the close warmth of the room.

On each side of a middle aisle, rows of tables were wedged together with chairs on either side. There was no privacy offered here. Diners would be elbow to elbow with strangers. However, the place was not crowded. I walked in quickly and claimed a place at the aisle end of a row, unwrapping my heavy woolen scarf and draping it over the chair, removing my coat, stuffing gloves in the pockets. Other customers were eating in their outerwear, even in this hot room, which is a strange custom of the natives that I had observed before. How can they expect to be warm when they venture back into the cold wind if they sit inside sweltering in their woolens? I draped my coat over the scarf-covered chair and sat down.

"Coffee?" asked a waitress. She was a square-shouldered woman with heavy breasts, overpermed blonde hair, and big black-framed glasses. I accepted the offer of coffee, ordered lox, bagels, cream cheese, and scrambled eggs without looking at the menu, and speculated as she walked away on whether she was wearing a girdle. No woman, even a young one, could have a bottom that flat coupled with such generous breasts unless she was wearing a girdle. I judged her to be in her thirties; she didn't have the delicacy of skin younger women have.

The waitress returned immediately to pour my coffee. "You from out of town?" she asked.

"Yes." Did I look like a tourist?

"How'd you hear about us?"

Now there was an embarrassing question. I'd feel like a ghoul admitting I'd come here because of the murder.

"Lemme guess? You read about the guy who died an' wanted to see where it happened?"

"Actually, the victim was a friend of my husband's," I said a bit defensively.

"Max was?" She looked surprised. "He was a regular here, you know. Came every Monday. Ordered the same thing. Sat right where you're sittin'."

"Here?" I was learning more than I wanted to know. "In this chair?"

"Yeah." She bustled off. I stared at a poster that demonstrated the Heimlich maneuver and wondered how many customers here had required it. Max hadn't, but possibly the fist in the stomach, as described by Punji, had been a fellow diner's attempt to administer it. Almost before I realized what I was doing, I glanced surreptitiously at the floor and the table, looking for bloodstains. How could I do such a distasteful thing? I don't stop to gawk at accidents or read the violent stories first in the newspaper.

A platter appeared before me, but now I wondered if I would be able to eat.

"He keeled over sideways," said the waitress, sounding chatty, as if she were gossiping with a neighbor. "Face first into the lox an' cream cheese plate next to him. Shook up the guy who ordered it. I can tell you that." She laughed, a sort of good-natured bray. "That sort of thing's no good for business. Likely to cut my tips. An' now my ma's scared an' wants me to quit an' move back to Jersey with her."

"I can understand that she'd be worried," I said.

"Well, it's not like people don't get offed in Jersey, too. Ma's got MS. She thinks someone's gonna break in an' tip over her wheel-

59

chair. Like anyone would think she's got anything worth stealin'."

"I'm sorry to hear about your mother's condition." Wouldn't that be terrible? To be confined to a wheelchair, anticipating attacks from criminals?

"Oh, she does pretty good. Runs this apartment house. Gets her own place free. Tenants go to her apartment to pay their rent. They don't pay, my cousin comes over an' hassles 'em. He's connected, so he don' take no shit from deadbeat tenants."

Connected? Did the waitress mean that her cousin was a Mob person?

"An' he knows all the union guys, so Ma don' have no trouble gettin' repairs done when the place needs 'em. Works out real good for her. Aren't you gonna eat your lox?"

"Oh. Oh, yes." I cut myself a bite: bagel, lox, and cream cheese. It was wonderful.

"Good, huh? You oughta come back for lunch or dinner. Try the pastrami. Your husband's friend, who got snuffed, he always came for the pastrami. Never left a scrap. My ma would have liked that. She can't stand people to waste food. Poor guy died before he finished his last sandwich. Damn shame."

"Did you see what happened?" I asked, forking up some of the eggs and enjoying them immensely.

"Well, I saw him keel over. I was headin'

that way when the guy with the lox plate jumped up and tried to Heimlich him. Course, no one knew then that he wasn't chokin'. Though you'd think the guy next to him woulda noticed he wasn' coughin' or nothin'. Then some other guy hauls off the lox guy an' lays Max out on the floor. 'This man's not breathin',' he says an' starts blowin' in his mouth an' poundin' on his chest. Puff, push, push, push, or whatever. You want some more coffee?"

"Yes, please." After her graphic description, I needed it. I felt as if a bite of bagel might get stuck in *my* throat before she could pour again into my cup.

"So then the boss comes back from the cash register an' says to the guy givin' artificial respiration, 'What the hell did you do to him?' an' the artificial respiration guy, who turns out to be a doctor — kind who does nose jobs, but still that's a doctor, right? — He gets huffy an' says he's tryin' to save a life here an' don' bother him. An' the boss says, 'Man's bleedin' onna floor.'"

"Dr. Heydemann was bleeding, and no one noticed it until then?" I asked.

"Max was a doctor, too?"

"Research scientist," I replied.

"Well, he wasn' bleedin' a whole lot, but by then it was seepin' out from under him."

She pointed to the aisle floor with her shoe, a sensible shoe, I might add. Why

61

would a woman wearing a girdle be able to overcome vanity to the point of wearing sensible shoes? Maybe the girdle supported her back, while the shoes supported her arches. Waitressing must, after all, be a physically taxing job.

"So the boss calls EMS," she continued, "but the guy, your husband's friend, is dead by then. For all I know, the Good Samaritans killed him."

"But I thought he was stabbed."

"You'd have to ask the cops. They didn' tell us. Ask a hunnerd questions, don' answer none."

"And no one saw who killed him?"

"Place was mobbed. It was lunchtime." The waitress strode off to wait on an elderly man who had taken a seat across the aisle and two rows back from me. I was left to wonder how a man could be murdered in a crowded restaurant and no one see the murderer. I pondered that conundrum as I continued to eat my lox and cream cheese, which were so-o delicious. I suppose lox is carcinogenic. I believe all cured meat has nitrates, which turn into nitrites, which cause cancer, or the other way around. Jason would know. For that matter, and because of my husband's research interests, I know more about such things than anyone who likes to eat would want to know. Wasn't pastrami a cured meat, too? Maybe Dr. Heydemann had cancer as a result of eating pastrami, and a minor hemorrhage had killed him when well-meaning fellow diners administered fatal, life-saving measures. Wouldn't that be ironic?

"Actually," said my waitress, returning to scoop up my empty plate, "this is probably the safest place in town. What are the odds of another murder happenin' here in our life-times?"

"What indeed?" I replied and handed her my credit card.

"Pay up front," she instructed, "an' we don't take credit cards, so you'll wanna leave the tip in cash before you head up to the register."

5

Blue Mountain Coffee and Arsenic

Jason

My first interview of the morning was with Frances Striff. Instead of taking me out to breakfast, she provided Blue Mountain Coffee and Viennese pastries in her office. While I breakfasted with good appetite, as a result of my run, Dr. Striff had tea and dry toast. I couldn't see that she needed to diet, so she may have preferred Spartan fare. Her personal appearance was certainly Spartan: a brown pants suit that hung off her gaunt frame, no makeup, blunt-cut hair, and lace-up shoes that would have done her great grandmother credit. Of course, I have seen my own fashion-conscious daughter in footwear that is equally grim, but hers, she once assured me, was stylish. I doubted that Frances Striff worried about fashion. I made a mental note of these things because Carolyn likes to hear about my day but becomes discouraged if I can only tell her what scientific topics were discussed.

"I guess you've heard about Max Heydemann," Striff said, setting her teacup into its saucer with an angry clink. "You can bet that whoever takes his place won't even try to hire another woman. Max did try, but I'm the only one who could stick it out. Probably because I look like one of the boys and mind my own business."

"Maybe you should consider academia," I suggested, at a loss as to how to respond to her description of herself. "Women are doing very well at a number of universities."

"When I hear of one that offers lucrative stock options and a generous retirement plan, I'll consider it. In the meantime, I've sacrificed two marriages to this company, so now I'm avoiding legal commitments, making a bundle here, and piling up retirement money. Maybe I'll get out early and take an adjunct professorship somewhere so I can do whatever I want in the lab and travel when I feel like it. Isn't that why you're considering us? The money?"

Frances Striff's personality was as blunt as her haircut. "Actually, I'm interested in the toxin research," I replied.

"Well, I wish I could tell you about mine, but as of five last night, we can't say anything about anything related to Hodge, Brune to anyone, even you. But please don't take that as evidence that we're not interested in hiring you. After Max's recommendation, upper management is salivating at the prospect.

"Except for the unlovable Vernon Merrivale, former scientist, present security fanatic for R and D. The man's paranoid, and I've heard him say that academics are notoriously loose-lipped about their research. He thinks that about women, too. The man's always skulking around my labs asking questions." She took a bite of her dry toast, which she had popped out of an ancient toaster on her desk after pushing the pastry plate in my direction. "So-o-o. I can't talk to you, but —"

"Am I to take it that this new wall of silence is related to Max's death?" I asked.

"Oh, no. The police think some street crazy knifed him. Merrivale is just using Max's death as an excuse for more security measures. We already have to be debriefed after outside conferences to be sure no one asked us nosy questions or got into our briefcases where we'd stashed secret papers that shouldn't have left the company. It's worse than having a high security clearance with the government."

I was, at this point, beginning to wonder if I really wanted to consult on any regular basis with Hodge, Brune. Free discussion among colleagues is not only one of the joys of science but also an impetus to new ideas — a sort of intellectual cross-pollination. But even if I didn't take this position, I felt I owed it to Max to find out what had been worrying him and see if I could do something about it. "Did Max say anything about a problem before he died?"

"What problem?"

"I don't know. He . . ." Since Max hadn't even been willing to talk about the matter on the telephone, I felt bound to keep his confidence by being at the least circumloquacious. "He seemed . . . worried . . . that last time we talked."

"Did he? Well . . ." She considered the topic. "At the Thursday meeting he was acting strangely. He'd stare at each of us as we talked and then ask odd questions. It was almost as if he thought people were fudging their results. It made me nervous, I can tell you, and I've never falsified data in my life. Made us all uneasy. Calvin Pharr got testy and actually took a belt from his flask at the meeting. Usually he's more discreet, by which I mean he only drinks in his office," she added dryly.

I must admit I found the idea of a scientist drinking on the job highly unusual. That would certainly be a problem to a research director, although I couldn't see how my "connections and expertise" would be of any use in this situation. Dealing with alcoholism would seem to be a medical problem and quite outside my experience.

67

". . . Vasandrovich was frowning, and poor Fergus McRoy started babbling when he was put under the gun," Striff continued, "but that's typical Fergus. The man's a good scientist, but he's a first-class worrier. What was so unusual was Max's attitude. I've never seen him act like that before, suspicious and nitpicking. Did he tell you —"

"It was just a feeling," I replied quickly. Given the extreme secretiveness now imposed on the scientists here, I might never find out what Max had wanted my help on.

"So do you want to tell me about *your* research?" Frances Striff asked. "Merrivale can't object to that."

What scientist doesn't want to talk about his work? "I've got three students doing an interesting arsenic pollution problem."

"Really?" She leaned forward to listen, dropping the remains of her toast into a wastebasket. For the next thirty minutes I told her about ground and water pollution by arsenic, the result of smelter operations in the past, and what we hoped to do about it. When I finished and had answered a number of intelligent and provocative questions, she pulled a telephone forward and punched in a number, saying, "You've got to talk to Calvin Pharr. He'll love this. He and Sean Ryan do heavy metals. Calvin, Frances Striff here." In minutes she had changed my schedule and was leading me to another office, saying before she departed, "I'm your host tonight. What do you want to eat?"

"Something unusual," I suggested vaguely. "My wife is a culinary writer; she —"

"I know just the place. Patria. Nuevo South American. My partner and I love it. Might as well let the company pay for a return visit. Your wife won't faint if I bring a lover along, will she?"

"No, of course not." I must admit that I wondered whether the lover was male or female, and what Carolyn would think if it were a woman. Even so, Patria sounded familiar to me. Carolyn must have mentioned it when she was looking at the Zagat guide to New York restaurants. She'd be pleased.

"Arsenic?" Calvin Pharr was saying. He was a fat man with a square, bald head. "I've got just the problem I want to talk to you about." He reached into his drawer and pulled out a flask, then thought better of the impulse and replaced it, saying, "I just remembered I can't talk to you about anything scientific. Hell! Listen, I hope you sign on so we can have a two-way conversation. Max would kill Merrivale — that's the prick in charge of security — if he knew what was going on now."

Max and this Merrivale, whom I had never met, hadn't gotten along? Did that have anything to do with Max's death or the problem he wanted to discuss with me? I shook off

69

that thought as bizarre. "Maybe you'd like to hear what we're doing in El Paso."

"Absolutely. I purely love heavy-metal pollution. New Jersey is a gold mine, which I could probably get fired for saying, even if everyone in the country knows it."

I had another fruitful conversation with Pharr, although he evidently forgot about his previous discretion and took swallows from his flask at twenty-minute intervals while we talked. When we had finished discussing arsenic, I asked him, as I had Frances Striff, whether he knew of any problem that had been bothering Max Heydemann.

"What? You mean like a premonition of his own death?" he asked dryly, then thought better of his response. "Sorry. That was a serious question, wasn't it? Which makes me wonder why you asked and what you know that I don't. Well." He took another hit of brandy.

Given that it was not yet noon, I had to surmise that Pharr, no matter how brilliant on heavy-metal chemistry, really was an alcoholic.

"I heard him yelling at someone in his office. That was unusual for him. Max wasn't the noisy type. He could cut you up into little pieces and spit you out with words, and he did to a few us, but I can't remember him yelling at anyone."

Us? Max had attacked Pharr verbally?

About his drinking? Or about something else? "Who was he shouting at?" I asked.

"Dunno. I was on my way out to a long, liquid lunch and didn't stop to listen."

"When was it?"

"Friday? I think so. It must have been Friday."

The day before Max called me. How could I find out at whom he had been angry? "What was the fuss about?"

"Dunno. Why are you asking?"

"I liked him."

Pharr received a phone call and said he had to head for his lab. Before he left, he called someone named Morrie to come and get me. Pharr had hardly left when a man with thinning hair and a rumpled suit appeared in the doorway and asked, "Dr. Pharr?"

I introduced myself after saying that Pharr was out.

"OK, you'll do," said the man and took the second visitors' chair, from which he stared at me wearily. "You know any reason anybody'd have to kill Dr. Heydemann?"

I shook my head, because I really didn't know anything concrete about the matter.

"How about his wife? Did they get along?"

"May I ask who you are?"

He scratched his ear. "Sorry. Worski. Detective." He pulled a shield from his pocket. "The wife?"

"I've only met her twice, but they seemed to have an amiable relationship."

"Kids? Did he have problem kids?"

"I don't know if he had children."

"How long you been with the company, anyway?" he asked, looking irritated, as if I were withholding vital information.

"I'm not with the company. I'm being interviewed for a consulting position."

"Well, shit."

"How exactly did he die?"

"His heart was punctured by a long, narrow, pointed instrument. Like an ice pick, only longer. Perfectly placed."

"Does that sound like the work of a crazed street person?" I asked doubtfully.

"Maybe. Could have been a pro. Who the hell knows? An' what do you care if you hardly knew him?"

"I liked and respected him." I considered telling this policeman my concern and decided that I should. "And before Dr. Heydemann died, he called me and asked for my help on some serious problem."

"What problem?"

"He didn't say. He seemed to think his phone was tapped, or someone was listening. At least that's what I assumed, bizarre as that sounds, because he said he didn't feel that he could discuss it on the phone."

"Well, these people are worse than doctors claimin' doctor-patient privilege when it

72

comes to discussin' what the company does. No big surprise to hear he was paranoid. Makes you wonder what they *are* doin'. Makin' illegal drugs or something? You know anything about illegal drugs?" He gave me a narrow, suspicious look.

"The company has made its name in research on environmental toxins."

"Yeah, but how do they make their *money?*"

"I would have assumed the same way," I replied.

"Well, I'm not assumin' anything, an' no one is tellin' me anything. Christ. Guy got stabbed in a crowded restaurant over a pile of pastrami, an' no one saw a thing. No one around here knows a thing. No one at his house knows a thing. His wife's sedated. We can't even talk to her."

Detective Worski rose, handed me his card, and told me to call him if I discovered what the victim's problem had been. I agreed.

6

Green Tea on Commission

Carolyn

When Jason and I travel, we each carry hundred-dollar bills and travelers' checks. The occasion of buying New York's fifteen-dollar subway and bus pass seemed a likely opportunity to use one of my hundreds. Therefore, I stealthily slipped the bill from my handbag as I stood in line. When I slid the money into the opening, the tall African-American in his bulletproof glass enclosure said, "WE DON'T TAKE HUNDREDS, LADY," his voice booming over the loudspeaker system. I gulped, feeling all eyes turn in my direction as I stuffed the bill into my purse and fumbled for a twenty. That bill he accepted, I received my pass, and then he counted out my change: "SIXTEEN, SEVENTEEN, EIGHTEEN . . ." As I hastily thrust the five one-dollar bills into my handbag, I imagined that every purse-snatcher in the city had been listening and was now heading in my direction, bent on violent robbery.

Only the subway car ad for 1-800-DIVORCE took my mind off my fears as I rode, white-knuckled, toward Loretta Blum's office. Under the telephone number the ad said, "Finally an affordable lawyer. We take Visa, MC, and Diner's Club." I remembered someone telling me that holders of Diner's Club cards experience the highest percentage of divorces. Perhaps that credit card company offers a special, low interest rate for the maritally challenged.

Do you picture people before you meet them? I had pictured my agent rather vividly: an older woman, slim and chic, gray-streaked hair, charming. In person, Loretta Blum was younger than I, sported a wide circle of dense, jet-black curls, and was screaming at someone named Simon on the phone when I was ushered into her office by a young woman with a pierced eyebrow.

"What the hell are you thinking of, Simon? You keep her away from the damned computer, you hear me?" She waved me to a seat. Evidently Simon's answer was not satisfactory because she threatened, if he didn't get Rachel under control, to provide him with a second and more radical bris. Was Rachel an author? I wondered. And why didn't Loretta Blum want her near the computer? Perhaps Simon was someone from the agency sent to monitor the activities of the troublesome Rachel.

"She puked on the keyboard?" shrieked Loretta. "Put Ellie on. I want that computer cleaned up and locked up immediately, and, Simon, don't you dare put any disks in the drive, you hear me? No disks! The last thing I need is some damn virus or crash."

Ah, Rachel was drunk and endangering the work stored on the computer. Perhaps Simon was a husband, lover, or son, who was prone to introducing disks into Rachel's computer, disks that had not been scanned for viruses and caused disastrous hard-drive crashes that deleted whole novels. Jason won't let the children use his laptop for just that reason. However, they have their own computers; whereas, I was never allowed to use my father's typewriter, and he did not provide me with one of my own until I was a college student. Ah well, old resentments do persist in one's psyche.

My agent, as yet unintroduced, slammed down the telephone. "Kids!" she snarled. "I should have drowned them at birth." I must have looked confused because she shrugged. "I got two on vacation, one with the flu, and my mother-in-law won't come over to watch them. She says they don't treat her with respect. Hell, I'm happy as long as they don't burn the house down."

"I'm Carolyn Blue," I said, trying not to think about her threat to provide Simon, evidently her son, with a second circumcision. Would my agent be considered a "castrating mother"? Would her mothering techniques

76

produce a serial killer? Men are extremely testy about their genitalia (pun intended).

"Right," said Loretta. "*Eating Out in the Big Easy.* Have some green tea." She poured a singularly vile liquid into a dainty china cup and pushed it toward me. "How's the book coming?"

"Well, actually —"

"Don't tell me you've got problems, writer's block or some damn thing. I don't want to hear that. You've got the advance. Now you write the book."

"Unfortunately, I had a very stressful, even dangerous week in New Orleans. I'm finding it extremely difficult to write about —"

"So get over it, whatever happened. And I don't want to hear about it. You think you know hard times? My mother was born in a concentration camp. My Uncle Bernie got her into this country. Only one to survive in the German part of the family. Now *that's* something to be upset about. That's hard times. She named me Loretta because someone told her she looked like Loretta Young. That was some movie star from way back when. My poor mother, she thought looking like a movie star when you got numbers tattooed on your arm was pretty neat, so she named me Loretta. You can bet I didn't name any of my kids after movie stars. Maybe I should have." Having established her superiority in the recognition of genuine hard times, she slapped her hands down on her desk and stared into my eyes.

"So you'll write the book. You've been paid; you write the book. You're a professional now. Stress?" She snapped her fingers. "We all got stress. Get over it.

"Now, we're meeting the editor for lunch this week, and he'll want to hear all about it: the recipes, the restaurants, all that gourmet stuff. Believe me, Rollie won't give a rat's ass about your personal problems. All he cares about is food, and books about food, and people who want to talk or read about food. So when we go out to lunch with Rollie, you tell him about all the great stuff you ate in New Orleans. I wouldn't give you two beans for that town myself, but Rollie likes it.

"And let him do the ordering. I don't have to let him order for me, but I'm Jewish, thank God. You're not, right? If you are, don't tell him. He's got nothing against Jews except we don't eat stuff gourmets love. He orders you pig liver or some disgusting thing, you love it. Got that? And don't order a cocktail. He thinks cocktails ruin the *palate*. The man's a pain in the ass, but that's OK. You drink wine with whatever he gets you to eat. Let him pick the wine. He'll love you."

"About the New Orleans book," I persisted when she stopped to take a breath. "Perhaps

I could replace it with one called *Eating Ethnic in the Big Apple*."

Loretta Blum actually gave my suggestion two or three seconds of thought before she resumed her monologue. "Good idea."

I felt a welling of relief.

"Tell Rollie about it. Run it by him. First, *Eating Out in the Big Easy*. Then, *Eating Ethnic in the Big Apple*. Catchy. You got good instincts. I bet he'll go for it. You got a synopsis with you?"

"No, and I meant to substitute it for —"

"Forget that. The contract says New Orleans, but it can't hurt to negotiate for a second book. Maybe they'll give the first one some publicity if they've got another one in the pipeline.

"Now, about stirring up some interest in the book and in you. After all, no one knows you from Jane Doe. We need to get your name around, so I had a great idea. I wangled you an appointment tomorrow with a guy named Marshall Smead, works for a syndication company. You already had some columns on food published in newspapers, right? That's how I found you. No reason you shouldn't do that regularly, make a little money, get your name spread around. It's not big bucks, unless you get real well known. I wouldn't even handle that — syndicated columns. It would be a deal between you and the syndication company, if you can swing it." She began to stir through the litter of papers on her desk. "Address. Where did I put that address?"

When her phone rang, she picked up and snarled, "I'm talking to someone in here, Marsha. What are you doing out there? Getting your brain pierced to go with your belly button? I said no calls." She listened briefly, then said, "Put him on. I'm gonna kill him. . . . Simon, why are you still bothering me at work? . . . So Ellie's throwing up, too? What do you expect from me? I'm here. You're there. Call your father. See how he likes it. . . . OK, put Ellie on. . . . Ellie, I forbid you to throw up anywhere but in the toilet. You got that? In the toilet . . . Don't tell me you're sick. You're not. You're throwing up because your sister did." She hung up, retrieved an address written on the back of a business card, read the printed front, and muttered, "Who the hell is that?" Then, thrusting the card at me, she said, "Tomorrow at ten. Think you can find the address? Take a cab. Then you won't have to worry."

I stared down at the scrawl on the back of the business card of someone she didn't remember. Marshall Smead. His office was on the twenty-first floor of some building that I took to be farther downtown. The idea of writing a regular food column sounded appealing. What would I call it? "Eating Out

80

with Carolyn?" "Other People's Cooking?" That was the only kind I really like these days. "Have Fork, Will Travel?" I felt an overwhelming desire to laugh but doubted that my bossy agent would be amused.

In fact, I didn't get the chance, because she was off on a new subject. "Now, about your clothes."

I glanced down at my tailored, blue wool dress. It looked perfectly appropriate to me. Not as flashy or as expensive as her red and black suit, which would have been stunning had she been built less like a cement block.

"You need something with more flair. You know what I mean? Something that says *designer rags.*"

"I really don't think my advance will cover *designer rags*," I said dryly.

Loretta Blum snorted with laughter. "You never heard of buying wholesale? You know who to go to, you can dress sharp without touching the inheritance from your grandmother or whatever. So you'll go to see my uncle, Bernie Feingold. He's in the rag trade. I'll call and tell him you're coming; he'll take care of you." She ripped from a pad a note page that was engraved with her name and wrote down another address. "Don't put it off. Better you go before your appointment with Smead.

"Absolutely turn up looking like you been in the big city more than once in your life

81

when we have lunch with Roland DuPlessis. After food and wine, he notices clothes. You'll see when you meet him. Fat as a pregnant cow and dressed like some fag artist type. You never know what he'll turn up wearing, so don't stare. Wouldn't hurt to say something nice about his outfit if you can do it with a straight face."

She stood up. "So that's it. Go get a few outfits from Bernie, then go home and think about a sales pitch for Smead tomorrow at ten. Tell yourself, it's not just a little extra money; it's free publicity. You're gonna get paid for having your name in the paper. You can even plug your own book when it comes out. Pure gold. One of my best ideas. I'm counting on you to follow through. OK?"

Numbly, I agreed, put down my teacup with its disgusting brew virtually untouched, and allowed myself to be sent away. Loretta Blum was overwhelming, to say the least. With any luck, I'd never have to meet her again in person after the lunch with the food editor. She did seem to have the success of my career at heart — if she had a heart. She certainly didn't want to hear my problems. Or even the problems of her children. I hoped my next appointment, lunch and a museum visit with some scientist's wife, proved to be more pleasant. I wouldn't be visiting Uncle Bernie today, no matter what my agent advised. Mrs. Vasandrovich this af-

ternoon and Mr. Smead tomorrow would just
have to put up with me in my country
cousin clothes.

7

The Caesar Chicken Burrito as an Objet d'Art

I love museum restaurants. The food is usually acceptable and often very good, but best of all, a museum restaurant allows one to sit down on something other than a bench. Walking in one of those revered temples of art is worse than an uphill climb on a rocky path. The slow pace and the marble floors result in aches, pains, and exhaustion. Therefore, falling into a chair in the restaurant is pure luxury, delicious relief. One does not have to rise and move on after three minutes in order to make way for other weary art lovers or to prove that one is an art lover oneself.

I had my first bruschetta in the balcony café at the History of Women in the Arts Museum in D.C. The bruschetta was wonderful, and the interior views of the elaborate old house that hosts the collection, lovely. One day at MoMA, the Museum of Modern Art in New York, I sat down in their austere black, gray, and silver café with its fascinating modern chandeliers.

From my chair I could gaze out huge windows at the sculpture garden while I feasted on thick, nicely herbed tomato soup and finished with a delicious chocolate tart. In the garden, snow was falling on the ground, on the black metal sculptures, and on the black and white birches. It was as beautiful a scene as any museum-quality painting.

Carolyn Blue,
"Have Fork, Will Travel,"
Spokane News-Ledger

Carolyn

I arrived at Hodge, Brune, half frozen. A cold wind whistled off the water surrounding the island and howled through the stone canyons of the city, crystallizing my blood. (Although I meant that metaphorically, Jason once told me about research involving fish that live under the arctic ice. They have ice crystals in their blood. Isn't that a strange thing?) Jason, unfortunately, was nowhere in sight at Hodge, Brune, and according to a secretary, the husband of my hostess, Dr. Vaclav Vasandrovich, was now occupying the office of the late R and D director, Max Heydemann.

Having profited from a colleague's death,

85

was the new director considered a suspect by the police? I wondered. Probably not. I have heard of some very unpleasant scientific quarrels but no murders motivated by chemistry.

The secretary advised me to wait in the R and D office, where the visitors' chairs were more numerous and comfortable. I dutifully shuffled off on icy feet and approached a second secretary, who looked decidedly tearful. She was obviously another of the late director's many admirers. After telling her that I was here to meet Mrs. Vasandrovich, I took a seat beside a grammatically impaired man wearing an olive green topcoat.

"I ain't got all day," he said to the secretary.

"Dr. Vasandrovich is still on the telephone," she replied.

That was obvious. I could hear him through the door, shouting in a foreign language. Russian, I think. When I was an undergraduate, my roommate took Russian and frequently begged me to quiz her on vocabulary lists.

The man in the olive topcoat, which looked like army surplus to me, or possibly some trendy new style, muttered angrily to himself. "It's obviously a long distance call," I said by way of consolation. "It must cost a fortune to call Russia."

"Russia, my ass." He eyed me with disfavor. "Vasandrovich is probably callin' his bookie in Coney Island. Or he jus' don' wanna talk to the police."

Upon discovering that I shared the sofa with a policeman, I introduced myself and asked if he was investigating the death of Dr. Heydemann.

"I'm Worski," he said. "Did you know Heydemann?"

"No, but my husband did. In fact, he came here to be interviewed by Dr. Heydemann for a position and was exceedingly upset to hear of his death, which I gather was not only tragic but bizarre." Detective Worski did not find any death in New York City bizarre. He had seen it all, or so he said. "But how did a street person manage to get into the restaurant, much less stab someone without being noticed?" I asked.

"Who says it was a street person?" retorted the detective. "Your random murder — that's not the usual way of it, lady. This Heydemann, the killer got him with something like an ice pick, only longer an' thinner, an' he knew just where to put it. Does that sound like some homeless schizoid? No way. But try to get these people to talk to you about why he might have been killed. You'd think they was sellin' plutonium on the black market the way they clam up about company business. Worse today than yesterday."

I stared at Detective Worski, aghast. "Do

you think someone *here* killed him?"

"Naw. More like they hired it done."

"A professional assassination?" And my husband wanted to work for this company? "Dr. Heydemann did go to that particular restaurant every Monday," I confided. "If someone wanted to find him in a public place, that would be an obvious choice, although it seems peculiar to me. Wouldn't a site less public be preferable?"

Worski shrugged. "Hit men got their own fetishes. Anyway, thanks for the tip, Mrs. Blue. That's more than anyone else bothered to tell me."

We both turned when the office door opened and a distinguished man with thick silver hair, dark skin, and startlingly blue eyes waved the detective into his office, apologizing in an offhand manner for the delay.

"Yeah," said Worski, rising with effort from the soft cushions of the sofa. "This lady says you was talkin' Russian in there."

The man, presumably Dr. Vasandrovich, asked, "You speak Russian, madam?"

"Not really," I replied, embarrassed, and introduced myself.

"Ah. Jason Blue's wife. And my own dear Sophia is late for your afternoon together. I must scold her for her tardiness, and you, dear lady, for mistaking the language. I was speaking Czech, to my Aunt Elizabeta, as a matter of fact. Still, perhaps it is a natural mistake, for my name must sound Russian to you, whereas I am actually Polish and Czech. A graduate of Charles University. You may have heard of it."

"Of course," I replied. "Founded in 1350 in Prague by a Holy Roman Emperor."

He gave a slight bow. "I am gratified by your knowledge of my country's history. Well, Sophia, finally you are here. This is Mrs. Blue. Your absence has kept not only Mrs. Blue but the very impatient Detective Worski waiting."

Maybe I should have visited Loretta Blum's Uncle Bernie after all. Compared to this very sophisticated, very tall lady, I did indeed feel like a country cousin. Mrs. Vasandrovich swept me away, ignoring her husband's reprimand, courtly though it had been. She declared it a shame that my appointment had kept us from eating somewhere more chic than the museum restaurant, which was now our only option in the short time left. Obviously, we had to see the *Picasso in Clay* exhibit, to which she would be so pleased to introduce me, Picasso being a special favorite of hers, as he was with most art connoisseurs, etc., etc., etc.

I found myself rather irritated to be blamed for Mrs. Vasandrovich's missing an elaborate lunch when she was the one who was late. My hostess and I ended up in the cafeteria line at the Metropolitan Museum of

Art because there were no tables available in the restaurant. Mrs. Vasandrovich was unhappy with the choices. I spotted a Caesar salad with chicken on French bread and reached for it, only to have a burrito-like packet wrapped in plastic shoved in front of my choice by a stout cafeteria employee wearing a hair net.

I sighed and took the burrito, along with a small bottle of white wine and a $2.75 cookie. The cookie was delicious, but at that price it should have been. The burrito was filled with chicken bits and an approximation of Caesar salad, but the dressing — well, in my cooking days, I had done much better and still could in a pinch. The wine was a disaster. Mrs. Vasandrovich, who invited me to call her Sophia, toyed with her lunch and discussed the tragedy of Max Heydemann's untimely death, the violence of life in the United States, and the qualifications of her own husband for the position that he now filled on an interim basis. She assured me that her husband would give mine every consideration in his search for employment with Hodge, Brune, particularly because Max had thought so highly of him. "Max was Vaclav's mentor, you know," she confided. "They were as close as father and son."

Since Max had been in his fifties, and Vaclav looked to be of the same generation, I found her description rather peculiar, but I did manage to keep my thoughts to myself.

Sophia then told me that Max had been responsible for bringing Vaclav to the United States while the Czech Republic was still in communist hands. Having seen in her husband such great potential, Max managed to arrange his escape right under the nose of the communists, who would never have let Vaclav go had they known of his intention to defect. Of course, Vaclav would never have left her behind to be imprisoned, but Max had arranged for her escape as well. Sophia herself had been most unpopular with the detestable red regime because of her noble, in fact royal, lineage. An excellent scientist, Max, she concluded. Vaclav was taking his death very hard.

I was by then eating my lovely cookie, all creamy chocolate and crunchy nuts, and feeling much more charitable, so I asked with genuine interest, "Hapsburg or Premyslid?" referring to her "royal lineage."

My question evidently won Sophia's heart. She beamed at me and exclaimed, "You know Czech history?"

"Some," I agreed as I pressed a finger onto the last crumbs of my large cookie and lifted them to my mouth.

"My family is descended from the true Bohemian kings," she replied proudly. "We predate that upstart, John of Luxembourg. Ottakar II is my progenitor on my mother's side."

"Ah, the one who brought in the German settlers in the thirteenth century. A canny political move at the time, but the source of much ethnic strife thereafter," I murmured and winced over a sip of vinegar masquerading as wine.

"Yes, well, he was a very successful king." She touched her lips with a napkin. "Much more admirable than any of the Hapsburgs, who weren't even Bohemian, or for that matter John of Luxembourg, who was responsible for the massacre of our nobility on the field at Crecy. What a shame my ancestress, Elizabeth, was forced to marry such a foolish man."

"Ah, but you have to be fascinated by a king who would lead his knights into battle even though he was blind. And he *was* the father of Charles, the Holy Roman Emperor, who was certainly a credit to the Bohemian crown," I replied.

"Indeed." She nodded enthusiastically. "But I regard the brilliance of Charles's reign as a credit to his Premyslid blood. His father, through neglect, left Prague in ruins." She pushed her goblet away, having evidently found the wine as detestable as I did. "I noticed that you were talking to that ill-dressed policeman. Have they caught the crazy person who killed poor Max?"

"I think they're leaning toward the idea that it was a hired assassin," I replied.

"Really?" She looked taken aback but recovered her aplomb quickly. "How interesting. A scandal in the making, perhaps. His wife, Charlotte, his second wife, was simply a nobody, even by American standards, before he married her. A failed ballet dancer."

Now that was interesting, I thought. I'd never met a professional ballet dancer, failed or otherwise.

"Who knows what such a woman would do?" said Sophia. "His children do not care for her, which is understandable. Their own mother came from a fine family. Family is most important, don't you think?"

"Um-m," I replied, wondering how she would characterize mine.

"I tell you this in confidence, but I saw her, Charlotte Heydemann, in a hotel with a young man. Perhaps the lover killed Max!" She stopped talking long enough to notice that I had finished my lunch. "Shall we go now to enjoy the Picassos?"

She certainly did, exclaiming over every silly plate and pitcher. Picasso must have been hooting with laughter when he made those ugly things: plates with fish and vegetable lumps on them, garishly painted; and the pitchers, whose curves were the breasts and bottoms of fleshy women. And I had to nod politely at Sophia's many admiring exclamations. What fun the exhibit would have been if Jason and I had gone together.

We'd have been helpless with giggles . . . well, not Jason, but he would have been amused.

I do love modern art. It so often exhibits a marvelous sense of humor. We saw a picture that afternoon, part of the regular collection, called *The Critical Eye*. The artist had painted a scene in which a real cow was examining a portrait of a cow while a number of serious, black-clad scholars seemingly awaited the real cow's critical opinion. One man held a notebook to take down the cow's impressions while another had a mop in case the cow soiled the museum floor. Sophia was not amused.

But the afternoon wasn't a total loss. The news that Mrs. Heydemann had a lover was certainly intriguing. Detective Worski would be interested, if anyone thought to tell him. In fact, perhaps it was my duty to do so, but how to get hold of him? Maybe he was still at Hodge, Brune. I called, and he was. At first, he seemed surprised and not too pleased to hear from me, but when I mentioned the story I'd heard that afternoon, he said, "Good lead, Mrs. Blue. Murders usually lead back to sex or money."

I had read that somewhere.

"And family members are first-class suspects. Thanks for the tip."

"You're very welcome," I replied, not sure that my husband would thank me for getting involved.

94

8

Ominous News in Patria

Jason

When I returned from lunch with several Hodge, Brune scientists, the atmosphere at company headquarters had changed from one of restrained grief to one of near panic. Upper management and senior scientists huddled in twos and threes in offices and hallways, talking in undertones, falling silent when lower echelons or outsiders approached. I was evidently an outsider, because the prevailing alarm was never explained to me.

The seminar that I was to give that afternoon was postponed, and I was suddenly shuffled off to spend the afternoon with Fergus McRoy, a nice enough fellow, although neither of us really knew why we had been thrown together. McRoy's interest was in coal and its by-products, and company paranoia prevented him from discussing his research. In fact, he seemed distracted, and Striff had described him as nervous during the last meeting with Max, so I studied McRoy as we talked but saw nothing more sinister than anxiety in him. Was that anxiety

95

indicative of a guilty conscience?

I had rather expected to spend at least some time after my seminar with Vasandrovich, who had become interim director of R and D. It did not happen, which made me suspect that the company, all protestations to the contrary, was no longer interested in working out a contract with me. McRoy also expected to see Vasandrovich and even mentioned that he might have to leave me abruptly. Neither of us was summoned, so we ended up talking sports, as men are prone to do when at loss for more interesting topics. McRoy was a soccer fan, not an interest on which I had much to say.

I arrived at the Park Central earlier than expected to find my wife napping but quite willing to awaken, hear about my day, and tell me about hers. Her tale centered on her take-no-prisoners agent and her afternoon with Vasandrovich's wife, a woman with whom Carolyn had not been charmed beyond some interesting medieval family connection. I, in turn, said that something was going on at Hodge, Brune, beyond or perhaps even connected to Max's death, and we discussed what it might be. Carolyn suggested that people were afraid of losing their jobs when a new R and D director was brought in.

These downsizing and housecleaning operations that go on in contemporary industry make me appreciate universities and the tenure system. One may have some anxious early years in academia but, if granted tenure at a compatible institution, life can be very pleasant thereafter. Of course, too much ease can be stultifying, which is why I left a very good position. My colleagues thought I had lost my mind, but I wanted new challenges instead of an easy slide into middle-aged complacency.

"We're eating at a place called Patria tonight with Frances Striff and her companion," I told Carolyn. "I assured her that you wouldn't be horrified at the presence of her lover."

"Of course I won't," Carolyn replied. "On the whole, it sounds rather exciting, and Patria is very chic."

"Even if the lover is another woman?"

"They're a lesbian couple?" she asked, intrigued.

"I have no idea, but Striff has had two failed marriages and is quite plain. Even I noticed that, so I thought —"

"Don't be ridiculous, Jason. I'm sure science is responsible for many divorces, and *plain* fends off sexual harassment. Being a woman in the world of science isn't the most comfortable position."

"There are many successful female scientists," I replied rather defensively.

"How many at Hodge, Brune?" Carolyn demanded.

What could I say? Dr. Striff herself had pointed out that she was the only one. Our speculations about her companion proved to be moot. In fact, my description of Dr. Striff was embarrassingly off the mark. If she hadn't approached us in the lobby, I wouldn't have recognized her. Wearing makeup and a very skimpy black dress, she looked more like a former model than a frumpy scientist. Carolyn raised an eyebrow at me after the introductions. Striff's companion, Paul Fallon, was a charming fellow, possibly younger than she, whose profession, if any, I never learned, but he and Carolyn hit it off immediately with common interests in things cultural. Fallon had seen the *Picasso in Clay* exhibit and remembered as many ugly ceramics as Carolyn: plates of bacon and eggs, a pitcher depicting a fat man in a green hat. We became a very jolly group over a round of mangolitas, a concoction of champagne and mango juice, not to mention bits of mango that tended to lodge alarmingly in the throat.

Once I had developed a strategy for avoiding mango strangulation, I divided my attention between the restaurant decor, on which my wife was busily making notes, and my menu. I am a fairly well-traveled individual, but few scientific meetings are held in South or Central America. Therefore, but for the explanations, the menu would have seemed to be in a foreign language. What, for instance, is *fufu?* Obviously, I was in for an exotic experience.

Carolyn was discussing dishes with a hovering waiter, who could evidently recognize a food professional when he saw one. I reluctantly passed up the Oysters Rodriguez because of the *fufu* and Huacatay sauce in the description and chose an eggplant empanada. I know what an empanada is, a small pastry. They are served in El Paso, although usually with fruit rather than eggplant inside. This empanada came with "adobo roasted lamb tenderloin and *sarsa* salad." Both Carolyn and I agreed that my appetizer was excellent — rare lamb, crusty empanada, and a fine chili tang, which came, I presume, from the *sarsa.*

She ate half of mine, and I finished off her Pastel de Choclo, a mushroom potpie with corn bread on top, spicy shrimp on a skewer, and a sweet sherry vinaigrette on some leaves. Although I've never been a fan of corn bread, one can hardly go wrong with mushrooms.

I had no trouble choosing the Seafood Parihuela as a main course. How could any seafood lover pass up grilled lobster tail surrounded by clams, mussels, rock shrimp, bay scallops, and calamari? It was served on a white bean cake and cooked with tomatoes, *chorizo* and *panca* pepper. Carolyn remarked that the sauce had a lovely beany flavor, which was quite true.

She was more venturesome and ordered Sugar Cane Tuna described as a "coconut glazed loin with *malanga* puree, chayote, and dried shrimp salsa." Other than the tuna, I probably failed to identify the ingredients. I thought I was sampling a sweet potato puree, but perhaps *malanga* is something else entirely. Whatever it was, it contrasted nicely, as my wife pointed out, with the chopped vegetables marinated in lime and the crust on the rare tuna, which was rich and sweet. This unusual fish was served on a frosted aqua platter. Carolyn liked the platter so much that I was struck with the idea of buying her something similar for Mother's Day. Maybe if I do, she'll cook me another meal like the one she prepared from her new cookbook.

God knows what Frances and Fallon were eating. We weren't well enough acquainted to exchange portions, and they weren't interested in discussing ingredients. However, our waiter was, and some other fellow, when Carolyn had filled many pages with notes, came over to ask if we were happy with our meals. We chemists nodded, mouths stuffed with alien food. Fallon said the Churrasco Nica was better than ever (it appeared to be beef), and Carolyn absolutely beamed at this new representative of management, swallowed, and asked for copies of the menu. She was also sampling from their alcohol offerings — not only the mangolita but also a jojito, which was a rum drink with lime and mint. I had Cabro, a Guatemalan beer recommended by Fallon. My wife said that it tasted like sweat.

Over our appetizers (we all ordered from the three-course prix fixe menu), Frances and Fallon argued about who had discovered the place. Fallon said that his hairdresser had recommended Patria. I wondered what a hairdresser could do for him that my barber couldn't at a more reasonable price. Frances insisted that she had read about it in the *New York Times* and suggested they go, and didn't he remember the fellow on the subway who had been complaining in song about the cultural inadequacies of males?

Any conversation was difficult because of the noise. The two-story room was huge, with towering, green-framed windows and, over the door, a lush collection of plants and a mosaic. Of this, we had a good view because we were seated on the balcony above the main dining room and bar. Carolyn was particularly taken with the waveform banisters and the twisted spindles that held them up. She lamented not having brought a camera to take a picture of the place. Frances looked taken aback. Evidently, taking pictures of the interior of a restaurant would not have been chic, although, as I said, I was astonished that Frances Striff could look chic.

Over the entrées, Carolyn asked Frances whether she thought Vaclav Vasandrovich would be welcomed as the new R and D director.

"Good God, you had lunch with his wife, didn't you?" Frances replied and began to laugh.

Fallon murmured to me that Sophia Vasandrovich was a notorious snob. Then Frances got control of her hilarity and advised Carolyn not to judge Vaclav by his wife. "I think the poor man was initially impressed by her royal ancestry, but none of the rest of us are. I suppose, if we can't have Max, Vaclav will do as well as anyone."

Sighing at the thought of Max's death (he had been a man I thought might become a close friend), I turned back to my lobster. Carolyn and Fallon began a spirited argument about which Picasso sculpture was funnier, the pregnant goat or the lollipop-head baby in the stroller. My wife takes great delight in modern sculpture, while I prefer Bernini, Michelangelo, or even Canova, although his male figures are on the effeminate side. Carolyn maintains that the models were just younger.

When we were presented with the dessert menu, my wife ordered That's da Bomb, which I promise you was the name on the menu. She is, unquestionably, a chocoholic, and That's da Bomb is a chocolate dish.

However, she was taken aback when it arrived because it looked rather like a space machine: chocolate mousse in a chocolate shell with hazelnuts, ice cream landing legs, and a crispy, chocolate cookielike thing in the shape of an isosceles triangle thrusting up from the ship. Mine wasn't much less bizarre because she talked me into ordering the Chocolate Cigar. The cigar itself contained chocolate mousse wrapped in a chocolate almond cake with mocha ice cream, but the cigar also came with a ring — not edible — and a book of lighted matches that wafted the smell of caramelized sugar under my nose.

Fallon had lime jalapeño sorbet, which does not sound very appetizing, but he seemed to enjoy it, and Frances had a pear tart with pistachio and blue cheese ice cream. Carolyn had been considering that dessert — for me — until I refused to try it unless the blue cheese could be eliminated from the ice cream. I personally prefer to have my blue cheese on a salad, or even a cracker, but in ice cream? That sounds like something you'd use as a threat when your child refused to eat his broccoli.

Frances had taken two bites of her dessert and laid her spoon down when I decided to introduce the subject that had been nagging at my mind all evening. "A lot of people at Hodge, Brune seemed worried this after-

103

noon," I said around a spoonful of the ice cream. "Is something going on that I should know about?"

Frances looked hesitant. Fallon said, "The man is thinking of hiring on. He should be told what just happened."

Carolyn looked alarmed and blurted out, "Has someone else been murdered? If so, I think we should go straight home, Jason."

"You haven't seen your editor yet. You have to stay until Friday," I replied.

"Not if you're in danger."

"It's not that," said Frances. "We had some very disturbing news today. Another company just announced the development of a process we've been working on for five years, one we were ready to patent."

"That's a relief," Carolyn murmured. She was nibbling on the wing of her spaceship.

"It won't be to our stockholders, if it gets out," said Frances grimly.

"May I ask what kind of process?" I asked.

"It has to do with a method for eliminating pollution from coal-burning power plants."

"That should be a very lucrative break-through."

"They've filed for an international patent," she said gloomily. "Did it just before making the announcement, the thieving bastards."

"You're sure it's your process?"

"Pretty sure."

"What company?"

"Some small Ukrainian outfit no one ever heard of. For heaven's sake, the Ukrainians don't even care that their coal miners keep getting killed. Why would they care about air pollution?"

"No doubt because they stand to make a fortune if their, or your, process works," I replied thoughtfully.

"It works."

"Without costing a fortune?"

"That's the great thing about it," said Frances. "The power companies won't be able to say they can't afford it, and our stock has already been rising on the rumors that we're about to make a big announcement. When this gets out, shares will plummet, and there goes my early retirement."

"And people at the company think the research was stolen from Hodge, Brune rather than being a parallel effort that neither of you were aware of?" I asked.

"I'm guilty," said Fallon, grinning. "I don't want Frances to retire and move away to some leafy campus in some uninteresting section of the country, so I engineered a stock disaster."

"Not funny, Paul," Frances snapped. "A lot of people are going to be hurt by this unless we can prove that they stole from us. Take Charlotte Heydemann, for instance. I imagine a lot of what Max left her is in company stock."

"You know Mrs. Heydemann?" Carolyn asked, suddenly interested.

"Of course. Max finally lucked out in the family sweepstakes with her. She adores him, as opposed to his crazy first wife and their obnoxious offspring."

"Really?"

Now why was Carolyn interested in Max's family? I wondered. That question was eclipsed when it occurred to me that Max's death might somehow be connected to this expensive piece of industrial espionage. Carolyn calmly continued to demolish her That's da Bomb. She hadn't seen the implications and, when back at the hotel, I mentioned them, she said, "Now, Jason, industrial espionage? That's crazy."

Of course, my wife has never had to deal with industrial paranoia about the open discussion of science.

"I imagine the police are more likely to look at the family situation, especially if it's as dysfunctional as Frances seems to think."

I eyed Carolyn narrowly. "Well, you don't need to look into it, my love," I said. "You didn't even know Max." The last thing I wanted Carolyn to do was put herself in danger. However, *I* intended to make some inquiries, and not about Max's family. Perhaps I now had the answer to what had been worrying Max when he called me over the weekend.

9

Besting the Syndicate

Carolyn

Before I went downtown to keep my appointment with Marshall Smead, I again stopped for breakfast at the deli where Max Heydemann was killed. Again, Thelma of the black-rimmed glasses and bouffant hair waited on me. I had thought of a possibility for relieving my husband's mind about industrial espionage, at least as it might relate to Max Heydemann's death. Although Jason hadn't mentioned that piece of deduction, I know my husband well enough to make accurate guesses as to how his mind works, by application of relentless logic to socially unlikely situations.

"Good morning, Thelma," I said and gave her my order for coffee, juice, and a roll, no butter, no cream cheese.

"You sick?" she asked.

"Just mindful of my waistline," I replied. "I made a recent trip to New Orleans."

"Not much theater there," she remarked, apropos of nothing, unless she wanted to remind me that I was now in the theater center

107

of the country and should take advantage of my opportunities. Jason and I planned to. We had tickets to an off-Broadway play, whose premise was, according to the Internet review, "In the beginning God made Adam and Steve." I anticipated that it would be outrageously contrary to the principles of political correctness, and political correctness, which can be admirable, does become wearing at university campuses. A bit of outrageousness had sounded good to both of us.

When Thelma returned with my breakfast, I asked my question: "Did you ever notice Max meeting any Eastern Europeans here?"

She looked surprised. "He never met anyone here that I saw. How come you're asking about Eastern Europeans? That's like Russians?"

"Just idle curiosity," I replied. Then mindful of the company fear about stock plunges, I added, "Actually, one of his closest colleagues and friends was Czech. I was hoping that they got to spend some time together before Max died."

"Not here," said Thelma and strode off to wait on an elderly, bearded patron.

Probably because I arrived on time and he kept me waiting forty-five minutes, I was predisposed to dislike Marshall Smead before I ever met him and even more so at first sight. He looked . . . devilish. V-shaped eyebrows and hairline, which would probably leave him, in a year or two, with a tuft of hair in front, a bald spot around it, and the remaining hair too far back to be noticeable except from the rear. Perhaps that's why he was so rude, because he was anticipating the future temptation to comb that remaining forelock in silly strands across the barren field of his head. And I might add that I did not judge him solely on his looks and inability to keep appointments on time; when I entered his office, he was glaring at me, as if I, not he, had been late.

His first words were, "Is your name really Blue?" While I puzzled over that, he added, "Don't bother to answer. Whatever your name is, you should change it."

I replied that I had no plans to change my name or my marital status, for that matter.

"Let's see your portfolio," he snapped.

"What portfolio?"

"If you don't have a portfolio, why are you here?"

"Because my agent, Loretta Blum, sent me, and she said nothing about a portfolio."

"I thought you'd written food columns for newspapers."

"I have. Three. For the El Paso paper."

"Oh, great! I'm overwhelmed. Three columns for a small-town newspaper."

"The metropolitan area is over two million." I didn't mention that I was including Juarez, Mexico, in what we laughingly call the El Paso Metroplex, a little joke that would undoubtedly go unappreciated among Juarenses.

"And I suppose you forgot to bring your three columns along?"

"I didn't forget. I had no idea I'd need them."

"How do you figure I'm going to judge your work if I can't see any of it?"

"Look, Mr. Smead —"

"Look, Mrs. Blue, you're wasting my time. Call for an appointment when you have something to show me. Better yet, just send me something." Then he got up to open the door for me, his first, and not very convincing, sign of courtesy. After all, he was showing me out. And I was delighted to leave and furiously angry at both Mr. Smead and Loretta, who had gotten me into this embarrassing situation without the least forewarning of what would be expected of me. Just send him something indeed!

"That was short," said his secretary, smiling at me. "I'll walk you out."

Good grief! Were they afraid I'd refuse to leave the building?

"I'm taking an early lunch today."

"Are you?" The sight of her soon-to-be-unused computer sparked a delicious idea. "I'd like to use your computer while you're gone." She looked at me askance. "Mr. Smead asked me to write him a column. If I do it here, I can leave it and save myself the trouble of coming back." Since I never planned to speak to him again.

"Well . . . I guess." She looked dubious and glanced at the closed door to his office.

"Shall I bring him out to give you permission?" I asked generously.

"Oh, no," she replied and left as fast as her high heels could tap-tap out the door.

Teeth gritted, I dropped my coat over her chair and sat down to write. "Advice for a First-Time Visitor to an All-You-Can-Eat Sushi Restaurant." I paused only a second before continuing.

Five minutes into my off-the-cuff column effort, someone came in and asked, "Where's Marshall?"

"In his office, if he hasn't slipped out the back way," I replied, continuing to type.

"Carolyn? What are you doing here?"

I looked up to find Paul Fallon walking toward me. "I'm writing a column for Marshall Smead," I said, continuing to type ferociously.

"No kidding. You should have told me last night you'd be coming here today. I had no idea you did columns as well as books." He was now standing behind me.

"I had no idea you . . . well, do you work here, or are you visiting?"

"I'm the VP." He had been reading over my shoulder and started to laugh. "That's delightful, Carolyn. I'll look forward to seeing the rest." Then he walked into Smead's office without knocking and closed the door. I recovered from my surprise and concentrated on the column, which I was sure Marshall Smead would hate. Had Paul Fallon hired the ultrarude Mr. Smead? I wondered. After changing the title, I was just printing out copies when the two men left Smead's office.

"What are you doing here?" Smead asked sharply.

"You asked for a sample of my work. Here's a column." I placed it in his hand and picked up my coat. Paul Fallon hastened to assist me while Smead looked surprised.

"Take a good look at it, Marshall," said Fallon. "It's great! How about lunch, Carolyn?"

Because Smead seemed so unhappy to discover that his boss was asking me to lunch, I immediately accepted, just to spite him. I had originally planned to return to the hotel for a snack and a nap before the memorial service for Max Heydemann, about which Jason had called from Hodge, Brune before I left the hotel.

"Send that column on to my office, Marshall," Fallon called over his shoulder as we left. "I want to see the rest of it." To me he said, "How would you like to eat at a very popular restaurant behind a butcher shop?"

"Sounds like meat for a column," I replied blithely.

"Was that a pun?" asked Fallon.

Keeping Your Head in a Japanese Restaurant

1. DO NOT visit a Japanese restaurant with a sushi bar if you believe, as my Aunt Beatrice does, that raw fish bits introduce death-dealing parasites into your body.
2. DO NOT attempt to converse in Japanese with your waitress on the basis of having listened to language tapes from the Japanese for Commuters series. She will giggle behind her hand and rush off on her little feet to tell her father that the elephantine, round-eyed barbarian at table three is too stupid to speak properly even the simplest Japanese phrase. Then the whole family may gather by the cash register, staring and giggling.
3. If you are so venturesome as to order *uni,* DO NOT smell before tasting unless your salivary glands are stimulated by swamp gas.
4. DO NOT complain about the miniature size of your sake cup. Remember that the Japanese are a small people who do

113

not tolerate alcohol well. You can always order a second carafe of sake, but chances are you won't need to. At one swallow per cup, it takes a while to finish the first carafe, or whatever they call that little stoneware jug.

5. If you do order two jugs of sake, DO NOT become amorous and pinch your waitress's bottom. She will report any sexual overtures to her grandmother, who will dash out of the kitchen swinging her ancestors' samurai sword and attack you in the name of family honor. Since she is only four foot six, you may be able to fend her off, but you will be charged the dreaded family-honor gratuity on your bill and be banned forever from the restaurant.

6. If you are unable to handle chopsticks with dexterity, by all means pick your sushi up with thumb and forefinger. This method may earn you the disdain of management, but it is preferable to leaving the restaurant with wasabi and soy sauce stains on your clothing. Neither condiment is easy to remove.

7. While eating sushi with your fingers, you will discover that the sticky rice adheres stubbornly to your skin. Use your chopsticks to scrape it off, then ask for a cut lemon to remove the fishy odor. It is not polite to suck the rice off by putting

your fingers in your mouth, and politeness aside, you will be embarrassed to find rice adhering to your chin, where it is harder to remove.

8. DO NOT sample the wasabi (green paste served on a small plate). Any amount introduced into the mouth unaccompanied by soy sauce and food will cause flames to shoot up your sinuses and out your nose. Then other guests will crowd around to stare, assuming that you are the floor show.

9. DO NOT pick the little seeds off your eel. You will insult the chef who has gone to great pains to concoct the eel sauce, and it is only sensible to remember that a sushi chef always has large knives at hand.

10. When eating a hand roll, clutch it firmly in the fist to keep the contents from trickling out the bottom of the cone; then open wide and empty it into your mouth. The seaweed cone is reputed to be edible, but it isn't.

11. By following these simple instructions, your visit to the sushi bar will be a safe and exotic experience. Raw fish is delicious, no matter what your Aunt Beatrice says.

> Carolyn Blue,
> "Have Fork, Will Travel,"
> *Louisville Star Times*

10

"You're Not Hired Yet!"

Jason

When I arrived at Hodge, Brune, having stopped for breakfast, I had already made plans. If I was to find how a little-known Ukrainian company had managed to steal the results of a long research project here in the States and how, if at all, that theft related to Max's death, I needed to know who had information on the project to sell or trade. Such knowledge would rest with the men on the team that had developed the process. The only Hodge, Brune coal chemist I knew was Fergus McRoy, who had said nothing about industrial espionage the afternoon before. If Frances Striff knew what had happened, surely he had. Consequently, I went in search of him, avoiding receptionists, secretaries, and chemists who might have other activities in mind for me.

I found Fergus in a state of extreme anxiety. "Have you heard what happened?" he asked. "No, of course you haven't. I didn't hear until the end of the afternoon. I was supposed to have an appointment

116

with Vasandrovich. I told you that, didn't I?"

"Yes. I expected one myself."

"Right. I'd forgotten. Sit down." He waved toward a chair.

"I guess you mean the Ukrainian thing," I added as I accepted his offer.

"Then you do know? I'm the project leader, and no one told *me*. How'd you —"

"Gossip last night at dinner," I replied.

McRoy dropped his head into his hands. "Five years of work," he moaned. "My biggest project. How the hell could it have happened? You know some bunch of Ukrainians couldn't have come up with it. It was my idea! Mine! And why isn't anyone talking to me about it? There are all these meetings going on, and I'm not invited."

This did not seem like a man who had sold the company out, but I've been fooled by colleagues before. I told myself to reserve judgment. "Well, my advice, Fergus, is that you start thinking about who on your team could have —"

"— given my project to some other company? Ruined my future? Taken the food from my children's mouths?"

"And gotten paid very well for it, I would imagine, so you should think about those who knew enough to turn the research over." I reached across his desk and pushed a legal pad in front of him. "When I've got a problem, I always find it helpful to get it down on paper."

McRoy stared miserably at the sheet and mumbled, "I can't believe any of my people —"

"It could have been someone who had access to the research. Not even a scientist," I suggested.

He shook his head in disbelief, but finally he began to write. Every time he stopped, I made new suggestions, for I had thought quite a bit about the matter while I jogged through the frigid streets near the hotel, zigzagging around other early risers. Scientists, lab assistants, computer programmers, computer repair people, secretaries who might have typed up reports, or conversely people above him in the management chain or colleagues who might have shown a particular interest in the project. On the basis of my suggestions, McRoy managed quite a long list, but he assured me that security was tight. The detestable Merrivale saw to that, although he, Fergus, was beginning to appreciate the man's vigilance.

"Does anyone on this list seem to have more money lately than you'd expect?" I asked.

"I don't know who has money," he said woefully. "I work here. I live at home."

"You must have lunch with colleagues."

"Fiona packs my lunch."

"Don't you socialize after working hours with these people?"

"Not really." He grimaced. "There's the Christmas party of course, but I don't remember anything out of the ordinary."

It occurred to me that had anything out of the ordinary taken place at the party, Fergus McRoy might well have missed it. "Anyone from this list quit just recently?"

He ran a finger down the page. "Waller. He was a lab tech. Went to some gas company in Louisiana. You think he —"

"It's a possibility," I said. "Does he seem like a good source for someone wanting to steal the process?"

"Well, he didn't have the combinations to the safes. And he was rotten on the computer."

"Could have been faking that," I suggested.

"I suppose." He studied the second page of his list. "Angie Mottson. She got pregnant and left."

I frowned. "Many young women these days work until just before delivery. What was her financial situation? Could she afford to leave when she did?"

"Her doctor said she had to quit . . . some kidney problem and high blood pressure. Fiona, that's my wife, insisted that we send flowers. If I bought those flowers for someone who sold me out —"

"You need to talk to these people. Ask them questions."

"What would I ask?" McRoy looked completely bewildered.

"Do you want me to help?" I wasn't sure what I'd ask either, but McRoy looked pitifully grateful for my ill-considered offer. While running and thinking, I had barely gotten to interrogation techniques before my ears went numb and I had to turn back to the hotel.

"Let me make you a copy of the list." Fergus called his secretary to do the job before I could stop him. She was, after all, on the list. If she were the culprit, she'd be forewarned that he was conducting an investigation himself, one in which I was involved. However, she didn't seem to be at all alarmed when she returned with the photocopies. In fact, she was gossiping with another woman who followed her in.

Fergus took the copies and passed one to me while the second woman was saying, "Dr. Blue? My, I've had a time chasing you down. You were supposed to be talking to . . ." She looked at what was evidently my schedule, although I didn't have a copy. "Well, no matter. Dr. Vasandrovich would appreciate your coming to his office."

"What about me?" asked McRoy eagerly.

"He didn't mention you, Dr. McRoy," she replied and held the door for me. Evidently, it was to be a command performance. McRoy gave me a conspiratorial look, as if to say he would begin talking to suspects immediately.

Mindful that Vaclav Vasandrovich was on the list of people who had access to information on the coal project, I thought about things I might ask him, tactfully, during our meeting. There was, however, little time for idle, if intrusive, chitchat. He apologized for not having seen me earlier. I said that I understood, considering the bad news the company had had from the Ukraine. He frowned at me, seemingly surprised that I knew. I asked if he, with his Eastern European connections, had any idea who might have passed the information on. He replied that I needn't worry about the problem, that the company would survive, and an investigation into possible espionage was already under way, headed by their security officer, Dr. Merrivale.

Then he changed the subject by informing me that a group of senior scientists would be gathering for lunch in the boardroom with Vice President Charles Mason Moore before the memorial service for Max. If I'm not mistaken, his eyes glistened with tears when he mentioned Max. I found myself moved as well. A memorial service may bring closure to some mourners, but there is a finality that makes us face, once and for all, the fact that the one memorialized is incontrovertibly dead.

"The body has been released by the police?" I asked.

"Not that I know of. The burial will be later," said Vasandrovich gruffly. "God knows why they have to keep him so long. The trauma to family and friends is terrible. We at the company organized this service in the hope that it would bring some comfort to all. But as I was saying, we would like you to attend the luncheon and, of course, the memorial, if you wish to."

"Yes," I agreed. "As intermittent as our acquaintance was, I was an admirer and, I hope, a friend."

"Those who wish to say a few words will be invited to do so. You are welcome to join in. Max spoke very highly of you."

"That's gratifying," I murmured. What a strange man Vasandrovich was, on the one hand rather cool and formal, on the other sorrowful to the point of tears over the death of his superior.

"Then, if you feel you can do it on such short notice, I was hoping you could give your seminar after the service. I'm sorry that it had to be postponed, although I'm sure you understand."

"Under the circumstances, of course."

"Then can we count on you for the lunch and the seminar? Possibly the interest of your research will serve to take the minds of our scientists off this tragic event."

"Certainly," I answered. "My papers and slides are in my briefcase. I'll be glad to oblige, and to attend the luncheon as well. Max spoke several times of Dr. Moore. I look forward to meeting him."

Vasandrovich said, "Don't expect too much. He has a lot on his mind."

With that, I was dismissed and hastened away to begin making casual visits to people on McRoy's list. I learned that the gone-south lab tech had saddled himself with a demanding Southern belle who swore to divorce him if he didn't immediately move to warmer climes. Would my wife tire of warmer climes and demand that we move back north? Carolyn is not a complainer, but I know she's finding the climate of El Paso burdensome. She has to spend an inordinate amount of time rubbing lotion into her skin to keep from peeling, and in New Orleans last month, she absolutely basked in the rain.

The pregnant secretary, according to McRoy's secretary, had been given maternity leave, although not yet delivered of her child, and was lounging at home in bed with a visiting nurse and company medical insurance to cover her vacation. "Some people have all the luck!" the young lady exclaimed. I wouldn't have considered high blood pressure and possible kidney failure "all the luck," but perhaps this young, unmarried woman had never heard of preeclampsia. When Carolyn was carrying our son Chris, she had been warned of the possibility. However, the urine tests had been switched with someone else's, and the high blood pressure had been temporary.

A computer person, eager to talk, as such people often are, told me, over his special blend of African coffees, that research data on computer hard drives was locked in safes nightly. Only the big shots had access, which was a "pain in the ass" because the disks had to be reinstalled each morning, sometimes causing crashes, data loss, and bouts of painfully itchy hives for him personally because of the stress.

At that point in my investigation, Vernon Merrivale swooped down on me and hustled me off to his office, which was furnished with agonizingly uncomfortable furniture, except for his own cushy leather chair. The room also had no windows, cameras in all corners scanning back and forth, and locks on everything. He had to press a fingerprint pad before he could get into his own office.

"Your wife was seen talking to a police detective yesterday in Vasandrovich's outer office," he said accusingly.

I must admit that his tone immediately irritated me. "So what?" I snapped. "I talked to one myself."

"About what?" Merrivale demanded.

"Max's death, of course. He asked me questions because I happened to be there. That was probably the case with my wife, as well." *Or not,* I thought, but kept that possibility to myself. I could imagine my wife running into the detective, discovering that he was investigating the murder, and quizzing him rather than the other way around.

"Since you and your wife are here at the invitation of the company, we would appreciate your not talking to the police."

"Why?" I asked. "When the police ask questions in the course of an investigation, good citizens try to be helpful — or ask for a lawyer," I added dryly. "I hardly think Carolyn or I would need a lawyer since we were aboard an American Airlines flight in midair at the time Max was killed. On the other —"

"Exactly. Therefore, you have no information to offer the police," said Merrivale triumphantly. "So don't volunteer information on matters you know nothing about, and tell your wife to stay out of it, as well."

Why was Merrivale trying to impede the investigation? I wondered. I had no time to pursue this question because he continued by saying sternly, "Why are you asking people about the coal project?"

"Because the research has evidently been stolen," I replied.

"I don't see that that's any of your business."

"Then you'd be wrong. Max called me last weekend to say he had a problem he couldn't discuss on the telephone but on which he hoped to recruit my help."

"Did he mention the coal project specifically?"

"No."

"Then what makes you think his concerns had anything to do with the Ukrainians?"

"That's the only problem I've run across except his untimely death. Surely, you've had the thought yourself that they might be connected."

"In what way?"

"If I knew that, I wouldn't have to ask questions." I thought a minute. "Well, actually I would. Even if Max's death *was* unrelated, he did want my help on something. If this was it, I want to give that help. I thought very highly of him."

"Coal isn't your field."

"No, it isn't, but he mentioned my connections."

"You have connections in the Ukraine?"

"Not there specifically, but in other areas of Eastern Europe."

"But they'd be academic?"

"Mostly."

"Not likely to be of much use," said Merrivale. "My information is that you've talked to several people connected with the coal project."

"Yes, I chatted with various people this morning."

"Amateurs in the field of industrial security, bumbling around, asking questions, can only impede the professional investigation."

"Has it occurred to you that Max might have had suspicions about who was responsible for the leaks or sale of information and was killed to keep him from revealing the person he suspected?"

"I assure you, Dr. Blue, I do not need your assistance to formulate rational hypotheses about this case, and I must ask you to keep away from the investigation. It is not your concern."

"I beg your pardon, Merrivale, but as Max wanted to bring me in as a consultant, I feel honor bound to —"

"You haven't been hired *yet*, Dr. Blue. Keep that in mind." Vernon Merrivale eyed me coldly over a high-bridged nose and stood up, indicating that the interview was at an end.

I have to admit that I was happy to leave, not that I was intimidated by Merrivale, but I resented having to sit in an uncomfortable chair that was unusually low to the floor. Had he ordered the legs shortened in order to look down on visitors to his office? I wouldn't be at all surprised.

And what was *he* up to? As the man in charge of security at Hodge, Brune, he should welcome anything the police could discover and encourage cooperation with them. Instead, he almost seemed to be engaged in a cover-up. Why?

11

Salade Niçoise in
a Butcher Shop

Ah, those French! They invented haute cuisine. They invented the bistro. They even gave us the word *restaurant*. In the eighteenth century, *restoratives* or *restaurants* were soups sold in Paris by Monsieur Boulanger. Within several years, the word having become popular, another culinary entrepreneur, Monsieur Beauvillier, was selling not just soup but a menu of popular dishes to visitors who knew better than to eat at a Paris inn.

And the French at home and abroad continued to be the purveyors of good food. In New York during World War II, when meat was rationed and hard to come by, wonderful beef could still be eaten at Au Cheval Pie by those hardy enough to brave the screaming arguments, smashing bottles, and physical assaults the owners launched at one another. But where did the volatile French restaurateurs, Marcel and Louise, get their meat?

One night, a mysteriously muffled figure

actually stalked through the dining room with a live sheep in his arms. Perhaps there were farmers of French descent throughout the Northeast willing to make special trips into the city in order to up-hold the honor of French cuisine in hard times. Or perhaps the owners of Au Cheval Pie had a network of lamb and cattle rustlers.

Carolyn Blue,
"Have Fork, Will Travel,"
Salt Lake City Post-Telegraph

Carolyn

Paul Fallon took me to a place called Les Halles, so named for the market in Paris, which was torn down by the city fathers to make room for the Pompedieux (that amazing museum that looks like a chemical factory. I remember thinking, when I first saw it, that the museum, with its exterior pipes painted in bold primary colors, must have been de-signed by Joan Miró; it wasn't.) Les Halles is now just a subway stop in Paris but also a bistro on Park Avenue between Twenty-eighth and Twenty-ninth Streets in New York, a reasonable walk from the building that housed the syndicate. However, we took a cab. Perhaps Paul hadn't noticed that I was

130

wearing flats. Men tend to think that women wear heels unless they're home barefoot and pregnant in the kitchen.

And it was, indeed, a butcher shop with glass cases full of meat and crowds through which we wove our way to the dining room in back. The dining area was even more crowded and roaring with conversation, bustling waiters, and clattering crockery. Paul had a reservation at a tiny table. Every other seat was filled. I wouldn't have been surprised to see people sitting on one another's laps.

When I looked at the menu and ordered salade niçoise, Paul said, "You can't order a salad. This is a meat place. Have the cassoulet or the steak with *pommes frites*. Or they serve a wonderful sausage here with garlic enough to ward off a vampire. Do you read Anne Rice?"

"No," I replied, "and I'm in the mood for salade niçoise. Because of those tiny green beans. I can't get them at home. Besides I have to attend a memorial service. I can't go reeking of garlic."

"Well, I can," said Paul, and he ordered the sausages. "We'll share a cab. Maybe my breath will take Charlotte's mind off her grief."

I had to laugh. "Are you sure she's grief-stricken?" I asked. "Has anyone found out yet who killed Max?"

He looked surprised. "Well, I doubt that Charlotte did it."

"You've never heard rumors that she has a lover?"

"Have you?" When I nodded, he looked surprised. "I can't imagine who said that. Care to confide?"

"I had lunch and visited a museum with Sophia Vasandrovich."

"And she said Charlotte had a lover? No way."

Our lunches were served at that moment, and Paul attacked his meal with gusto. I could smell the garlic across the table and see the glistening fat as he cut into his first sausage. In truth, it looked delicious. Perfect for an icy day with a stiff wind blowing through the crowded streets. Why had I chosen a cold plate? But then I looked down at my salad and those lovely little green beans, perfectly cooked. I moved the anchovies to the side and began to savor ripe, peeled tomatoes, sweet and moist (where did they get them this time of year?); meaty black olives; raw, thinly sliced onions; hard-boiled eggs with no green ring inside the whites (I have problems doing hard-boiled eggs, and what an embarrassing thing that is for a woman who was once reputed to be a gourmet cook); and last, flaked tuna, oily and flavorful, not the wimpy kind packed in water. *Oh Carolyn, what about your waistline?*

my conscience asked.

Paul was grinning at me. "You're really enjoying it, aren't you? Does that mean you don't want to sample my sausage?"

"Of course I want to sample your sausage, but I don't know you well enough to ask." He cut off a piece and deposited it on my plate. "Um-m-m," I murmured appreciatively.

"Sorry for not taking my advice?"

"Not a bit," I replied, popping a black olive into my mouth and following it with a deliciously red wedge of tomato. "Do you want to sample my tomato?"

He laughed and shook his head. "I'm more into red meat than red vegetables. Anyway, we were talking about the big question: Who killed Max? Believe me, I'd pick Sophia over Charlotte any day."

"Why Sophia?" I asked.

"Don't tell me she wasn't dripping furs and jewels. She probably had him killed so Vaclav could take his job at Hodge, Brune and rake in the big bucks." He took a long draught of beer while I sipped my white wine. "Or maybe Calvin Pharr did it after Max warned him about his drinking."

"You mean this Pharr person got drunk and killed his superior?"

"Nah. Hired it done. If Calvin had showed up at the deli, Max would have recognized him, or at least someone would have remembered him. He's really bald and really fat, so

133

you could hardly miss him. In fact, he'd have a hard time getting into the aisles between the tables."

"Max was seated at the end on a cross aisle," I replied.

"How do you know that, pretty lady?"

I didn't much like being called "pretty lady." To me it seemed either condescending or flirtatious. "Because I had breakfast at the deli in question and talked to one of the waitresses," I replied.

"What are you, an amateur detective?"

"Of course not," I replied uneasily, knowing that Max's death wasn't really any of my business.

He grinned at me. "It's that writer's curiosity. You've all got it."

"Even food writers?" I asked dryly.

"OK, so we've got Sophia and Calvin. Who else had a motive? Well, his children and his first wife. *She* hated him."

"Really?" That was interesting.

"But she's probably locked up at the very fancy country-club-type sanatorium her parents spring for every time she goes off the deep end. Still, that leaves the kids: Junior, better known as Rick, who keeps running up debts at Dartmouth, and his charming sibling, Fluffy, who doesn't even bother to go to school."

"Max had a daughter named Fluffy?" I asked, astounded. "If he thought of that name, she did have a motive for murder."

"Actually, I think Fluffy was the name of Charlotte's cat. Junior wrung its neck when Max refused to pay any more gambling debts. The daughter's name is — what?" Paul Fallon popped a French fry into his mouth as he tried to remember. "Ariadne. She hated it. I've forgotten what she calls herself now, but she's expensive to maintain and has the morals of an alley cat. They say she's already had two abortions, and Max refused to pay for the second. Then Charlotte stepped in and wrote the check. Probably thought she'd get stuck with a cocaine baby while sweet Ariadne went on screwing her way through the smart set. She even had a shot at me during one of the gala company Christmas parties, but Frances rescued me before Miss Heydemann could get her itchy little fingers on my zipper. Are you horrified?"

"Fascinated," I replied. "Who'd have guessed at all this scandal?" *And widely known at that!* "So why did they kill their father?"

"Money. Maybe they heard he was going to change his will, so they had him assassinated. Or Rick went into the restaurant in drag and did it himself."

As I whisked a piece of tuna through the lovely vinaigrette and savored the morsel, I shook my head in amazement at the breadth of his imagination.

"You don't buy that scenario? Well, maybe

135

Max was mad at Charlotte for crossing him on the abortion and threatened to disinherit her, so she hired a hit man before Max could get to his lawyer."

"You should be a novelist instead of a vice president."

"That one sounds more likely to you?"

"Not really."

"OK, so he was killed by the thieving Lithuanians."

"Ukrainians? Now that would really make a good plot."

"I give up. Maybe Blind Harold did it." He called to the waiter and ordered cheesecake, without even asking me. "New York is the birthplace of cheesecake," he told me.

"Nonsense. Cheesecake was being baked in Europe in the fifteenth century. Now, who's Blind Harold?" Since Fallon was paying, I didn't protest being cheated out of the delights of picking my own dessert. Probably the cheesecake would be good. New York might not be the originator, but its renditions are famous.

"Blind Harold was this old guy Max gave five dollars to every Monday before he went into the deli. Maybe he forgot to come up with the money, so Blind Harold followed him in and killed him. Was Max missing five dollars when his body was found?"

"I don't know, but if Harold is blind, how could he find Max in a crowded restaurant, much less drive the — whatever it was — into the right place?"

"Maybe he's not really blind. Just because his eyes are weird and white when he takes off his dark glasses doesn't mean he hasn't been faking it all these years."

I had to laugh, but when I did, Paul Fallon beamed at me and took my hand. "You have one nice laugh, Carolyn," he said.

I snatched my hand away without even being subtle about it. Within the last month or so, I'd had one man get the wrong idea about my availability, and I really didn't want to find myself in that position again.

"Whoa!" said Fallon, looking surprised. "I'm not coming on to you. I'm just a guy who touches people. Bad fault, hmm?" He waved to the waiter and paid the bill. "If you go to work for us, promise you won't charge me with sexual harassment."

I was thoroughly embarrassed and once again felt like the country cousin in the big city.

"Well, let's get to that memorial service. That is, if you're not afraid to share a taxi with me."

"No problem," I retorted. "You can sit in front with the driver."

"I am properly chastened." He helped me into my coat and then led the way through the throngs of customers still waiting for seats in the packed restaurant.

12

In Memoriam

Jason

Luncheon in the board dining room was excellent, but then I love raw oysters, and six were served to those who wanted them. I met more chemists and listened to talk about the subject on everyone's mind, the fact that some little-known, Eastern European company had beaten Hodge, Brune to the patent on a very lucrative antipollution process. It was obvious that Vernon Merrivale, the security chief, was trying to keep people from talking about the subject in front of me and to me. Also, I finally met Charles Moore, the vice president. Although I did not sit by him at the table, I found him to be a very serious man, little given to smiling or idle conversation. He addressed a few comments and questions my way and remarked that the company was very pleased that I had been able to spend the week here. Then he fell into discussion with Vasandrovich, and I turned my attention elsewhere, although not without thinking Moore's enthusiasm for my visit rather lukewarm.

After the meal he stopped me at the door and asked that I come to his office for a conference following my seminar. As I rode to the memorial service with several other chemists, I considered the probability that Moore's message that afternoon would be Hodge, Brune's inability to offer me a contract at this time. So be it. My connection had been Max, who was now gone. Since I dislike teaching the summer session, I'd have to scare up some grant money.

The memorial service was held at a midtown club, very well appointed and sedate. Had Max been a member here? It didn't seem to fit his Brooklyn background, and I wondered idly whether he had been religious. That was not a topic that had ever come up between us. Much as I had liked and admired the man, I really knew very little about him personally or what in his life could have led to his untimely death, unless it was connected to the theft of proprietary information from the company.

I got a surprise when Carolyn came in, cheeks red with cold, in the company of Paul Fallon. She explained that, New York being such a small world, Fallon had proved to be the vice president of the syndicate where she had had an appointment that morning. I replied that I'd heard connections were all in the publishing world. Carolyn murmured back, "What good's one friendly connection when the man who interviewed you is a rude, snide, obnoxious —"

"I hope you're not talking about Marshall," Fallon interrupted; he had been waving Frances Striff over to join us.

Carolyn flushed, but Frances remarked that she couldn't stand Smead herself. "The man thinks all women are incompetent and doesn't even have the good manners to keep his attitude to himself."

When my wife gave Frances her own special glowing smile of approval and sisterhood, Fallon groaned. "I hope that doesn't mean you've crossed us off before I even get to read the rest of your column," he said to Carolyn.

"Not at all," she replied. "I intend to send Mr. Smead several examples of my work, all written in whatever spare time I have while I'm here. No doubt, you'll be able to find them in his wastebasket if you want to see them, Paul."

Then we were called to our seats by the appearance on the podium of a man I had not met. Whether or not Max was religious, this man evidently was, for he spoke of Max's great soul and the hope that he would find as much happiness in the life hereafter as he had in his work and in his personal life. At that moment, the speaker smiled at a woman in the front row. She wore a wide-brimmed hat with a veil, but I could see the gleam of her chignon through the veil and knew it was Max's wife, Charlotte. Her thin body, entirely clothed in black, almost disappeared from sight in the cloak of her widowhood. I glanced at Carolyn, sitting quietly beside me, and hoped that I would have a long life with her before death separated us.

Many members of the audience rose to speak of Max, as I myself did, saying that I wished there had been more time to know him better because he had been a person to be admired. Some mentioned the brilliance and innovativeness of his mind, others the great influence of his guidance on their research. Vasandrovich had tears in his eyes as he spoke of how Max had changed his life by bringing him to this country and how much Max's friendship and support had meant. I noted that Vasandrovich's wife sat stiff and expressionless through her husband's remarks and wondered whether she would have preferred to stay in Czechoslovakia. Carolyn had said she was of royal Bohemian blood, so she may have felt that she left her identity behind when she came here.

It was an interesting service, over and above the grief that shrouded the room, and I listened to and watched carefully each speaker in turn, looking for clues to the mystery of his death, I suppose, and to what had been bothering him that last weekend when he called me. There were shocking things said, as well, for his children were there, his son, Rick, and daughter, Ariadne. Max had never mentioned them to me, and I began to see why, for they spoke of their father with barely concealed enmity. What a source of sadness and disappointment they must have been to him, for I did not see Max as a man who would have been indifferent to his children.

The son was slender and condescending in a black suit that evidently cost ten times anything I own; I wouldn't have realized that, but Carolyn poked me and whispered that she saw London tailoring there. How do women know such things? This Rick stood up and said that although his father had not been an understanding man or a generous one, he hoped that Max would make it up to him and to his sister Ariadne in death. The girl said that Max had been beastly to her mother, deserting her when she needed him most. At this, she looked directly at Charlotte Heydemann as if she blamed her for the divorce. Still she, Ariadne, had loved him, she claimed — he was her father, after all — and she hoped he realized in the end that he owed something to a daughter who had had little from him but criticism and unkindness. Then she sat down, her face mirroring satisfaction, her body fashionably clothed but thin to the point of boniness.

Carolyn murmured, "Anorexia." I found

myself wondering whether the young woman's unpleasant personality was formed by a pathological fear of food and whether she thought she looked beautiful in her skeletal way. Appalled, I flashed to my own daughter, wishing I could call and ask what she'd had for lunch, just to be sure Gwen hadn't begun to waste away since Christmas break.

When the service was over, we joined the receiving line to offer sympathy to the family. Carolyn murmured, "Someone ought to look into those two children. They probably killed him for his money." Then she sailed right by said children in the line with me in tow, only able to mumble a few words as we passed, and up to the widow. Charlotte had lifted her veil and, at the sight of the barely controlled anguish on her face, Carolyn put her arms around Charlotte, whom she'd never met, and said, "You don't know me. I'm Carolyn Blue."

"Of course, Jason's wife. I'm pleased to meet you," Charlotte murmured.

"I'm so sorry for your loss, Mrs. Heydemann," Carolyn continued. "My husband thought the world of yours, and if there is anything I can do for you while I'm in New York, please let me know."

Women never cease to amaze me. I don't think I could hug a stranger in public no matter how much sympathy I felt for her.

Charlotte Heydemann bit her lip and muttered something about the kindness of strangers, and Carolyn replied, "I'm sure you have as many friends here as your husband. You need to cling to them now."

Charlotte shook her head sadly. "Haven't you heard? Widows become outcasts. We're no longer burned on the pyre, but we are excluded from the lunch-in-town and the day-shopping circuit."

"Then have lunch with me," said Carolyn. I could see that she was speaking on impulse; we didn't have that much time left in New York. She evidently realized that herself because she said, obviously regretful at the thought, "Well, I have tomorrow, but I don't suppose, with all you have to see to . . ."

Charlotte lifted her chin. "Tomorrow would be lovely, Mrs. Blue. The coroner —" Charlotte seemed to choke on the words. "They're keeping Max's body."

"I'm so sorry. That's terrible."

Charlotte nodded. "I hate it, and the will won't be read until Friday, so if you really have tomorrow free —"

My wife's face lit with a smile. "I'll look forward to it. Where shall we meet?"

"Well . . ." Charlotte thought a minute and said, "Sfuzzi. We can eat light, but still, Italian is always comfort food." She smiled at me. "She's every bit as lovely as you said, Jason."

"Did he say nice things about me?" Carolyn asked, giving me an affectionate look.

"Indeed, he did. We could go to the Guggenheim afterward if you have the time. There's a *Picasso in the War Years* exhibit that's supposed to be delightful."

Carolyn looked doubtful. "I just saw *Picasso in Clay*."

"Oh well, that's just one of his pranks. You'll love the hats on the women in the Guggenheim show. A friend in our . . ." She swallowed hard. ". . . in my building loved it."

"Good. That's what we'll do," said Carolyn decisively. Then she glanced back. "We're holding up the line. Is twelve-thirty all right?"

"Perfect," said Charlotte. "Jason, Max and I were so looking forward to taking you and your wife to the opera Monday night. I hope you got to go. I heard the Ryans were tapped since Patsy was the only company wife who claimed to like opera."

I smiled. "I don't think Sean did. Charlotte, I can't tell you how . . . how very —"

"I know," she said, patting my arm, and it was as if we'd said it all about the loss of Max. "Thank you for coming today. Max was so determined to bring you into the company. I hope it will work out."

"We'll see," I replied, thinking but not

saying that I doubted it would.

Once we were free of the line, Carolyn leaned to whisper in my ear, "Who's that strange man?" She darted her eyes expressively. "He keeps lurking about eavesdropping on people's conversations."

I followed her glance and spotted Merrivale, who was indeed standing close to Fergus McRoy and listening to his conversation with Francis Striff and Paul Fallon while trying to look as if he hadn't even noticed them. However, Striff noticed him, took Fallon's arm, and walked away, after slanting Merrivale a poisonous look.

"Goodness, what was that about?" Carolyn asked. "I thought Frances was going to kick him in the ankle, and that redheaded fellow talking to her caught sight of him and blanched."

"The eavesdropper is Vernon Merrivale," I murmured, "head of security. He's running the investigation into the industrial espionage."

"Really?" said my wife. "Well, the way people react to him, you'd think they're all guilty, and I seriously doubt that Frances is. She's the one who told us about the problem in the first place."

"Yes, and Merrivale wants us to keep our mouths shut about it, especially where the police are concerned."

"Wants who to keep their mouths shut?" she asked.

146

"You and me."

Carolyn turned astonished eyes on me. "Of all the nerve. I can talk to anyone I want. Who is he to . . . well, did he mention me specifically?"

"He said you'd been talking to one of the police detectives."

"I was sharing a sofa with the man. What was I supposed to do? Ignore him?"

I sighed, checked my watch, and told Carolyn that I needed to get back to Hodge, Brune because my seminar was scheduled in less than an hour.

"Goodness, can't they even wait until the man's buried before returning to business as usual?"

I was surprised at the sharpness of her tone. "Are you saying you think I should refuse to give the seminar?"

"No, of course not, Jason. I guess I'm still peeved at those two . . . two . . . Did you see the look the daughter sent Charlotte? They must have been a trial to her."

"Stepchildren often are," I replied in a low voice. "Can you get back to the hotel on your own?"

"Of course," she replied. "I'll just catch a bus or a subway. I'm getting quite good at it. Do you think it was all right to ask Charlotte to lunch?"

My wife looked doubtful, so I said quickly, "I think it was a very kind thing to do. Probably just what she needed."

"But still, I didn't get Mr. Merrivale's permission," she added snidely. "Maybe you should ask him what I can talk to her about."

I chuckled and replied, "I'll definitely ask him and get back to you."

Grinning, she brushed her lips across my cheek. "You do that. Are we going to be on our own tonight?"

"As far as I know."

"Good. I'll choose the perfect restaurant for a romantic dinner." She gave me a smile that still, after all these years, stirs my blood and then headed for the front door. Before she reached it, she stopped to talk to the detective I'd met my first day at Hodge, Brune, possibly the same one Merrivale had been complaining about. Ah, Carolyn. I could only hope her remarks would be tempered by discretion rather than prompted by pique.

Vasandrovich paused beside me and said there was a limo waiting for us behind the building. The last thing I saw as I turned to follow him was the sad face of Charlotte Heydemann as she left the hall talking to Calvin Pharr, who looked quite sober and almost as unhappy as she. Still, I wondered how much cognac he had consumed that morning in preparation for the services. I did know his wineglass was refilled a number of times in the company dining room.

13

A Ride-Along

Carolyn

I must admit that I was surprised to find the police in attendance. "Hello, Detective Worski. Did you know Dr. Heydemann personally?" I asked when I spotted the detective I'd met in Vaclav Vasandrovich's office. Worski was still wearing that peculiar green overcoat and was now accompanied by a tall black man who was better dressed.

"Never miss the memorial service of a murder victim," Worski replied. "Surprisin' what you pick up when people start talkin' about the deceased."

"Really? Has anyone ever confessed at one?" I asked.

"Not that I've heard," said Worski. "You know of any, Ali?"

The black man said, "Why ask me? I've spent more time in white-collar crime than homicide, so I don't attend a lot of memorial services looking for evidence."

We were out on the street by then, and I asked where I might find the nearest subway entrance, a question that earned me the offer of a ride to the hotel in their unmarked police car. Was the arrogant, security-conscious Mr. Merrivale watching me? I wondered. Was he fuming because I chose to defy him by talking to the police? Too bad. I also chose to accept the ride and was soon sitting in the backseat.

"Well, Mrs. Blue," said Detective Worski, "you still like the wife for the murder? I saw you talkin' to her."

"Oh, absolutely not," I replied. "She's very nice and much too miserable about her husband's death to have killed him. But those children. If they didn't kill him, they probably wanted to. Did you hear them?"

"Oh yeah," said Worski. "Glad they're not my kids. Still, when there's money involved, it's usually the wife. She gets the biggest cut. You think he's leavin' a lot?"

"I have no idea, but I'm having lunch with her tomorrow, and she mentioned that the will's to be read Friday. If you have a formal will reading, that probably means there's a substantial estate. Wouldn't you think?"

"Well, if you're havin' lunch with her, keep your ears open, Mrs. Blue."

I couldn't really tell whether the detective was humoring me in a jocular way or seriously asking for my help.

"Here's my card." He slid a wide-palmed, short-fingered hand inside that green overcoat and plucked out a business card, which he handed me, even as he negotiated a rather terrifying traffic maneuver between two taxicabs, both of which honked angrily. "You give me a call if you hear anything," he added.

I took the card and slipped it into my handbag. "Actually, I had lunch with someone who knows all the gossip: Paul Fallon. Maybe you should talk to him."

"What did he think? He got any ideas about who might have done it?"

"Well, he doesn't think Charlotte Heydemann did, but he mentioned the children. They've evidently been every bit as greedy and unpleasant to their father as they seemed today and weren't on the best of terms with him, mostly over money. Also they resent the breakup with his first wife, their mother."

"How about her?"

"He said she's probably in a mental institution. Evidently, she spends quite a bit of time there."

"Interestin'. I'll have to look into that. Anyone else?"

"Oh, he mentioned the Vasandroviches, because Dr. Vasandrovich has stepped into Max's job and they might need the money, but I think he was joking about that."

"Vasandrovich. That's one of a lot guys at that company I didn't like."

"What did you think of a man named . . . what was it? . . . Calvin. Calvin Pharr, I think. He evidently has a drinking problem that Max warned him about, although that doesn't seem a good reason for murdering someone." I had shifted to the middle of the backseat, the better to carry on the conversation. "And I suppose there's the espionage angle, although really — killed by Ukrainian spies? That's a bit far out."

"I'd like to hear about that," said the black man, speaking for the first time.

"I don't believe we've been introduced," I murmured. He'd been so quiet, I'd almost forgotten he was there.

"Sorry. My partner, Mohammed Ali," said Worski. "Great name, huh?"

"Really," I agreed. "Detective Ali, are you by any chance —"

"— related to the boxer?" he finished for me. "No, ma'am."

"Well, actually I was thinking of an Egyptian ruler . . . sometime in the last hundred years, I think. The one who invited forty of his enemies to dinner and poisoned them all."

Detective Ali turned around and stared at me. "Do I look like an Egyptian?" he asked.

Indeed, he was very dark. "Well, Aida, the opera heroine, was supposed to be dark-skinned," I said, feeling a bit foolish.

"Wasn't she Ethiopian?"

"What the hell are you two talkin' about?" Worski demanded. "It don't sound like it's

152

got anything to do with our case. Why don't you tell him about this espionage, Mrs. Blue? It's the first sign of interest he's shown since we partnered up."

Embarrassed at my faux pas, I was a little more forthcoming about what I'd heard from Frances Striff at dinner last night than I might have been otherwise. "But I doubt that would be connected to his murder, do you think?" I finished lamely.

In reply Detective Ali gave me his card and suggested that I call him if I heard any more about the Ukrainian connection. "Nobody's talking to us about anything connected to company business over there." Then he murmured something to Worski about the Russian Mob. Worski snorted.

I wished I'd held my tongue. With Hodge, Brune being so secretive about the theft of their research and their security person making threats, I had undoubtedly done my husband a disservice by mentioning it. Should I call Jason and tell him what I'd done? Well, no, I couldn't do that. He was giving a seminar. Maybe tonight when we had the evening to ourselves for a change.

14

Tea with the VP

Jason

My seminar was well received, even attended by Charles Moore himself, who congratulated me afterward on a very interesting piece of research and reminded me of our meeting at 4:30. As he left the seminar room, Vasandrovich approached me and said, "I hope that you and your wife can join Sophia and me this evening. My wife so enjoyed meeting yours. Mrs. Blue evidently has what, in an American, is a surprising interest in and knowledge of Czech history."

"Carolyn mentioned a discussion they had about medieval history." But I doubted that she'd relish the prospect of being entertained this evening by the Vasandroviches. "Actually, we —"

"Ah, please don't tell me that you have made other plans, Dr. Blue. I feel quite remiss in not having entertained you before now."

I wondered, perhaps unfairly, whether his sudden interest didn't stem from the vice president's compliment on my seminar and

154

reminder of our scheduled meeting.

"Sophia has managed to procure four tickets to the opera. *Il Trovatore*. She tells me we can expect an excellent cast. Of course, we'll have dinner somewhere close by. I hope the restaurant will please your wife who, I believe, is a culinary writer."

"I'm sure she'll be delighted." At least with the opera. Carolyn loves *Il Trovatore*. She is particularly fond of the aria "Il Balen," sung by the Count de Luna, and, for that reason, holds the peculiar opinion that the villain, rather than the hero, Manrico, should win Leonora. Not that it matters. Whoever wins the lady will die with her in the last act, as is expected in grand opera. Vasandrovich expressed his pleasure at my acceptance and went off just before a tall black man, who introduced himself as Mohammed Ali, accosted me. *Mohammed Ali?* Had some poor lunatic managed to get into the building? I wondered. He looked respectable enough.

"No," he said, "I'm not related to the Egyptian who poisoned forty enemies."

"Actually, I was thinking of the boxer," I replied. "What poison did the Egyptian use?" Toxins always catch my interest, even when mentioned in such unusual circumstances.

"I don't know. Ask your wife. She thought I might be related to some Middle Eastern murderer."

I had to laugh. Trust Carolyn to introduce

155

an arcane piece of history into a conversation. "Where did you meet my wife?" I asked.

"Detective Worski and I gave her a ride back to her hotel. Now what's this business about industrial espionage, and why would a bunch of Ukrainians want to steal research about coal?"

Obviously, my wife had not bowed to Merrivale's demand that she keep her mouth shut about company business, and in response to such a specific question, I could hardly remain silent either. "It's a process for stopping pollution from coal-fired power plants," I replied. "Because of global warming and the spread of environmental laws, such technology would be extremely valuable."

"Excuse me, but I'll have to put a stop to this conversation. It involves proprietary information," said Vernon Merrivale, who had spotted us talking from down the hall.

Caught in the act, I thought.

"He doesn't work for Hodge, Brune," said the detective, "so —"

"But he has an appointment to keep," said Merrivale and gave me a hard look. I glanced at my watch and saw that I was, indeed, due in Charles Moore's office.

"I'm afraid that's true," I said to the detective.

"Another time then," he replied. "We are

conducting a murder investigation here." He stared at Merrivale. "And we expect cooperation. Or is Hodge, Brune trying to cover up something about Heydemann's death?"

I left Merrivale to answer that question, about which I was beginning to wonder myself, and went to my appointment. Charles Moore, ensconced in a large corner office with a breathtaking view of the city, offered me a cup of English tea, which I accepted reluctantly. I am not an enthusiastic tea drinker, even when assured that this blend was one of the best he had found in his lifelong search for fine tea. We had a brief discussion on recent medical research that revealed the protective properties of tea and then got down to the topic that evidently brought me to his office. Moore wanted to assure me that, despite the disarray in which the company found itself, there was still interest in employing me as a consultant. "Max thought very highly of you, Dr. Blue," said Moore.

"And I of him," I replied. "His death came as a great shock, but perhaps not so much after I considered the telephone call he made to me over the weekend."

Moore's glance sharpened. "I'd appreciate hearing about that."

"He said that he was worried about some problem the company faced and was hoping for my input."

"He told you what the problem was?"

"No, he didn't feel free to discuss it on the telephone. Strange, don't you think?"

"Perhaps not," said Moore. "What input did he want from you? Did he say?"

"Only that he hoped to avail himself of my expertise and academic connections. I'm surprised Merrivale hasn't told you about this."

"What connections?" Moore asked, taking no notice of my mention of his security chief. "Was Max specific?"

"No, but in the light of the Ukrainian debacle, I assume he meant connections in Eastern Europe."

"Which you have?"

"Yes, but I certainly don't have any particular expertise in coal research, so I may be wrong in my assumptions."

"No, I think that you're right. What I'm about to say to you, Dr. Blue, must be in confidence. Are we agreed?" Intrigued, I nodded. "Max feared just what has happened, the theft of our research, and he expected to nail down over the weekend who was responsible. We were to meet Monday morning, but he postponed until that afternoon, and then . . ." Moore sighed. "And then he was killed."

"Good lord!" I thought over what I'd been told. "Someone mentioned (I think it was Calvin Pharr) that Max was overheard shouting at someone in his office. If you de-

termined with whom he had an appointment —"

"We've tried."

"Surely his secretary —"

"She was out with the flu, and the temp
who replaced her must have been in the copy
room at the time the argument occurred because she heard nothing."

"Have you talked to the police about this?"

"That's exactly what we don't want to do,"
said Moore. "Too many people know already.
It could have a disastrous effect on our stock
if it gets out. We've sunk a lot of money into
this project over a five-year period, and we
want to salvage our investment before the
news hurts us more than we've already been
hurt. Merrivale will handle the investigation;
the man's a pit bull when he gets on the
scent, although unfortunately he has a personality to match." Moore smiled ever so
slightly, the first smile I had seen from him.
"And any help you can give us will be much
appreciated. If you could, discreetly of
course, make inquiries of your connections in
Eastern Europe . . ."

"Of course," I agreed. "Anything I can do
to find out why Max was killed." I stopped,
having had a thought that would not please
Moore. "On the matter of the police, however, I'm afraid they already know about the
theft. A Detective Ali questioned me just before I came up here."

"What did you tell him?"

"Why the research would be worth stealing, although nothing specific about its nature, with which I'm not familiar."

"Yes." He sighed. "Well, it can't be helped. I'll have to talk to them myself and beg for their discretion. I hope I can count on the same from you, Dr. Blue."

"I understand your concerns, although it seems to me that you might make more progress if you took the authorities into your confidence and used their resources."

"I rather believe our resources are more extensive in this area than theirs. After all, it has to be someone here who assisted in the theft."

"Yes." *And the murder,* I thought, not happily. "I'll see what I can find out."

"Good. I'll assign you an office, a telephone, a fax, whatever you need."

"I'm afraid this is somewhat outside my area of competence, both the research and investigating a crime."

"Well, we all have that problem, don't we?" said Moore. "Still, we must do what we can."

As I left his office, I was glad to remember that my wife considered the idea of industrial espionage outside the realm of sensible consideration. Her remarks to the police had probably been facetious in nature. In fact, I could easily imagine her laughing about bizarre theories of espionage and murder. That being the case, I hardly needed to tell her what I'd just heard and put her into danger, not that I felt threatened myself. I was just going to make a few calls, which no one but Moore and I and perhaps Merrivale need know about.

The thought of Merrivale reminded me that he evidently hadn't passed on to Moore the news of my last conversation with Max. Why would he keep that to himself? This was obviously a complex situation, which I did not fully understand. Still, I'd make inquiries, and if I found out anything, I'd report directly to Moore, in whom I had more confidence than in the security chief. Then Moore could take the information and the investigation from there in whatever way he thought best. I'd be out of it, and Carolyn, if she felt the need to think about the murder, could think about Max's obnoxious children.

15

How to Pronounce Gelato

What place could be more enchanting than Italy with its splendid churches and castles, majestic Roman ruins, fabulous works of art, glorious music, charming people, delicious food and wine, and, most enchanting of all, its gelato? Everywhere in Italy from the humblest corner grocery to the most sophisticated *ristorante,* one can purchase that paragon of ice creams, gelato. So smooth, so rich, so intensely flavorful. Made fresh every day. One's first taste of gelato is a transcendent experience. And the second taste. And the third.

Can we Americans, you might ask, enjoy gelato in our own country, where Italian restaurants abound? The answer is yes. Americans can eat gelato, without ever crossing their own borders. Therefore, in a New York restaurant that serves delicious Italian food, wouldn't one expect to be able to order gelato? Certainly. Instead of looking puzzled, wouldn't one's waiter, even if he had a peculiar accent (Serbian? Guatemalan? Bornean?), have immediately assured us, when asked, that the house served gelato?

One could excuse him for not recognizing the word *grappa,* even though it has become exceedingly chic and, in its more expensive manifestations, can even be considered acceptable for human consumption. It no longer *always* tastes like a petroleum product. My husband is very fond of it, but he had to call the headwaiter in order to learn that the restaurant had grappas for every taste. He chose one.

But in the matter of gelato (which is pronounced with a soft *g*), our waiter looked blank. I tried a few of the simpler flavors on him: *cioccolato, fragole, caffe, pistacchio, limone.* He looked frightened. Italian ice cream, my husband translated. "Oh, gelato!" exclaimed the young man. He pronounced it with a hard *g.* Of course. They had vanilla, he assured us.

Would it really be gelato, I had to wonder, when so egregiously mispronounced. Gelato has eggs and cream in it, not to mention the freshest fruits, the tastiest nuts. I didn't want plain old vanilla ice cream. Used to more exotic flavors in my gelato and suspicious that I might not get the real thing, I gave up and ordered tiramisu, the choice of which our waiter approved, probably because he knew how to pronounce that.

Carolyn Blue,
"Have Fork, Will Travel,"
Toledo Star-Signal

Carolyn

I can't say that I was pleased to hear we were having dinner with the Vasandroviches, although his tears at the memorial service had given me a better opinion of him. Still, as Jason said, who could pass up *Il Trovatore*? And I had hopes that the snobbish Sophia would pick a famous restaurant.

Instead, we went to a place I had never heard of: Coco Opera. It was charmingly decorated: brick walls, wood floors, fat columns of a mottled dark red, red drapes with gold fringe, elaborate Venetian carnival masks on the walls and opera posters on the columns, even sheer screens with excerpts from opera scores hanging from the ceiling. No question we were meant to attend the opera after dinner. Of course, Sophia had hoped for something more famous, "but last-minute reservations are so hard to get, you understand," she explained, "even when you have good connections. We're fortunate that I was able to obtain the tickets to *Il Trovatore*."

We all agreed that we were fortunate indeed and studied our menus. I ordered roasted salmon, which was rare and moist, set on top of creamy mashed potatoes and surrounded by grilled zucchini and cherry tomatoes whose bite contrasted nicely with the delicious sweetness of a wonderful balsamic reduction sauce.

My husband ordered, of all things, liver. The dish was called Liver Venezziana, and the dreaded liver arrived cut into small pieces, perfectly medium rare, as Jason had ordered it, accompanied by sliced caramelized onions and grilled polenta, which Jason described, smiling, as grilled grits. The whole swam in a dense liver sauce, which was slightly sweet. At his insistence, I ventured to dip a bit of bread in the sauce. I believe Sophia was shocked.

She certainly looked askance when I discovered that I had forgotten to put a pen in my handbag and had to ask the headwaiter for the loan of his in order to take notes. Our waiter, although anxious to please, was not knowledgeable either about the menu or Italian cuisine in general. I gathered that he, I, and the restaurant were a source of embarrassment to Sophia, even though the food was very good, and the wine . . . well, it was a so-so Chianti. Then Jason had a terrible time ordering grappa, and I was forced to select tiramisu for lack of a more exotic dessert choice. Cheesecake, which the waiter was pushing, is not on my list of Italian delights. The tiramisu, however, was just as good as he insisted. I felt that I was consuming rich, sweet, coffee-scented air.

Evidently, while Sophia and I were making the obligatory trip to the ladies' room, Vaclav had a little talk with Jason, because as we walked over to the opera, Jason asked me why I had been talking to the police again about Max Heydemann, whom I didn't even know. "Not just Merrivale but other Hodge, Brune executives seem to have security concerns about us now," Jason said dryly.

"Really? Well, if they don't want me talking to the police," I said tartly, "they shouldn't leave me stranded in the company of the police." Too late to confess my indiscreet revelations to Detective Ali; obviously my secret was out. "Since no one thought to offer me a ride back to the hotel from the memorial service, I accepted one from both the detectives on the case, and — surprise, surprise — I talked to them while we were in the police car."

Jason laughed. "Ah yes, Detective Ali, the one you thought might be related to a mass poisoner." He still didn't seem to be particularly worried about the company's perception that I might be a security risk. And I felt that any citizen has a perfect right to talk to the police if she wants to. I rather liked Detective Worski, even if his overcoat was frumpy, and Detective Ali was very well dressed and amazingly lacking in the cynicism of his partner, but then he was the younger man.

The opera was a delight. I do love *Il Trovatore*. There's hardly an aria or chorus that you couldn't sing in the shower if you were so inclined. I rarely do, but I've been known to hum arias in the kitchen. Of course, Manrico treats Leonora abominably in the last act, accusing her of being unfaithful, and that when she's dying from the poison she took to prevent the Count de Luna from having his way with her in return for the release of her imprisoned and ungrateful true love. Opera plots do sound nonsensical when you try to summarize them. Still, the music is thrilling.

But before we got to that piece of high melodrama, we encountered another at intermission, for a strange-looking woman with wild eyes and wilder hair, wearing an expensive gown and diamonds, shrieked across the gaggle of operagoers to Dr. Vasandrovich, "Congratulations, Vaclav. You got the job, didn't you?"

Vaclav looked horribly embarrassed, as well he might, but the woman ploughed through the crowd in our direction, calling, "The demise of my ex is cause for celebration, don't you think, Vaclav? For both of us! Let me

167

buy you a drink! You too, Sophia. Wouldn't you like to be seen drinking at the Met with someone like me, from such a *fine family?*"

Jason and I were speechless. Vaclav, too, but Sophia collected herself and said, purring, "Melisande, how lovely to see you."

Over the strange woman's shoulder I could see a young man shoving people aside as he headed toward us. He looked familiar.

"You're surprised?" the bejeweled woman purred back, her voice a nasty imitation of Sophia's, accent and all. "I'll bet you thought I was back in the sanatorium, didn't you? Not at all. I wouldn't have missed this for the world. I can't think of anyone who deserved killing more than Max."

The young man clutched her shoulder. "What are you doing?" he hissed.

She ignored him. "Well, I did miss the memorial service, didn't I? No one thought to invite me. I'd have had some remarks to make about Max. Stop pulling on my dress, Ricky."

I had recognized the young man: Max Heydemann's son.

"Oh, and Vaclav, you can tell that tacky chorus girl he married that she's not going to get his money. No, indeed. We can count on Daddy to see that my children get what's coming to them."

"Mother, let's go." Rick put his arm around her. "Dad will have done right by us."

168

"Max neglected you for that bitch, and now they'll both pay."

The intermission bell had rung, and Vaclav was edging away, but she screeched after him, "You tell her that. You hear me? If Max hasn't done the right thing in his will, she'll spend the rest of her life in court trying to pry a crust of bread out of the lawyers."

"Shut *up*, Mother."

"Don't you shush me," she snarled back. "You owe me *money*, dear Ricky, and I expect to be repaid."

We hastened after Vaclav and managed to disappear into the grand tier, where the starburst chandeliers were rising like receding galaxies, but I hated to miss a word that might be passing between those two.

To Sophia I whispered, "Was that —"

"Melisande Heydemann. Max's first wife," Sophia whispered back. "She's obviously overwrought, but as I told you, she does come from a very prominent family."

As *Trovatore* soared to its tragic conclusion, I confess to some distraction. Surely, if Max's children hadn't had him killed, his ex-wife had. Or perhaps she followed him into that deli and killed him herself. And for what did her son owe her money? Maybe she had financed the hiring of an assassin, and Ricky had done the hiring. She was a truly frightening woman. Talk about dysfunctional families!

Because I couldn't sleep when we got back to the hotel, I took hotel stationery from the desk drawer and diverted myself by writing a column in longhand about the waiter who had served us that evening.

"Where are you going?" Jason mumbled from bed as I opened the door to the hall.

"Downstairs to fax this column to that rude Marshall Smead," I replied.

16

The Designated Baby-Sitter

Carolyn

When Jason woke me up on Thursday morning, it was still dark. "What's wrong?" I asked, alarmed. "It must be the middle of the night."

My husband replied that it was eight o'clock and snowing. Accordingly, I squirmed back under the covers, unable to believe he'd awakened me to give me a weather report, and at eight o'clock! That meant I'd had less than seven hours' sleep.

"Carolyn!" He gave my shoulder a little shake. "I can't find my telephone book."

"Who do you need to call?" I mumbled. "Maybe I know the number."

"It's in Eastern Europe."

"What in the world for?"

"The Ukrainian espionage thing."

"For heaven's sake!" I opened one eye and stared balefully at my spouse. "Surely after seeing Melisande Heydemann, you don't think the Ukrainians killed Max."

Jason shrugged. "I didn't say that."

But did he think it? Or was he just trying

to help Hodge, Brune on the possible loss of their research efforts? "Did you look in the inside zipped pocket of your briefcase? No, actually, you put it in mine because you didn't have room in yours with all those slides. Did they like your slides?" I was sliding away myself — into sleep.

"They loved my slides," he assured me and leaned over to kiss my forehead. I assume he found the address book, but I wasn't able to get back to sleep, after all. Grumbling, I rose to shower and dress. At eight-thirty I was calling my agent's office to complain about being sent, unprepared, to Marshall Smead. The secretary said Loretta wasn't in yet. Hadn't I noticed that it was snowing? Then she suggested that I come over in an hour or so. They'd fit me in. She hung up before I could protest.

I pulled on the fur-lined boots I had brought with me, bundled up, and headed out into the snow to get breakfast. Because the hour was earlier, the deli was crowded with red-nosed, overcoated New Yorkers, wolfing down huge platters of hot food. Max's ill-fated seat on the aisle was open; maybe all the customers knew someone had died there. I took it and was again served by Thelma, who asked me how the memorial service had gone.

"His children were horrible," I replied. "Only interested in inheriting money from him."

Thelma nodded. "How sharper than a serpent's tooth it is/To have a thankless child!"

Good heavens, I thought. *A waitress who quotes* King Lear. "His widow seemed very nice. She was a professional ballet dancer before she married Max."

"Second wife, right?"

"Oh, yes. I had the misfortune to meet the first Mrs. Heydemann last night. She's a terrifying woman."

"So who do they think killed him? One of the wives?"

I had to laugh, remembering Jason's plans for the morning. "I suspect that my husband thinks it's some industrial espionage thing. Can you believe that?"

"How come?"

"I don't know. Evidently someone in the Ukraine stole their research before they could patent it. Jason's going to call friends in Eastern Europe. They'll probably think he's crazy." And there I went again, talking about Hodge, Brune's secrets.

"How come he knows people in Eastern Europe?"

"Oh, professors. They all know each other."

"Yeah? Well, not likely they'll know anything about the killin'. Mark my words. It was one of the wives. Marriage makes people crazy." She laughed her raucous laugh. "Wouldn't catch me doin' the bride thing."

Then she was off to another table, leaving me to wonder if her declaration meant that she was a man hater or just commitment-shy.

When I'd finished my breakfast, I headed for Loretta Blum's office, resenting every step I took in the blowing snow. Nonetheless, I intended to give her a piece of my mind about the horrid visit with Marshall Smead, a disaster for which I considered her responsible. After that confrontation, I was off to look at area rugs farther downtown. Our house has tiled floors, and I wanted to put something pretty and softer underfoot. A few hours of rug shopping, and I'd return to dress for my twelve-thirty appointment with Charlotte Heydemann. But in this weather, would she make it to the restaurant? Would I?

I found Loretta's office in a state of war. Her two daughters were still sick, and her mother-in-law had agreed to look after them, but not their brother, Simon. Consequently, Simon, a sullen twelve-year-old, was sitting next to Loretta's desk (Marsha, the much-pierced secretary, refused to keep him in her anteroom) playing a noisy electronic game. His mother screamed at him to turn it off several times while I was voicing my complaints about Smead, but Simon ignored her.

Finally, Loretta gave up on her son and, catching the drift of my anger, said, "Oh, that's vintage Smead. He's a rude bastard, but did you get a contract? That's the important thing. Think publicity. Think —"

"I'm faxing him columns as fast as I can write them, and I really don't care what he does with them," I replied, taking malicious satisfaction in my anti-Smead campaign.

"Bad attitude, Carolyn. First rule of publishing: Learn to get along with the assholes."

"I'd rather get even, which I may do. Smead hates me, but his boss, Paul Fallon, whom I know socially, is interested in my work."

"Good girl. Second rule of publishing: Exploit your contacts. Contacts are everything. Call Fallon. Invite him to lunch. You can use my phone."

"I have to meet the widow of a friend of my husband's for lunch."

"What can *she* do for you? Does *she* have contacts? By the way, have you been to see Bernie? It doesn't look like it." She eyed my wool slacks and cable-knit sweater. "Simon, turn off that damned machine. You gotta get some decent clothes, Carolyn. We're meeting Rollie tomorrow at Le Bernardin. It's on West Fifty-first."

Well, finally a restaurant from my book on dining in Manhattan. I should be able to get a column out of that. Or two. Or three. I smiled, thinking about inundating the detestable Smead with columns.

"So go downtown to Bernie's. Tell you

what. Simon here's bored. You can take him along. He'll show you how to get there. How about that, Simon?"

"No," said Simon.

"Don't tell me no," she snarled. "I got a meeting in —" She looked at her watch. "Fifteen minutes. I'm going to be late. And you, Simon, Marsha won't let you stay, so you'll go with Mrs. Blue here. Take care of her. She's new in town."

"I told you I have a luncheon appointment," I protested. "And it's snowing out there."

"Simon doesn't mind snow, do you, Simon? Just drop him here before noon. I'll be back by then."

With that she left, pulling on her coat, leaving me to eye Simon morosely. "I'm not going to your Uncle Bernie's," I said.

"Wasn't my idea," Simon mumbled. "So, where are we going?"

"Rug shopping." I thought that might discourage him, and he'd insist on staying here with the reluctant Marsha.

"Man!" cried Simon. "Rug shopping? What did I do to deserve that?" But he was putting on his coat, then pulling a knitted cap over his ears. Evidently, I was stuck with him.

17

Telephone Detectives

Jason

Charles Moore was as good as his word. At Hodge, Brune the receptionist directed me to a small office equipped with telephone, computer, notepads, and a memo from Moore informing me that I was to be paid for this week at double my usual consulting rate, which was good news. Carolyn planned to look at rugs today. If she picked something extravagant, it wouldn't propel us toward the poorhouse.

The receptionist also provided a chart that showed the time differences between New York and various cities in Eastern Europe. I glanced at my watch, calculating that it would be the end of the afternoon in most of the cities I planned to call. Some of my contacts could be reached at universities; others would have to be called at home. Therefore, I chose to call first those who were more colleagues than friends. Friends would be less likely to resent being interrupted at home. Also on the first-to-call portion of the list were those who might not have telephones at home, always a problem in countries where the effects of communism have not yet abated.

As might be expected, I found people who were unfamiliar with the claim by the little-known Ukrainian company to a cutting-edge environmental process. A professor in Romania assured me that no cutting-edge environmental research was going on in the Ukraine, certainly not on coal pollution. "My dear Professor Blue," he exclaimed. "They mine coal and burn it; they don't worry about its effects. The miners die, the coal is used, but no one worries about smoke. Much worse are the effects of Chernobyl radiation. So that's what they worry about in the Ukraine."

A friend in Budapest assured me that no one in the Ukraine knew enough or had the funding or equipment to do the kind of research I was talking about. "They're bluffing. They have no process. Maybe they hope to do a bit of blackmail. Sell the rights to what they do not have. Tell your friends not to worry, my dear fellow."

It wasn't a bad theory. Word of the hopes for this research could have leaked, perhaps during the casual discussion that goes on at conferences, hints of great things to come by men who are drinking and chatting after long days of meetings, just the sort of careless talk that Vernon Merrivale deplored. In such a case, might not some impecunious scientist from a faltering economy go home to a dreary apartment and hatch a plan to take advantage of what he had heard? It was worth suggesting to Moore.

I picked up one more bit of information, negative, but still interesting. An industrial chemist in Krakow had actually seen the announcement and, intrigued, asked around about the company. He found the whole story exceedingly peculiar. This was a very small company, I was to know, very few people employed, scientists of no note, and no one knew where the capital investment had come from. One fellow, a colleague at his own company, said that the Ukrainian outfit, which consisted of one building in a poor area of Kiev, had only been in existence eighteen months, perhaps less.

If his information was correct, the Ukrainians could not have developed the process in such a short time and with minimal resources in space and personnel.

"Could there be government or university research behind this announcement?" I asked.

"If that were the case, my friend would be aware. He goes often to Kiev. Something does not smell good. I see this immediately, but not why your interest in this."

"I am making inquiries for friends," I replied. "Friends with an interest in such research problems. If you should come across the name of a scientist associated with the Ukrainian endeavor, my friends would like to talk to him."

"I do not think exists such a Ukrainian. But is like Russians, no? They invent everything and before everyone." He laughed heartily. "Some things never change." He inquired after the health of my wife, whom he had met at a meeting in Germany. We exchanged personal tidbits — Carolyn's new career, the birth of a child to his daughter, my surprising move to Texas — and parted on friendly terms.

Carolyn

Loretta's secretary managed to be away from her desk when Simon and I left. Therefore, I really had no choice but to take him with me, for I remembered very clearly what twelve-year-old boys are like. If I left him, he might disappear or cause chaos in his mother's office. Goodness knows what he might get up to.

"The place I want to go is on Twenty-third Street." I mentioned the address. Simon shrugged and led the way into the whirling, wet world outside, where snow clung to my coat and my eyelashes and squished wetly and with slippery tenacity under my boots. I put up my umbrella. Simon insisted that no one used an umbrella for snow. Much he knew. When I had to, I slipped into a doorway and shook the clinging snow from the umbrella, but I kept it open and thus prevented my coat from turning soggy.

He said we'd take a bus first; I had to pay for his ride, but I had my Metro pass, which was good on buses. So we rode across town, standing in a crowded aisle with my umbrella dripping on my boots, and exited to climb down into the bowels of the city to catch a subway that still left us many steep steps and two blocks from A.B.C. Carpet. During the subway ride, Simon studied the advertising cards displayed above the seats and asked in a loud voice, "Exactly what is an abortion?" The card said, "Need an abortion? We're here for you." Then a phone number for Planned Parenthood.

I knew just what he was up to and had experience in circumventing such embarrassing tactics on the part of obstreperous youngsters. "How interesting that you should ask that, Simon," I replied. "Are you familiar with the *Oxford English Dictionary*?" He turned to me suspiciously. "The stem *abort* is from the Latin *aboriri*, to miscarry or disappear." I had myself looked it up once in childhood, having heard some older girls whispering and giggling about abortions. Naturally, I used my father's compact *OED* because I loved the little square magnifying glass that came with it. "By the way," I added earnestly, "there is a fascinating book on the making of the *Oxford English Dictionary*, which, as you may know, is the most impressive lexicographic endeavor of Western man. The book is called *The Professor and the Madman*. It seems that a major contributor was, in fact, a madman, who spent many years in an asylum in England, although you'll be interested to hear that he was actually an American, a naval officer, if I remember —"

"Oh, forget it," Simon interrupted. An older lady across the aisle was listening to this exchange and laughing behind her hand when we exited the car.

As we walked the two blocks, Simon jumped into piles of slush that were accumulating on the sidewalks, while I stepped, flatfooted and with care, around them. "We're both going to catch something, a cold or the flu," I mumbled. I should have skipped this trip and gone back to my cozy, dry hotel room.

"*I* won't get the flu," Simon assured me. "I've had my flu shot."

"Kids don't get flu shots," I replied grumpily. "*I'm* not even old enough to need flu shots."

"I get them. I've got asthma."

Oh perfect, I thought grimly and began to

watch for signs that an attack might be imminent. I remembered all too clearly a time when I was a young mother and Chris had croup. The wheezing and gasping for breath had terrified me. "Do you have your inhaler?" I asked anxiously.

"Sure," and then he was running ahead of me again, making splatting jumps that sent dirty, semiliquid snow spraying from around his feet, often onto my boots and the bottom of my coat.

I considered what the state of my only coat would be when I met Charlotte Heydemann at Sfuzzi. I doubted that she, no matter how inclement the weather, would arrive with her hem splattered by muddy snow. "Stop that!" I said to Simon in my quietest voice.

For a wonder, he did. Perhaps he was so used to being yelled at by adults that a quiet command got his attention. What a relief to finally step inside that huge room at A.B.C. Carpet, with its dry warmth and its towering racks of hanging rugs. There were gangs of men who, at the command of sales folk, flipped the carpets onto the floor, building up wild overlapping patterns and then rolling them away. I would have felt overwhelmed by comfort if not for the strange, dusty, rubbery air that prickled my nose and brought on sneezes. I fished a Kleenex from my purse and gave said nose a good blow to clear away the odor.

Simon sneezed, too, but he wiped his nose with his hand instead of fishing for a handkerchief. Or perhaps, as the designated, if reluctant, baby-sitter, I was supposed to provide him with Kleenex. Too late.

Instead, I flipped hanging rugs until I found one with an indefinite green and blue pattern that had the faint lines and hues of a watercolor painting. When it was laid out on the floor for me, it proved to be both too small and, as Simon so succinctly put it, "bor-ing." But on the rack it had seemed huge and mysteriously lovely. Ah well. I looked at a carpet in green, yellow, and white with raised O'Keeffish flowers. It was gorgeous, although I had no idea where I'd put it, just that I wanted it very badly. And it was marked down! Really quite reasonable. Then it went onto the floor, and I saw that it was *very* small, and that dust had caught on the raised edges of the flowers, making the whole look bedraggled and secondhand.

"It's been very popular," said the saleswoman.

I looked at it askance. "Do you have a clean one?"

"We probably do, but truthfully, that model dirties up pretty rapidly."

Even though I didn't need that rug, I was disappointed. It had looked so pretty, so green and springlike, on the rack. It would have been a reminder, in stark El Paso, of landscapes more lush. I sighed and continued to look. Simon fidgeted, wandered off, picked out strange and dangerous-looking patterns in black and brown to show me, looked at rugs with cartoon characters embossed on their surfaces as if ready to leap off and grab some passing child by the ankle. He went to the front of the store to press his nose against the large windows. "Don't go outside," I called. Even though unfairly saddled with this child, I didn't want to lose him and have to explain the loss to his mother.

"If the snow doesn't let up soon, we won't be able to go outside," he called back. "We'll be stuck here. Marooned in a boring rug store on Twenty-third Street! Starving to death."

"It's not even lunchtime," I replied and pushed back more carpets. And more. But then I saw one I couldn't take my eyes off. "Oh my!" I said.

"A very popular design," the saleswoman assured me.

"Does that mean it picks up dirt like a magnet?" I asked.

"Cool!" said Simon, coming to look at my discovery.

"Even your son likes it." The saleswoman beamed at the two of us, while Simon and I, two strangers in the storm, exchanged a rueful glance.

"So buy it, and let's get something to eat,"

said my charge. "If you don't feed me, I'll starve to death. And then my mother will send out for some crappy chicken soup or something because I'm sneezing."

"When did you sneeze?" I interrupted anxiously.

"Same time you did. When we walked in here."

"That odor disappears within days," the saleswoman assured us.

"I think I'm going to have an asthma attack," said Simon. The saleswoman looked alarmed. "Something to eat would help," he added hopefully.

"We don't serve refreshments," she apologized.

"Just give me your card with the name and price of this rug," I suggested.

"You mean after all this looking, you're not going to buy one?" Simon stared at me with indignation.

"Doesn't you mother consult your father before she buys a rug?" I asked.

"Probably not. Probably he's the one who buys the rugs. How would I know? Nobody consults me about rugs."

I asked about shipping costs, length of time to delivery, and other practical considerations, all the while staring at the rug of my dreams with its op art, many-colored pattern. It was definitely large enough for the space and even contained some of the right colors, not to mention some colors that had never been seen in my living room. Oh well.

Once free from the rug store, the snow having abated somewhat, Simon began to make suggestions about places he'd like to go. I consulted my watch and reminded him that I had to be back at my hotel before noon. Dancing around me as I slogged over the slick sidewalks toward the subway entrance, Simon reminded me that he was hungry and he was my responsibility. Then I slipped! *Broken hip!* my mind screamed. But I did not break anything because Simon, skinny young fellow that he was, caught me.

"I saved you," he pointed out. "So shouldn't you —"

"What do you want to eat?" I interrupted. "It will have to be something you can carry back with you."

"A hot dog," he replied instantly. He even knew where to get one, so I bought Simon a huge hot dog doused with sauerkraut, smelling to high heaven, and dripping out of its wrappings. Then I took him back to his mother's office.

Alas, Marsha had left a note saying that she had taken an early lunch, and, good mother that I am, I did not feel comfortable leaving Simon by himself in the office. I consoled myself by using her absence to appropriate her telephone. When I'd fished my Metro pass from my purse during the ride

187

back with Simon, I also came up with Detective Worski's card, reminding me of two things he should know relative to the investigation of Max Heydemann's death. After all, the detective had said to call him if I learned anything useful. Therefore, I settled Simon in the chair beside Marsha's desk where I could keep my eye on him and called the detective.

He didn't sound very excited to hear from me. Perhaps he was busy. Nonetheless, I persisted. "Two interesting things happened last night at the opera."

"Hard to believe," said the cynical Worski, who evidently didn't care for opera.

"First, an official at Hodge, Brune remonstrated with my husband because I've been talking about the case to you. I thought perhaps that might be significant."

"Who?" asked Worski.

"Vaclav Vasandrovich."

"Yeah, him. No big surprise there."

"He doesn't want my husband to speak to you, either."

"OK."

"Not that the admonition says anything in particular about Dr. Vasandrovich personally," I admitted. "Secretiveness seems to be company policy, which I consider peculiar when a murder investigation is involved."

"Yeah. Same here."

"More important, I met Max Heydemann's first wife. Now there is someone who might

188

well have murdered him! She was absolutely jubilant over his death."

"At the opera?"

"During intermission. Noisily jubilant. And ready to go to court if her children don't inherit most of his money. But most important of all, detective: She's crazy!"

"Uh-huh."

"No, I mean psychotic crazy. Frequently institutionalized crazy. I'd have no trouble believing she paid to have her ex-husband killed. She could have done it herself."

I detected a definite interest in the detective's response to that information and felt the pleasant warmth of having been useful to the authorities, as any citizen is bound to do, even if that usefulness should bring the wrath of the frightening Melisande Heydemann down upon my head. Reconsidering my courageous public-spiritedness, I hastily added, "Please don't mention to her that I told you about last night." He promised that he wouldn't.

Only after I'd hung up did I notice Simon's eyes on me, round and fascinated. "Cool!" he breathed. "You know someone who got murdered?"

"My husband does," I admitted reluctantly.

"And you're helping the police?"

"Just with a bit of information," I replied modestly.

"And you know a crazy woman who did it?"

189

"I don't *know* that," I hastened to assure him. "I just consider her a . . . a suspect."

"That is so cool!"

It seems that, inadvertently, I had earned Simon's admiration. Not so his mother's when she discovered him finishing off his large, messy hot dog. I hurried off before she could turn her dismay from him to me.

How did a sausage between halves of a bun come to be called a hot dog? you might ask. As the result of a little research project, I discovered that a New York newspaper cartoonist drew a picture of a dachshund encased in a bun and labeled it a "hot dog." Then, as hot dog stands proliferated in the city and price wars ensued, the public began to question what was actually in a sandwich that could be purchased for five cents. Dog meat, perhaps?

Nathan's Famous, the hot dog emporium, pacified public concern by offering free hot dogs to interns from a Coney Island hospital. The crowds of white-coated customers made Nathan's "the place where the doctors ate" and the hot dogs the entrée of choice.

Carolyn Blue,
"Have Fork, Will Travel,"
Peoria Farm Sentinel

190

18

The Marriage of French
and Japanese

When eating in a famous New York restaurant, those of us from the hinterlands are understandably fearful that our clothing may not meet the standards of the house, that we may even be asked to leave for reasons of fashion deficiency. Stories have been printed about people who have been ejected. My favorite concerns the campaign against women in trousers conducted by La Cote Basque. Two ladies wearing mink coats arrived to exercise their reservations and were told that the one in trousers could not enter. Alas, the poor lady had a broken leg in a cast over which she felt trousers were appropriate. Management stood firm; no trousers; they must be removed. To be replaced with what? asked the embarrassed ladies. Wear your coat, said hardhearted management. Defeated, the crippled woman limped to the ladies' room, struggled out of her trousers — no small feat when one pant leg had to be dragged over the cast — and ate her lunch swathed in mink and perspiration.

The French are known not only for their wonderful food, but for their unwavering sense of propriety.

Carolyn Blue,
"Have Fork, Will Travel,"
Des Moines Clarion Monitor

Carolyn

When I arrived at the hotel, having sprinted up the subway steps, I found a message from Charlotte Heydemann. "Overcome by a desire to eat French. Got reservations for 1:00 P.M. at La Caravelle. French. You'll love it." I probably would, I thought with dismay after I'd researched it in *Dining and the Opera*, *Zagat*, and *Access New York City*. It looked wonderful and *very expensive*, and I had issued the invitation, so I would be paying.

Well, at least I'd have an extra half-hour to change. Hurriedly, I stripped out of my snow boots, slacks, and thick sweater and donned a dress, the very dress my agent had thought not chic enough for my editor and Le Bernardin. Would I be snubbed for fashion deficiency at La Caravelle? I then inspected my coat and used a washcloth to rub a few splashes, courtesy of Simon Puddle-Jumper, from the bottom. Jewelry, shoes, handbag, lipstick, French twist rapidly constructed, and I was ready to find a cab; I couldn't wear decent shoes in this weather and take the subway, so cab fare would add to the cost of my Good Samaritan instincts and natural nosiness.

Charlotte and I arrived simultaneously but in different taxis at the Shoreham on West Fifty-fifth and made our way to the restaurant. Quiet elegance, pink banquettes, murals of Paris: I was enchanted. The owner greeted Charlotte with an embrace. I was treated like a valued client, acceptably outfitted for their very beautiful dining room. As I studied the menu, I quickly decided that I would have to stop checking the prices.

Charlotte, looking it over with casual pleasure, said, "By the way, this is on me." Before I could protest, she added, "No arguments. I chose the place, so I'll pay. Believe me, it's worth it to me, a back-to-my-roots indulgence." She laughed softly. "I'm French. Well, my parents were. Oh, how they wanted me to become a great ballerina! But after all the financial sacrifices they made (my father owned a small French patisserie near Columbus Circle, never very successful), I just didn't have the talent. I loved dancing but never progressed beyond being one of the four members of the corps de ballet, mimicking each other's steps or twirling separately across the stage in turn. Are you very hungry, three-course hungry, or do you want something lighter?"

"Lighter," I responded immediately. At least, I didn't have to pick the most expensive things on the menu, since she seemed set on paying. I studied the appetizer list and found an intriguing entry: Little Flutes of Curried Escargots. The ingredients were unusual, to me at least: Oriental plus French. I presumed that I was seeing "fusion cuisine," the product of famous chefs raiding the menus of ethnic restaurants.

Charlotte mentioned a Japanese chef in the kitchen of this bastion of French comestibles, so presumably fusion cuisine snatched up not only recipes but also actual people. "And you have to try the Chair de Crabe de Caravelle," she insisted.

Again I tried to protest.

"You're a food writer. You can't leave without having sampled this dish," she announced. "It's dressed with a lovely herb sauce. Now, what about entrées?"

I laughed. "This is supposed to be a light meal. We still have the Picasso hats to view."

"Well then, I'll order the crab, you order the escargot, we'll share those, and then we'll have desserts. And wine. I know just the thing. A wonderful white burgundy."

"At least, let me pay my half."

"Absolutely not. It's *my* psyche that needs comfort." She did indeed look like a woman who needed comfort. I was sure she had been crying as recently as this morning. Even under the careful makeup, grief showed in the slight puffiness of her eyes and the drawn lines of her mouth.

We ordered, and Charlotte's forced merriment failed her for the moment. "It's so strange," she confessed. "The police have been back several times. Not to tell me about the investigation. To ask me questions. It's almost as if they think I had something to do with Max's death. That's so ironic. I'm the one most destroyed by this, and they think . . . well, I don't know what they think. Or why."

My conscience smote me because I had a good idea what lay behind the police's suspicions. Sophia's gossip about a lover, and my repetition of this tidbit, not to mention the perception that widows profited from the deaths of husbands who were well to do. Charlotte had told me that her family was not. "Perhaps they think . . . because you're the widow . . ." How could I put this delicately?

"That I stand to inherit a fortune because Max died? Well, I won't be penniless. I know he set up a trust for me, but beyond that, I have no idea what's in his will. Tomorrow's the reading, and obviously, his children are expecting big things." She shook her head. "The trust for me, that's because Max was

195

afraid his first wife's father would go to court, if anything happened to Max, and try to arrange for the kids to get it all."

"But surely he couldn't do that," I protested. "I mean he couldn't win."

"He's done it before. When Melisande, that's Max's first wife, was finally committed, her father went to court to take custody of the children away from Max, and he managed to get shared custody until she was out. You heard them at the funeral; they're dreadful, and they needn't have been. If Max could have kept them away from the D'Vallencourts, he might have made something out of them."

The herbed crab and the escargot flutes arrived, and we shared. The food was amazing, exotic, thoroughly unforgettable, the white burgundy the best wine I'd ever tasted. I've read that in the 1820s only women in New York ate at French restaurants. Men considered the food too effeminate for masculine tastes. I glanced around and noted plenty of male patrons today. How lucky for them that perceptions of manliness had changed.

"Her family is French, too," Charlotte continued as she bit into a spicy flute filled with escargot, mushrooms, and exotic flavorings. "Melisande's. Old money, unlike mine, the no-money family." Charlotte laughed. "When Max and I met (it was at a ballet benefit; I'm not even sure why he was invited, since he'd already divorced Melisande). Anyway, when we met, I couldn't believe he was interested in me. He was so wonderful, so funny, so brilliant, and there I was, a mediocre dancer nearing the end of an indifferent career."

"Charlotte," I said, "I'm sure he loved you dearly."

"He did," she agreed. "And I, him. I can't imagine life without him." She bowed her head, fighting for composure.

"I met . . . well, saw . . . his first wife last night. It's no surprise he wanted you. I can't imagine any man being saddled with a wom—"

"I thought she was locked away." Charlotte looked alarmed. "Where did you see her?"

"The opera," I replied. We were forking up ambrosial bites of the crab Caravelle. "We went with the Vasandroviches, and she accosted us."

"*Accosted.* That's a perfect word to describe being approached by Melisande. I'll never forget the first time she *accosted* me. I thought she meant to kill me. What did she want? Last night?"

"To celebrate Max's death, I'm afraid."

"That bitch." Charlotte's eyes filled with tears. "The best man who ever lived, and she's happy he's dead. I shouldn't be surprised. And I suppose Sophia couldn't say enough nice things about her. She's such a silly snob." Then Charlotte looked embarrassed. "Sorry. I think grief is making me catty and judgmental. Sophia's —" She seemed at loss for a kind word.

"No friend of yours, actually," I said impulsively, unable to leave Charlotte unaware of the gossip that Sophia was spreading about her, which I now totally disbelieved. "She told me —"

"What?" Charlotte looked curious. "What could she say about me? I've never done anything to her."

"She claims she saw you with a young man at a hotel."

Charlotte looked astonished. "A young man?"

"Whom she took to be your lover."

Then her face cleared. "That's rich. I know who she saw me with. My trainer. He does one-on-one sessions in the gym at the Westchester Suites Hotel on Park Avenue. I go every week to stay in shape. Since I stopped dancing, I have to work at keeping thin. Although now . . . with Max gone . . . Well, who cares about thin? But that does explain the questions from the police," she added bitterly.

"Not exactly." Then I confessed that, not knowing her, I had passed on Sophia's remark to Detective Worski.

"The one in the loden green overcoat? Poor man. He makes you want to take him to Bloomingdale's and buy him something decent to wear."

I apologized for having caused her added grief by repeating Sophia's gossip.

"I'm just glad to know where that came from," she replied, waving to our waiter for the dessert menu. "You can't miss the dessert here. There's the opera cake, which is amazing." The waiter said that wasn't available. "Well, what about the *tarte tiede a la banane?*" He smiled approvingly; most definitely that could be ordered, he replied. "Warm banana tart," she translated for me. "You'll love it."

What could I say? And I did love it.

After banana tarts and the last of the white burgundy and rich coffee, after the paying of the bill, which she would neither let me see nor share, we took a cab through another fall of snow to the Guggenheim, where we peeked out at Picasso's pregnant goat, dusted with snow in the sculpture garden, and I told Charlotte about the bizarre staging of *Mefistofele*, which forced the chubby tenor and soprano to climb up and down ladders while singing at full throat. We feasted our eyes on wild Picasso portraits of women wearing silly hats with stars sticking up at odd angles, and Charlotte laughed and then cried a little because Max would have loved *Picasso in the War Years.*

Finally, we said good-bye in a cab in front

of my hotel, promising to renew our acquaintance if and when I returned to New York. "Max did so want Jason to come aboard. I hope he does," said Charlotte in parting. I wasn't sure what I hoped. Hodge, Brune did not seem like that nice a place to work.

Once in my room I found a message asking me to call Marshall Smead. *Not likely*, I thought and sat down to write a column about hot dogs sold on a snowy street. I had just launched into a second on Japanese-French food and Picasso chapeaux when Detective Worski called me to ask what the story was on Charlotte Heydemann and Sophia Vasandrovich. Charlotte had called him to say that she definitely was *not* having an affair with her trainer or anyone else, and that Sophia Vasandrovich probably knew it, and that he might consider that it was Sophia's husband who was taking over for Max while Charlotte was left without the love of her life, so stop bothering her! I had to bite back a smile. Detective Worski sounded as if his feelings were hurt by her anger.

"I had lunch with Charlotte Heydemann," I said soothingly, "and believe me, she is not the sort of person to kill someone, certainly not a husband she adored."

"How do you know she adored him?" Worski asked. "Just because she said —"

"Women can tell these things."

"Great. And I can take that to court?" he asked sarcastically.

"As for Vaclav, he doesn't really have the job yet. He's *interim* director. Really, you should consider the first wife. Her maiden name was D'Vallencourt."

"Well, shit," said Worski without even apologizing for his language. "That's a very influential family."

"Which doesn't mean they might not be behind Max's death, for whatever reason: — hatred, revenge, arrogance, psychosis, greed —"

"OK, Mrs. Blue. I get the idea. You think I should go after the rich folks."

"Goodness, Detective Worski, I wouldn't try to tell you your business," I replied.

"Uh-huh. That's just what my wife was always saying. Before she divorced me."

He hung up, and I finished my second column, which I then took downstairs to fax. No doubt Mr. Smead hated getting longhand communications, although I have excellent and legible handwriting, if I do say so myself. He had probably called to say he wouldn't accept any more samples of my work unless they were typed. Just for spite, I faxed both columns to Paul Fallon, too, in case Smead wasn't passing them on.

Then I went upstairs and had a nice nap.

Little Flutes of Curried Escargots
Petites Flutes d'Escargots aux Epices de Madras

As a prelude to your next dinner party or a delicious hors d'oeuvre with cocktails, try this unusual recipe from Sharon O'Connor's Dining and the Opera in Manhattan. *It's on the menu at La Caravelle in Manhattan:*

- In a large sauté pan or skillet, melt *1 tbs. butter* and sauté *1 tbs. minced shallots* and *1 tsp. minced garlic* over medium heat until translucent, about 3 minutes.
- Add *1 cup (3 oz.) ea. thinly sliced white mushrooms and thinly sliced stemmed shiitake mushrooms* and sauté for 2 more minutes.
- Gently stir in *7 oz. canned snails, rinsed, drained, and minced.*
- Add *1 cup dry white wine* and cook to reduce until almost dry.
- Add *1 cup chicken stock or canned low-salt chicken broth* and cook to reduce again.
- Add *1/2 cup heavy whipping cream*, bring to a boil, immediately remove from heat.
- Stir in *1 tsp. curry powder, 1/2 cup peeled, seeded, and diced tomato, 1 tsp. minced fresh chives,* and *1 tsp.*

minced fresh parsley.

- Set aside and let cool.
- Preheat oven to 400°F.
- Lay *12 spring roll skins, cut into quar-ters,* on a lightly floured work surface.
- Place *1 tsp. of filling* on each spring roll skin and roll up one turn, fold in the sides, and finish rolling.
- Transfer to baking dish, and bake in preheated oven for 5 minutes.

MAKES 48 PIECES

SERVES 8 TO 10

19

A Greek Port in the Storm

Jason

Carolyn was napping when I arrived in our hotel room, but she had much to tell me as we dressed for dinner with Calvin Pharr and his wife: the wonderful rug she had found, which I would see Saturday; her indignation at being bullied into baby-sitting her agent's twelve-year-old son, even though she hadn't lost her touch in dealing with recalcitrant youngsters; her superb lunch with Max's widow at a very famous restaurant, better than anything Hodge, Brune had provided; the delightful Picasso exhibition at the Guggenheim, so much better than that silly pottery sideshow about which Sophia Vasandrovich had been so excited; and finally the two columns she had faxed to the abominable Smead before taking her nap. With all this information from my wife, there was no time to tell her about my own investigation, which was fortunate, because I didn't want to bring Carolyn into it.

The Pharrs awaited us in the lobby, Calvin having secured a drink from the bar, his wife,

Grace, who was much taller and much thinner than he, preoccupied with brushing snow from a long black coat that covered the tops of her black boots. To me, she looked like a Siberian army officer, although Carolyn later told me that three-quarters of the women she had seen in the city were wearing those long coats.

"It's a frigging blizzard out there," said Pharr in greeting. "Does this place have a restaurant?"

"I have no idea," Carolyn replied. It was obvious to me that she had hoped for better than a meal in her own hotel.

"Well, Calvin, I think we can at least make it across the street," said his wife. "There's a good Greek restaurant directly opposite."

"On your head if some crazy cab driver skids into us," said Pharr and threw back the rest of what looked like a martini. "Let's go."

As it happened, there were remarkably few cars braving the weather. We jaywalked straight into the warm precincts of Molyvos, a long, narrow establishment with rose velvet benches along the walls and those uncomfortable rush-bottomed chairs, so typical of Mediterranean restaurants, lining the aisle side of the tables. Carolyn may have been disappointed that she was not going to one of the restaurants in the book on dining in Manhattan, but the menu was promising. I was very happy with a selection of spreads that came with wedges of pita bread and with my lamb shank, cooked in clay and dropping off the bone. My wife was even luckier in her order of Rabbit Stifado, a stew in a rich wine sauce with sweet pearl onions and topped with crispy fried onion shreds. She said it was like *boeuf bourguignon,* but with rabbit. Three of us enjoyed a dry red wine called Agiorgitiko, of which I'd never heard, and Calvin ordered a bottle of retsina, which he finished on his own.

My wife's notebook was out from the first course onward. When our waitress told us she was new and didn't know that much about ingredients, Carolyn lured a male employee over to detail the ingredients in my dips. For instance, the eggplant spread, which I liked but didn't analyze for content, contained not just grilled eggplant, but yogurt, plum tomatoes, red onion, garlic, red wine vinegar, lemon rind, and lemon juice. And so it went. Calvin drank, Carolyn asked questions, and Grace told anecdotes about her experiences in other Greek restaurants, where servers had warned her, variously, not to dip her fingers in the bowl because it contained olive oil, not water, and not to eat the parchment that wrapped her lamb dish because it wasn't filo dough. "As if I'd never eaten in a Greek restaurant!" she exclaimed indignantly.

"Can I use those stories in a column?" Carolyn asked.

"Feel free," Grace replied. "Calvin, is that your third glass of wine? You'll have to order another bottle." Then she turned to us. "Calvin's an alcoholic; you've probably noticed. I've given up trying to change him. I just say, 'As long as you keep up your insurance payments, go to it, my love.'"

Calvin snorted. "And Grace is a one-glass-of-wine-a-night stockbroker. She makes more money than I ever will."

"Maybe if you'd stop drinking, you'd get a raise," she replied tartly.

"So many interesting professions among women these days," said Carolyn, always a diplomat. "What does Sophia Vasandrovich do?"

"Spend money," said Pharr. "How the hell Vaclav affords her, I'll never know. Maybe she had Max killed so Vaclav could get his job."

"Sophia's much too self-involved to plan a murder," Grace objected, "and too snobbish to deal with an assassin, whose family probably wouldn't meet her exacting standards."

"Right," Calvin agreed. "You're absolutely right, my love. And how would she ever explain it to Vaclav? The man loved Max. Cried when word came that Max was dead. Ol' Vaclav is one tough bastard, but he cried for Max."

"Still, you never know about people," Grace temporized. "Didn't they have a child

207

before they immigrated?"

"Yeah." Calvin poured the last of the retsina into his glass and signaled the waiter. "They had to leave the boy behind with Sophia's mother when they escaped. Max had made arrangements for the grandmother and boy to follow when the Commies let up the surveillance, but before the plan could be carried out, they disappeared."

Carolyn looked horrified. I remembered Sophia's cold face at the memorial service and speculated on whether she blamed Max for the loss of her son.

"I wonder if Vaclav would cry for Sophia," Grace mused.

Then we all ordered baklava, for which the restaurant was famous, baklava with sugared pistachio nuts and spiced honey. I could feel my mental processes becoming more acute as I ate my dessert and mulled over the significance of the Vasandroviches' lost child, of Vaclav's love for Max, of Sophia's spendthrift ways. The only conclusion I could reach is that Vaclav could not have been culpable in Max's death. But what of his wife? Even that seemed a stretch of the imagination. And what about Calvin Pharr, our host, who was now drinking ouzo, a strong Greek liqueur, on which he had started as soon as he finished his bottle of wine.

Finally he said, tossing off the final swallow, "Well, that's it. I loved Max, too, and he wanted me to quit drinking, so I am. Call AA, Grace. I'm on the wagon."

I looked toward Grace to see if she believed him. From the expression of shock on her face, I gathered that she did. Which perhaps eliminated Pharr as a suspect. Why would he have Max killed to keep his own job if he could accomplish the same thing by doing what Max had wanted in the first place? Or had the shock of what alcohol had driven him to changed his path? If, of course, he actually stopped drinking. Surely, for a man who started with cognac in the morning, abstinence would be no easy matter. Very likely, Max's death had indeed been linked to the stolen coal project, not to any personal motive beyond greed.

The Pharrs caught a cab; Carolyn and I pushed our way through snow to the door of our hotel, and she announced that she'd had two wonderful ideas for columns, one on pushy New York waitresses, the other on Golf Course Rabbit Stew. I couldn't imagine what the second entailed, but my wife intended to write both and fax them that very night. I suppose she did it. I myself went to bed, hoping the snow would abate enough overnight to allow me a morning run before going in to Hodge, Brune for double compensation and more questions by phone and in person. What an odd pursuit for a professor: investigation of a murder.

Golf Course Rabbit Stew

I first tasted Rabbit Stifado in a New York restaurant on a miserably snowy night. However, I had in my freezer at home two rabbits, if one could call such large animals (they were the size of small dogs) by the name I had always associated with Peter Cottontail, as read to me by my mother when I was a toddler. These rabbits were provided by friends of ours who live on a golf course in Santa Teresa, New Mexico. The husband, while having a margarita one evening by his pool, spotted a huge jack-rabbit hopping off the course toward a plot of shrubs that our friend had particular feelings for, having planted them himself. To protect his vegetation, he put down his drink, walked in to his desk, removed a pistol, for which he had a permit, walked back to the pool apron, and shot the rabbit. He then gave it to me with the mistaken idea that I might like to make some wonderful gourmet dish.

The second rabbit was killed, inadvertently, by his wife, who hit it with a golf ball and thereby lost a birdie on the eleventh hole. She was so indignant that she wouldn't have the rabbit in the house. Again, the husband gave it to me. And what was I to do with it? I'd never cooked a rabbit.

Here is a recipe for Rabbit Stifado that I found in a Greek cookbook. It may not be as good as what I had at Molyvos in New York, but, even made with golf course kill, it's very tasty.

- Cut a *medium-sized hare* into serving pieces. Wash well in *vinegar and water.* Place in an earthenware baking dish.
- Mix together *4 tbs. olive oil; 1 carrot, finely chopped; 2 medium onions, sliced; 1 stalk celery, finely chopped; 2 bay leaves; 2 whole cloves; pinch of thyme; 2 cloves garlic; several peppercorns; 2 wineglasses dry red wine; 4 tbs. vinegar.* Pour this marinade over the hare pieces and allow to marinate in the refrigerator for one to two days.
- Drain the hare pieces and sauté them in *1 cup hot olive oil* with *1 large onion, finely chopped.*
- Strain the marinade and add to the pot with *5 to 6 ripe tomatoes peeled and put through a food processor or mixer, 2 mashed cloves garlic, salt, and pepper.*
- Cover the pot and cook slowly for one hour.
- Peel and wash *2.2 lbs. tiny onions* and cut a small cross in their root ends. Put

211

them in the pot with the hare and continue to cook over low heat for another
hour.

SERVES 6 to 8

Carolyn Blue,
"Have Fork, Will Travel,"
Sacramento News Leader

20

Hot Dogs, Folklore, and the Old Testament

Carolyn

Loretta awakened me Friday with an indignant telephone call. She wanted to know why I would endanger her son's health and religious convictions by feeding him that disgusting hot dog, which undoubtedly contained prohibited pork and God knew what other dangerous things. Having been up late the night before, firing off columns to Marshall Smead in lieu of the requested telephone call, I was very sleepy and not a little confused by this unexpected attack.

"If he's not supposed to have them, why did he ask for one?" I mumbled.

"Because he's a kid," Loretta replied, as if any reasonable person could have figured that out.

Actually, she had a point. "I guess I didn't realize you kept kosher," I apologized.

"Oh, kosher!" she exclaimed dismissively. "It won't kill him to break the dietary laws, but think of what he might catch from those

213

things. Everyone knows they're made from floor sweepings, pork entrails, and parasites. That's why the Jews prohibited pork in the first place. Trichinosis."

"From what I've read — let's see; that was in *Folklore and the Old Testament* by Frazer — the Jewish prohibition against pork grew out of older pagan rites in which pigs were considered sacred and eaten only on high feast days."

"Horse hockey!" Loretta exclaimed. "I ought to report you to the Anti-Defamation League."

"Report the author of the book," I suggested. "It wasn't my idea."

"Have you been to my uncle's place? Today's the lunch with Rollie, and we're eating at a very classy restaurant."

"I know. Le Bernardin, and no, I haven't, but I'll try to get by this morning." I was tired of being nagged about my wardrobe, and I did want to make a good impression on my editor. But what would I do if I hated Uncle Bernie's fashion offerings? That would be seriously embarrassing, because Loretta expected me to buy something. I heaved a great sigh. This was turning out to be a wearing trip.

Loretta was asking, why the big sigh? Here I was being offered the chance to spruce up my image at fabulous wholesale prices, and I couldn't even be bothered. Tuning her harangue out, noticing the snow had stopped, I was relieved that I wouldn't have to feel like an arctic explorer while hunting for Uncle Bernie's establishment. And I'd now be going to two restaurants where I could sample recipes from *Dining and the Opera in Manhattan* without having to cook anything myself. The chance to avoid cooking was the greatest gift of all. Of course, that is not a proper attitude for a culinary writer, but so be it. "I'm going, Loretta," I said, breaking into her monologue. "If you'll let me get dressed and have breakfast, I'll take the first bus or subway that will deposit me at your uncle's place. Is that good enough?"

It evidently was, although Loretta urged me to take a cab. What if my selections needed alterations? Did I expect Bernie's people to drop everything so that I could be properly attired by lunchtime? I told her that I never needed alterations and hung up. Within a half hour I was at the deli, where I found not Thelma but Detective Worski. He sat down at my table, helped himself to a bite of my Nova and scrambled eggs, and said accusingly, as if her disappearance were my responsibility, "This waitress you told me about. She quit. She's not even at her apartment. Landlord said she moved out last night. Boss here says she quit last night."

I nodded. "Probably her mother's idea."

"What's that mean?"

"Her mother was worried about her working in a place where a customer was murdered. The mother wanted her to move back to New Jersey."

"Where in New Jersey?"

"Teaneck, I think she said."

"Got an address? No one else has one."

"I don't know her *that* well, detective. In fact, she didn't say anything to me yesterday about leaving, but . . . let's see . . . she told me her mother has MS and runs an apartment house in Teaneck. Maybe you could locate the mother by calling a local MS support group. All the diseases have support groups."

"You pick up anything else about her?"

"Well, she said her mother didn't have any trouble collecting rents or getting repairs done because their cousins were connected. I took that to mean that they had Mafia connections with enforcer/debt-collector types and corrupt labor unions. Isn't it amazing to think I may have actually met someone with organized crime ties?"

"Why the hell didn't you tell me about that in the first place?"

"It didn't seem relevant," I replied, surprised by his irritation. "Goodness, I told you about the ex-wife and the children. Now *that's* a clue."

"Huh!" said Detective Worski and rose, buttoning up his tacky overcoat. "Last thing I want to do is go lookin' for some woman in New Jersey."

Jason

Thinking of the telephone bills I was running up and grateful that the charges wouldn't be on my bill, I dialed a fellow in Dresden. He knew nothing about the announcement or the company in the Ukraine but said Kiev had been a favorite city before it began to glow in the dark. With a hearty laugh and best wishes to colleagues at my old university (he didn't seem to realize that I had moved), he rang off, saying he was entertaining his postdoctoral students at his apartment that evening with beer, bratwurst, and pointed questions about their research notes.

I renewed many contacts, some with people I hadn't spoken to in some time, some with people I didn't even know very well but who seemed glad to talk to me. The scientific world is somewhat inbred. If you don't know a researcher personally, you probably do know the scientist with whom he did graduate work or a postdoctoral fellowship or someone from his department. There is a traveling mathematician who has written papers with hundreds of other researchers. Now mathematicians have a number indicating that they wrote a paper with him or with someone with whom he's written a paper and so on over a whole network of interconnected men and women. Even I have an Erdich number because I collaborated with the postdoctoral fellow of a man who collaborated with the peripatetic math genius.

I'm afraid my thoughts had begun to wander as my calls yielded less and lunch with some air and water pollution experts approached. Then I got a call from the Polish industrial chemist with whom I had talked yesterday. "Dr. Blue," he began, accent thick and sibilant, "I have been intrigued by your inquiries and have done research among my contacts."

"That's very good of you," I replied.

"Yes. I have come on an interesting information, so strange."

"Really?"

"Yes. Company in Kiev, it have strange affiliations, perhaps of importance, perhaps not, but is unusual. You understand?"

I didn't but made interested noises.

"Yes, vice president of company is married to young woman whose father is man of power in Russian group which I believe you in United States call crowd."

"Crowd?" I confessed to being puzzled.

"Is not right word? I refer to group affiliated for criminal purposes."

A crowd of criminals? "The Mob?" I asked, astounded.

"Yes. I believe that is word. Mob. Yes. Russian Mob. Is most successful adventure in capitalism our old neighbor has yet initiated. Very violent, as I hear by others who know more of such things than I. One hears rumors of their activities in Poland, and my sources say their arms extend into your country. Yes?"

"So I've heard." The Russian Mob? "But would they be interested in scientific research?" I asked, questioning myself as well as my caller.

"If offers much money for little investment, why not? So, my friend, is this something useful for you?"

"I don't know," I replied, "but I certainly appreciate your passing it on to me."

"I am delighted to be serviceable. Poland wishes, as always, good relations with United States. Are we not military allies now as well as allies in world of trade? My company does business in your country and yours in mine."

"Yes," I agreed, although I know little about trade relations with Poland. "The world not only changes but becomes smaller."

"Is indeed so, and no doubt in smaller world I will see you again in future."

"I'll look forward to it." I hung up thoughtfully. The Russian Mob? Well, bizarre as it sounded, it was certainly something I would have to pass on to Charles Moore. I was to see him that afternoon.

21

Never Buy Retail

Carolyn

I found Bernard Feingold's establishment on the third floor at the address his niece had provided. It was a large, open place with people rushing around, racks of clothing rolling on and off the freight elevators, desks piled with paperwork and placed in no apparent order, conversation rising and falling, ironing boards in use, ladies with pins in their mouths, and one small sitting area in a corner fitted out with a worn living room set that looked as if it had come from a discount room store twenty or thirty years ago.

When I managed to catch the attention of a passing middle-aged woman who looked vaguely secretarial, she hustled me over to a tall man wearing a shirt, loose trousers, open vest, and bow tie. "From Loretta," she announced by way of introduction and rushed off to a typewriter on one of the desks. There were computers in evidence, but this woman did not use one.

"What is it, dear?" he asked, hardly looking

at me. "Loretta sent you? She needs something, my niece?"

Embarrassed, I explained my errand and Loretta's instructions.

"You don't mean to tell me you usually buy retail?" exclaimed the horrified businessman, evidently Bernard Feingold. "Never buy retail, dear." As he looked me over, I studied him, as well. Uncle Bernie was a man of indeterminate age — fifty, seventy, I couldn't tell — but he was very thin and round-shouldered, balding with tufts of colorless hair around his ears, skin splotched with large, irregular freckles or age spots, and wearing a pair of ancient, round spectacles from which one lens was missing.

"Size ten," he announced, having completed his inspection. "I see you looking at my eyeglasses, dear. I got one very good eye, so why would I pay for a lens I don't need? My brother-in-law, the optometrist, he charges me wholesale by the lens."

"I see." The conversation and the place were making me feel like Dorothy in Oz without the introductory tornado.

"Take off your coat, dear. What do you write? She's a go-getter, my niece. You got the goods, she'll sell them."

"Food," I said.

He raised flyaway eyebrows above his peculiar eyeglasses.

"A book about food. Maybe newspaper columns about food."

"Food is good. Who wouldn't want to read about food? Time was, I never saw enough. That was when I was a boy. Now Bernie Feingold always knows where his next meal is coming from. What occasion?"

"I beg your pardon?" Did he mean the occasion of his next meal?

"For the clothes, dear."

"Oh. Well, meals in famous restaurants." Now, that sounded snobbish.

"Lunch or dinner?"

"Both, I guess." Presumably, the company would entertain us again tonight. "Something warm, but . . . well . . . dressy. After the desert, I'm freezing in New York."

"Ah, the land of milk and honey. Where we Jews come from." He gave me a sweet smile as he beckoned employees to him and murmured instructions.

"Well, El Paso, Texas, isn't exactly the land of milk and honey," I replied. "More like the land of drought and killer bees."

He laughed. "The eye of the beholder, as they say. Israel . . . now Israel . . . most wouldn't say it's the land of milk and honey, but it looked good to the chosen people. What does your husband do, dear? Is he in the food business?"

"He's a chemist," I replied.

"Try this on." He handed me a green suit

223

with black braided lapels and jet buttons.

I knew I'd never wear anything like that. "What, here?" I asked. I'd seen models change clothes in front of people on shows about high fashion, but I certainly didn't intend to.

"No, there, dear. Ruth, show her the dressing room."

The dressing room was a curtained space in a corner. It didn't even have a mirror. It did have hooks where I could hang my clothes, so I tried on the green suit. It fit wonderfully and probably cost a fortune, but I didn't like it. What if he insisted that I buy it? If there had been a door to a hall in that curtained space, I'd have escaped, leaving his green suit on a hook. As it was, I had to re-enter the big room.

Bernie Feingold, benign and ageless, awaited me. "So your husband's a chemist. My son Sheldon, the doctor, he grew up in Brooklyn with a boy who became a chemist. Maybe your husband knows him. Turn around, dear, so I can see the fit."

What difference did the fit make when I hated the color? With a little salt on top, I'd look like a walking margarita. "There are lots of chemists," I replied.

"Not your color, dear. Bring me the periwinkle, Ruth, be a love. She needs a softer shade. Maxie Heydemann. My son's friend. Now there was a fine boy, even if he never got to be a real doctor. How many games of stickball those two played with their mothers shouting out the windows for them to come home to dinner. Mrs. Feingold, God rest her soul, liked the family to be on time for dinner."

"*Max* Heydemann?" Loretta's uncle knew Max Heydemann? This was Oz indeed. "My husband did know him."

"Here, dear. Try the periwinkle."

I staggered off to the curtained space and tried the periwinkle, a suit made with wool as soft as a baby's touch and a color straight from some alpine meadow. And it fit as if it had been tailored for me. *Goodness knows what it costs,* I thought with real regret. I wasn't going to put my husband in the poorhouse to have this suit. I hadn't even seen it in a mirror. Maybe I'd hate it. I walked out, feeling the smooth accommodation of the fabric to my stride.

"That's the one, dear. That one you should buy."

"What does it cost?" I asked in a small voice.

"Oh, I'll make you a good price. No worry there. You're my Loretta's client. Her mother was like my own child. So your husband knows Maxie? Here, try this on." He handed me a full-length wool dress, smoke gray with rose accents, so lightweight that I hardly knew when it passed from his hand to mine.

"I dress Maxie's wife, Charlotte. What a sweet shiksa she is. Not like the first one who was a schizoid with the mark of the devil on her soul. A Jezebel, that one. Evil-eyed."

I stared at him with a shiver and nodded. "I met her."

"Too bad. A nice lady like you. Much grief she gave our Maxie while he was married to her. Her and her whelps, no-goodniks, both of them. Bad blood drives out good. My mother used to say that. In Yiddish. She never spoke English, my mother. And that Sophia. She's a friend of Charlotte's. Thinks she's the queen of Bohemia." He grimaced, and I had to hide a smile. What an apt description of the lineage-proud Sophia. "Always trying to get me to lower my price. Like I'm not already giving her the dress at cost because Charlotte sent her."

Oh my. He'd think that of me when I found that I couldn't afford these dresses. He'd think I was trying to bargain him down. What was I to do? I liked Mr. Feingold! Better than his niece, truth be told. He directed me to the dressing room with the second dress, which I tried on, having caught a heart-stopping reflection of the periwinkle suit in a mirror propped against a long work-table. Oh, how I wanted that suit! And now I was probably trying on something else I'd long for and have to deny myself.

"Very nice, dear," said Mr. Feingold when I reappeared. "So how is Maxie? Turn around for me. Has your husband seen him?"

"Mr. Feingold, he's dead," I blurted out.

Bernie Feingold stopped studying his beautiful dress on my forty-something figure and stared at me. "Maxie's dead? That can't be! How? He's a young man."

"He was murdered. In a delicatessen."

Mr. Feingold's bespeckled face fell into lines of profound sorrow. "Murdered? I didn't know. And poor Charlotte. How is she doing?"

"Well, she's . . . she's pretty broken up."

"Of course, she is. She kissed the ground Max walked on, Charlotte, and why wouldn't she? Those two loved each other like teenagers, except she had to deal with his children. How they hated their papa for marrying her, and her so fine a woman, who made him so happy. Try these, dear. Maxie dead. How can it be that our children die before us?"

At his direction, Ruth handed me a black pants set. The slacks were flared from the knee with widening insets of material, and the top hung in a loosely fitted tunic decorated with insets of teal and, at the waist, a silver and turquoise belt that had a medieval look to it. Guinevere in pants. It must cost a queen's ransom, but I did have to try it on, to see myself in it just once. What a terrible idea on Loretta's part to send me here. Now I'd never be quite happy with my simple, sensible wardrobe. I gave the gray dress one last look and went off to try on another Bernie Feingold choice in the warm-but-dressy category. He was mumbling about Max as I slipped behind the flowered curtain.

"Well," said Mr. Feingold when I returned. "Very smart, and it doesn't overwhelm your coloring, dear. Take my word. It's good on you."

I took his word. I could see myself in the mirror. Another woman would have worn it with high, spiked sandals, but I, if it were mine, would wear flats. Even in imagination, I'll only go so far for the sake of fashion, and hobbling my feet is too far. At the moment, I was stocking-footed. And I had been right to tell Loretta that I wouldn't need any alterations, just an influx of cash.

"At least poor Charlotte will be well taken care of," said Bernie. "Max was a careful man, foresighted."

"We don't know that — that she'll be well taken care of, I mean," I said, turning wistfully before the mirror. "There's a trust fund for her, but the will won't be read until this afternoon, and who knows —"

"Oh, I know. Maxie and me, we got the same lawyer, Jake Blumenthal. Jake went to school with my boy and Maxie."

"No matter what provisions he made, the

first wife plans to have her rich father contest the will if her children don't get what she thinks they deserve."

"Jake draws you up a will, no one's rich father's gonna break it. Charlotte gets the most and controls the trusts for the children as long as she lives. That ought to put a stick in their spokes, worthless brats that they are. Now, you want to see more?"

"Oh no. These are lovely." I shouldn't have said that. "But how much . . ."

He went to his desk, pulled out a scrap of paper, scribbled figures on it, mumbled to himself, scribbled some more. *Oh me*, I thought. *I'll probably turn white when he names a price.* He named one. "For which outfit?" I asked. I could just about afford that. Oh, my goodness! I could justify that much! But which outfit was it that I could afford?

"For all, dear. For the three. I told you I'd make you a good price. For Max's friend's wife, for my niece, little Loretta, wouldn't I make a good price?"

"But Mr. Feingold —"

"So maybe I could come down a little, even throw in a bottle of my signature perfume, but I'd be taking a loss. Still —"

"Oh, I didn't mean that. I mean you're too generous. I can't let you —"

"I can see it's not the queen of Bohemia I'm dealing with here. Do I have to talk you into accepting my offer? You want me to raise the price a little?"

"Oh, Mr. Feingold," I cried and gave him a hug.

"Call me Bernie," he replied, beaming.

22

On Dining with a Famous Gourmet

Wonderful food and lovely decor are to be found in the restaurants of New York at the beginning of the new millennium, but surely they cannot produce the exciting stories and bizarre spectacles of the past. In the eighteenth century, Sam Francis, a well-known patriot and New York tavern keeper, was steward to George Washington, and Sam's daughter Phoebe acted as the housekeeper at Washington's Richmond Hill headquarters. While serving dinner, the girl found her sweetheart, a soldier on the general's staff, adding poison to Washington's favorite dish, spring peas. She carried the dish to the table but then had to choose between her country and her lover. She tossed the peas out the window, and they promptly killed all of the neighbor's chickens. The general survived, Phoebe was a heroine, but her true love was the first American soldier hung for treason.

If Sam Francis's various taverns were the

toast of New York in the eighteenth century, Delmonico's was the introducer of haute cuisine in the nineteenth century. Eighteen seventy-three saw the production of the famous (or infamous) swan banquet by Lorenzo Delmonico. It featured a huge, round, ballroom-filling table with a thirty-foot lake in the center where swans floated majestically until overcome by avian lust. The conversation of the diners was noisy, but it was nothing to the cacophonous mating of the swans during the banquet. What contemporary chef could hope to compete with that spectacle? And what did the prim Victorian matrons make of it?

Carolyn Blue,
"Have Fork, Will Travel,"
Bakersfield Valley Gazette

Carolyn

Even wearing my new periwinkle suit, I was nervous about meeting Roland DuPlessis. He was a noted gourmet; I was just a woman who liked good food and had once enjoyed cooking. Le Bernardin was a four-star restaurant; I wasn't sure I'd ever been in one. The room, when I was ushered in, featured paneled walls and pictures of ships at sea; I was a landlocked Midwesterner now living in the desert Southwest and about to be confronted with an elaborate fish menu. Fortunately, I don't object to fish, although I'm not as mad for it as Jason. Even so, I did have a lot to be nervous about.

On the other hand, Roland DuPlessis, when I met him, was strangely dressed. He was an immensely fat man, an Occidental Buddha wearing a beret and a vest ornamented with crewel embroidery under a tent-like sports jacket of emerald green. I, at least, looked wonderful. I noticed that the waiter thought so. Even Loretta gave my outfit a nod of approval before introducing me.

"I loved the proposal," said DuPlessis. "Country taste in the big city. What New Orleans recipes will you use?"

I certainly don't consider myself "country," but I held my tongue and named recipes. "Good, good," he said. "Send me copies immediately. I'll want to try them."

I hadn't tried them all myself. I hadn't even wanted to think about that trip. "About the New Orleans book —" I began.

"Menus first," said Roland DuPlessis, accepting his with a grand wave of the arm. "Ah, they have the black bass seviche. I'm sure you'll want that. Very Southwestern. Cilantro. Jalapeños. Loretta, what shall we choose for you?"

"I can choose my own, thanks, Rollie," she replied tartly.

"She's afraid I'll insist that she eat some ocean scavenger, some fearful shellfish." A chortling laugh rolled from his chest.

"I'm Jewish. I'm not eating shellfish to please you, sweetie."

"I think I'd like the Seared Tuna and Truffled Herb Salad," I murmured. Loretta glared at me, but I had the recipe for that in *Dining and the Opera*. It looked like something I could make without taking four days to do it, should I ever be overcome by a desire to cook, say for Jason's birthday.

"Excellent. Excellent," DuPlessis agreed. "I approve of truffles. Did you know that the French ambassador once insulted John Adams by bringing his own chef to a dinner at the vice president's house? The chef served game birds with truffles, much to the disgust of the Americans. We colonials didn't always like truffles; more's the pity. After the Civil War, Ward McAllister, arbiter of taste to the Four Hundred of New York society, said that truffles should never be served more than once at a dinner. Slow progress, but progress indeed. You should go to Umbria if you like truffles, dear lady."

I nodded. "La Rosetta in Perugia. I wonder what game birds were served with the truffles at the Adamses' dinner. During that period, a man named Niblo was offering all kinds of strange things: bald eagle, hawk, owl, swan, although swans were a popular banquet dish

234

in the Middle Ages."

Roland DuPlessis took my hand. I thought he was going to kiss it, so happy was he to find someone who had eaten at La Rosetta and knew snippets of food history. "La Rosetta would make a book in itself," he said enthusiastically. "But Loretta tells me you are thinking of a second book: *Eating Ethnic in the Big Apple*. Charming. Loretta, you can have the yellowfin carpaccio."

"You can't fool me, Rollie," she replied. "That's raw fish."

"No matter, it has fins, so it's not against your religion. Be adventurous, my dear. Expand your horizons. It comes with a divine ginger-lime mayonnaise. I like the ethnic angle," he continued, turning back to me. "Middlewesterner dines Basque, Indian, Thai, Senegalese. I'll make you a list of restaurants."

"He probably wants you to eat chocolate-covered termites," said Loretta, who had been studying her menu and ordered a Chinese spiced red snapper. "I like Chinese takeout," she explained.

"Always the Philistine," said DuPlessis.

"I'm only here until Sunday," I admitted. "I probably won't have time —"

"But you'll come back after the New Orleans book."

"About the New Orleans book —"

"She's dying to finish it," said Loretta,

kicking me in the ankle. We exchanged unpleasant glances as Roland urged us to order second courses.

"I want to try one of the desserts," I objected. "And I've done nothing but overeat since I got here."

"It is impossible to overeat if the food is good enough." He plunged a fork into the tuna carpaccio, which he had ordered for himself when Loretta refused it.

"You're living proof of that," said Loretta.

"Ha! Your rudeness is exceeded only by the beauty of your eyes, my dear Madam Blum. And you, Carolyn, how can you associate with a woman as crass as this, a person who refuses to eat shellfish or, say, an excellent loin of pork in a spicy plum sauce, and all in the name of a religion she probably doesn't practice?"

"Who doesn't? Simon's in Hebrew school preparing for his bar mitzvah as we speak. And don't try to come between me and my client, Rollie. We're very close."

I was certainly surprised to hear that.

"She even took Simon for me yesterday when I had a conflict."

"In that case, I hope you lowered your commission accordingly. An hour spent in the company of a child is as bad as a half day in a hot dog factory."

Oh, *why* did he feel it necessary to mention hot dogs? I foresaw another lecture from

Loretta on my insensitivity in exposing her child to the dangers of sausages filled with pork and other undesirable meat products. To head it off, I said, "My husband would love this restaurant. He adores fish."

"You should have brought him. *He* could have had the yellowfin carpaccio. Or is he afraid of raw fish, too?"

"Not at all. We eat sushi when we get the chance."

"They have sushi in El Paso, Texas?" Roland looked astonished.

"We even have Japanese people. But Jason couldn't have come." I hastened back into the conversation because I could see that Loretta was about to speak. "He's consulting at a chemical company, and unfortunately, a friend of his was murdered, and —"

"Max Heydemann," said DuPlessis.

I was dumbfounded. "You knew Max, too?"

"I certainly did. Max was the pastrami king of the city. Native of Brooklyn, graduate of Brooklyn Poly and Columbia, pastrami connoisseur. I've enjoyed many a bowl of chicken soup with matzo balls, many an order of Nova or pastrami in the company of Max. We did a research tour of New York delicatessens in our younger days. That was when he was married to his first wife, a dreadful woman whom he avoided by eating out. She never ate *anything* to my knowledge.

Absolutely anorexic. And her daughter as well."

"I know Max," said Loretta. "He's dead?"

I told the story. Roland said that he had a theory about the murderer. "A rival deli owner. Once Max made his choice, he never deviated. Every Monday, same place, same sandwich. What better way to ruin a rival than to murder his favored customer over a heap of the house's best pastrami? My second choice would be his abominable son, who once fished a live lobster from the tank at the Grand Central Oyster Bar and let it loose to roam the marble floors, causing a veritable cacophony of shrieking among the female diners. I believe the boy was ten at the time and hasn't improved his manners since then."

After that, we had dessert. I ordered the Chocolate Dome with a Symphony of Crème Brûlée on a Macaroon. I won't give you the recipe because it's really three dessert recipes in one, but it's heavenly, and you can find it in *Dining and the Opera in Manhattan* or on the menu at Le Bernardin.

Seared Tuna and Truffled Herb Salad

- To make the vinaigrette: In a small bowl, whisk together *3 tbs. balsamic vinegar; 1 canned black truffle, drained (juice reserved) and minced; 1 tbs.*

---

truffle juice; and *7 tbs. extra-virgin olive oil.* Season with *salt and pepper* and set aside.

- Season one *12-oz. tuna loin* with *1 tbs. minced fresh thyme, salt,* and *freshly ground pepper to taste.* Film a large sauté pan or skillet with oil and sear tuna over high heat until crusty on the outside and rare in the center.
- Slice seared tuna into ¼-in.-thick slices and arrange slices on 4 plates. Garnish with *4 cups assorted baby greens* and *1 cup mixed fresh herbs such as basil, dill, and parsley.* Drizzle vinaigrette over everything and serve.

It was four o'clock when I got home, and the subway ride, which was made charming by the sight of a baby in a stroller wearing a leopard-skin hat and sunglasses, gave me the opportunity to reflect on the things I had learned about the Heydemann family. I considered Roland (he had invited me to call him Roland between his second course and my dessert) DuPlessis's rival-deli-owner hypothesis facetious, but I did think Detective Worski would be interested to hear about Max's will and get another opinion on Heydemann's first wife and his son.

What the detective seized on, when I called, was the will. He wanted to know who had told me and how they knew the provisions, not to mention when the will was to be read. To protect Bernie, I said only that an acquaintance had the same lawyer, who had mentioned the bequests. Worski muttered something about client confidentiality, and hadn't lawyers ever heard of it? Who was this lawyer who went around blabbing the terms of wills?

"I don't think that's the point, Detective," I protested. "The point is that if Charlotte controls the trust funds for the children, they may try to kill her, they or their mother. I think you should provide her protection until this case is solved."

"Oh, great," snapped Worski. "And if she's the murderer, who am I protecting her from? Looks like she's the one with everything to gain. And say, your husband won't talk to my partner anymore. Ali wants to know about this espionage thing, mostly because he's into that white-collar stuff; I don't put much store by that theory."

"Nor do I," I agreed, "but Jason's been asked not to talk to the police."

"Well, he can't refuse."

"I'll tell him." Not a word of thanks for the information *I* had just provided. What a cranky person the detective was. Maybe his had been a very painful divorce.

I had another request that I call Marshall Smead. Instead, I wrote a column on ladies from the "hinterlands" eating in intimidating restaurants with known gourmets, which I then faxed to him. After that, I took a nap.

23

The Mob?

Oysters have always been popular in New York City, but in earlier years, the supply was more varied, more plentiful, and much less expensive. In 1776, two hundred canoes full came into port daily. In 1810, they were to be had from street vendors for one to three cents apiece. In the 1830s and '40s, oyster cellars on Canal Street offered all the oysters a patron could reasonably eat for six cents, although a patron who made a pig of himself could expect to be discouraged from further consumption by being given an oyster that had gone bad. By 1850, New Yorkers consumed more than six million dollars worth of the popular bivalves, and by 1880, Americans were eating 660 Manhattan oysters a year per person; New Yorkers preserved the delicacies fresh in barrels and shipped them to less fortunate parts of the country. And they were large! Thackeray said American oysters were so big that eating one was like "swallowing a small baby." But at the beginning of the twenty-first century, the oysters are smaller and can cost fifteen dollars a dozen. Many things change but not, it would seem, the taste for oysters.

Carolyn Blue,
"Have Fork, Will Travel,"
Las Cruces Pioneer News

Jason

I returned to the company offices around two-thirty after a long, pleasant lunch with a group of scientists whom I had not met previously — all air and water pollution men, an enthusiastic and jolly lot. Our lunch venue was an oyster bar that served sixty-five different types of beer and fourteen different varieties of raw oysters, although not all on that day. Nonetheless, the oysters were fresh and varied, the beer cold and robustly foreign, the booths deeply upholstered in soft, dark leather, the clientele almost entirely male, and Hodge, Brune picked up the bill.

My wife would have found the pleased complacency of our group decidedly amusing; nonetheless, we men do like, on occasion, to congregate where large-screen televisions show only sporting events, the atmosphere owes nothing to feminine tastes, and the conversation is decidedly Y-chromosome generated, in this case scientific. I found myself wondering, as I tossed down the liquid left in an oyster shell, whether Frances Striff ever comes here and if she enjoys it.

At any rate, I experienced a bolt of super-charged boredom at the prospect of returning to my small office to make more telephone calls abroad. Whatever my future connection with Hodge, Brune, I wanted to get back to my own labs, students, and scientific problems, which I could discuss as freely as I liked with anyone I cared to confide in. Avoiding questions from the police was a duty I found particularly irksome, yet I knew that Vernon Merrivale would have eyes watching me. He didn't have any power over me, to be sure, but I *was* in his territory. I was also aware that he considered my efforts on the company's behalf of no value and, in fact, likely to do more harm than good to his investigation.

"Dr. Blue. Dr. Blue." A young woman trotted down the hall after me. "Where have you been? Dr. Moore would like you to come to his office."

I turned and headed the other way, the young lady hurrying after me, evidently to see that I did not disappear again before she could fulfill her mission.

"Jason," Moore greeted me with his usual serious mien. "I was afraid you had deserted us." Merrivale sat in a visitor's chair, frowning suspiciously in my direction.

244

"I was invited to lunch by a group of your scientists."

"Excellent," Moore murmured. "I hope you enjoyed your break." Before I could respond, he hurried on. "I've read the report you sent late yesterday afternoon."

"Nothing much there," said Merrivale.

"What do you think of the idea that the Ukrainian announcement is a bluff?" I asked, ignoring the security director.

"To what end?" Merrivale demanded.

"To claim a percentage of the money you make on the process, I suppose. Or to let you buy them out."

"We've heard nothing from them," said Moore. "Even the feelers we've put out have been ignored."

I shrugged. "Well, yesterday that seemed the best idea I'd heard."

"The important investigation, *my* investigation, is at this end," said Merrivale. "We have to discover who let slip or sold our proprietary —"

"Of course, you want to know, but it won't repair the damage that has been done," I pointed out. "If they really have the process —"

"We'll prosecute," said Merrivale, his face flushing with outrage. "We'll destroy the spy and then the people who hired him."

"You said that was your best theory yesterday," Moore interrupted, addressing himself to me. "Have you learned anything else of note?"

"Perhaps one thing, and I'm not sure of its value. I had a callback this morning from an industrial chemist in Krakow. He tells me that he's found sources who say the vice president of the Ukrainian company is married to a young woman whose father —"

"For God's sake," Merrivale exclaimed. "Wives. In-laws. We're dealing with industrial espionage here, not family sagas."

"As I was saying, the wife's father is reputed to be a power in the Russian Mafia."

Both men looked at me as if I had lost my mind.

"A bizarre twist, if true," I admitted hastily, "but we must remember yesterday's speculation as to who was funding this company. Such a group would certainly have the means, if the project seemed profitable."

"Organized crime isn't *productive*," snapped Merrivale. "They don't *manufacture* things, and they go into legitimate businesses only to launder their dirty money."

"I'm sure you're right," I replied, "but they do engage in theft, threats, bribery, and extortion — or so I'd gather." I hadn't taken this avenue of speculation all that seriously myself, but no one likes to have his hypothesis sneered at. "Your research *has* been stolen, unless this is an amazing and unlikely scientific coincidence. And these criminals may have threatened or bribed an employee of yours into providing the information. Lastly, they may be planning to extort money from you. Just because they haven't doesn't mean they may not yet do so. Theft, threats, bribery, extortion: all within the purview of a criminal organization." I sat back and held a steady gaze on Merrivale. *A cogent argument,* I thought. *Probably wrong, but perfectly logical.*

"Bizarre," said Moore. "But I can't fault the logic."

Exactly, I thought.

"It doesn't matter who's pulling the strings," Merrivale exploded. "We can find that out when we catch the traitor in our midst. We need to ascertain —"

"How did you get along with Fergus McRoy?" Moore interrupted.

"Seems a nice enough fellow," I replied. "He's certainly upset about the theft of his brainchild. He's conducting his own investigation."

"Smoke screen," snarled Merrivale. "He's covering up."

Moore waved a hand to quiet his head of security, looked pensive for a moment, then spoke, each word carefully thought out and articulated. "We have some reason, no evidence mind you, to think that Fergus himself might be suspect."

"Why?" I asked. Of course, that had occurred to me, although instinct told me it was unlikely. But then instinct would undoubtedly lead me to believe that no one I know would have engaged in industrial espionage. I frankly found the concept as incredible as my wife did, although I could not rule it out and so had helped in this investigation.

"Fergus is well paid," said Moore slowly, "but not as well paid as some. And he has seven children. The raising of so many children is a considerable expense. And his wife does not work. She is a homemaker."

"And no one seems to think he's in financial straits," said Merrivale. "So why isn't he?"

"In other words, you think he'd be vulnerable to an offer?" I concluded for them. "That may suggest motive but hardly constitutes evidence."

"Motive explains the inexplicable," said Merrivale.

"Um-m-m." I really didn't care to comment, nor was I impressed. Merrivale's investigation had not progressed beyond wild guesses.

"So what we have in mind," said Moore, "is a social evening between you, your wife, and the McRoys. It's all arranged. They'll take you out to dinner and a play."

"And you'll question him," added Merrivale, "and report back."

"Gentlemen, I am neither a qualified interrogator nor a spy," I protested. "I —"

"We're only asking you to spend an evening with the man," said Merrivale impatiently. "Hell, it's a free dinner and theater tickets."

"*Waiting in the Wings*," said Moore. "Oscar Wilde's last play, I believe. It's had fine reviews."

I felt like walking out on them, but Merrivale was already placing tickets in my hand. "They'll pick you up at six. That should give you plenty of time to quiz the two of them before you have to head for the theater. Then, if you haven't found out anything, suggest a drink afterward. Nothing like alcohol to loosen a man's tongue. Maybe he'll let something slip. Or she will. Big spending plans or something."

I looked at Merrivale with intense dislike.

Moore, evidently sensing my reluctance, said, "I'd appreciate your opinion, Jason, because I'd hate to think we are holding under suspicion a man who has worked with excellent results for Hodge, Brune for some years."

Put that way, I rethought my impulse to refuse. Maybe it was McRoy, not the company, who needed my help. Perhaps I was obliged to give this plan a try.

By the time I got back to the hotel room and told my wife of our prospective evening out, it was five o'clock, and we had only an hour to prepare. Her first question was: "What restaurant?" She was already reaching for that book I had bought for her birthday. I had to admit that I didn't know. "Well, I hope they pick something I can write about for a change."

"It seems to me that you've been writing constantly since we arrived."

She laughed. "Only since I met Marshall Smead. I just ignored another call from him. Oh, Jason, you'd have loved Le Bernardin. Wonderful, wonderful fish dishes."

"I'd be green with envy if I hadn't had as many raw oysters as I could eat for lunch."

"That would turn anyone green," she retorted gaily, "and not with envy. Ugh." She was putting on a stunning gray dress as I changed my shirt.

"Do you think this is all right for a night at the theater?" She twirled for my inspection.

"My God, you look beautiful, Carolyn. I haven't seen that before, have I?"

Immediately she looked contrite and explained about her agent's Uncle Bernie, the three outfits, and what they cost. "I know it sounds like a lot, Jason, but they're worth ever so much more than —"

"Just the one you're wearing is worth that price," I replied. "And don't give the money a thought. They're paying me double my usual rate."

"They are? My goodness! I could have bought something else."

"Well, no need to go overboard."

"Oh, Jason, I heard something truly frightening at Mr. Feingold's," and she told me about Max's will and her fear that Charlotte was now in danger of being killed by his ex-wife or children because she controlled the trust funds.

Amazing! The Russian Mafia. Murdering offspring. We needed to get away from this city. Maybe I *didn't* want a job with Hodge, Brune. I'd have to give the matter careful consideration, if the job was offered. Perhaps it depended on my catching Fergus McRoy in some damning slip of the tongue over dessert.

24

The Apprehensive Host

Carolyn

The company was paying Jason double his usual consulting fee? I had to think better of them for that. In fact, it might not be so bad to spend several months each summer in New York. The children would love it. And after all, I was quite sure now that the murder of Max Heydemann had had nothing to do with Hodge, Brune, so Jason would be in no danger.

All these thoughts floated through my mind as I showed Jason my two other outfits while we waited for the McRoys to call from the lobby. I even held out high hopes for the restaurant to which we'd go and for the play we were to see, *Waiting in the Wings*. The review in a magazine about New York provided by the hotel was quite favorable. Lauren Bacall and Rosemary Harris were starring. What luck that the McRoys had managed to get tickets. And where were they? Six-thirty had passed, although they were to have picked us up at six.

Jason began reading an article that compared lifestyles of different types of monkeys, one species in which the males practiced rape, another in which the females controlled the males with sexual favors — lots of them. And if that didn't work, they tore off male genitals. Jason read me choice tidbits, and I wondered what a zoo would do about such behavior, which seemed much too sexual and violent to be viewed by the children who customarily flocked to zoos. And where were the McRoys? At this rate, we'd be lucky to consume one course before we had to hasten to the performance at the Eugene O'Neill Theater. Was this my penance for refusing an entrée at Le Bernardin? We might get no dinner at all, and I was hungry.

"What if they never arrive?' I asked anxiously.

"Well, I've got the tickets." Jason displayed them.

"But dinner," I protested.

"I thought you were worried about your waistline."

Men are so insensitive. Here I was starving, and my husband saw fit to remind me of my waistline.

Our telephone rang at 6:45, just as I was taking a tentative sniff of Bernie Feingold's signature perfume. Good grief! It was awful! I hastily capped the small atomizer and dropped it into my purse for later disposal. Then we rushed downstairs to confront our windblown, flustered, apologetic hosts. It seems that they have seven children — seven! Can you imagine? And the baby-sitter had canceled at the last minute, making it necessary for the eldest to baby-sit the younger ones, a solution that the McRoys found worrisome, since they rarely went out evenings and had never left the children to fend for themselves. But they — Fergus and Fiona — were so sorry to be late, and now there was nothing for it but that we eat at a restaurant right next to the theater. They hoped we didn't mind. They had no idea whether or not it would meet my standards, my being a cuisine expert. By the time we actually got to the place, which was called the Garrick Bistro, I was feeling sorry for them.

That feeling blossomed as the evening progressed. Fergus, poor man, was distraught. We had no sooner ordered — Seared Sea Scallops and Wild Mushroom Ragout with Truffled Gnocchi for me and Shellfish Bouillabaisse on Lemon Pepper Linguini for Jason — than Fergus announced that the company suspected *him* of being behind the industrial espionage that had led to Max Heydemann's death.

"I would never betray Max!" he cried.

"Of course you wouldn't," his wife murmured soothingly.

"It was my project, my big chance! Would I throw that away? Never. Here I've been alienating everyone on my team, trying to discover how the research got away from the lab, and all along they suspect me."

"Your team?" I asked, confused.

"No, Moore, Merrivale, and Vasandrovich."

"Well, I could tell them that Max's death had nothing to do with industrial espionage," I replied, hoping to calm him. "It was obviously a family dysfunction that resulted in murder."

"You think so?" Fergus looked as if I was about to save him from drowning.

"Of course," I replied. "Didn't you go to the memorial service? You could feel the waves of enmity coming off those children of his. And his first wife — Jason and I saw her at the opera, and she was celebrating his death. She made no secret of that."

Fergus nodded. "She's crazy. And the daughter's a slut."

"And Ricky — the would-be actor — is always in debt and in trouble with his father," Fiona agreed. "So you see, Fergus, you don't have to worry."

All the while we had been dipping a fennel-flavored bread into an excellent olive oil infused with herbs. We also had an amazingly good South African Shiraz, although I hadn't even known they made wine in South Africa. I wrote down the name: Rust en Vrede. Vrede sounded Boer. I found it hard to imagine phlegmatic Dutch farmers making tasty wines whose grapes had been picked, perhaps, by towering Watusi tribesmen. No doubt that is a mistaken picture of wine making in South Africa.

"But no matter who killed Max . . . and I'll never believe it was anyone at the company . . . he was loved. Wasn't he, Fiona?"

"He was," she agreed and asked me what herb that was in the olive oil.

"Tarragon," I replied.

"So no matter who killed him," Fergus persisted, having fallen into anxiety once more, "we've still had our research stolen, and I'm being blamed."

At that point, our dinners were served.

"Why would they blame you?" asked his wife reasonably. "It makes no sense."

I ate a scallop and almost gagged. What *was* that? I poked suspiciously at my ragout. Jason sent me a questioning look.

"Pure prejudice," said Fergus. "It's because we have seven children."

Gingerly, I tried another scallop. And that *was* a scallop. Well, of course. The first thing had been a lump of gnocchi. I'd forgotten about that component of the dish and was very relieved to discover my error. "Surely, it's against the law to discriminate against people because of the number of children they have," I remarked. "Like age discrimination. Or sex discrimination."

"I see," said Fiona. "We have seven children, so they assume we need the money."

"What money?" I asked. My scallops were delicious, firm, perfectly cooked, and bathed in a citrusy sauce with greens and mushrooms in it.

"They think I sold the company secrets. That has to be it," said Fergus.

The man was beside himself with anxiety. And my husband looked terribly uncomfortable. Surely, he didn't think this poor fellow guilty of anything.

"Well, that's just foolishness," said Fiona stoutly. "Fergus makes plenty of money. As long as the stock market keeps rising, we'll never have any serious financial problems. The market is his hobby. Other men watch Monday night football. Fergus reads the *Wall Street Journal* and logs onto the financial sites on the Internet." She patted his hand. "You should take your financial records in and show them, dear."

"How can I do that? They haven't come right out and accused me of anything."

"Then maybe you're worrying for nothing." She was eating steadily through her dinner while her husband fretted.

"What do you think, Jason? Do they suspect me?"

"Well, I . . ." Jason looked even more uncomfortable.

"Jason hasn't said a word to me about anyone suspecting you of anything, Fergus," I answered, jumping in with reassurances.

"There, you see, Fergus," said his wife. "All's well."

The music system in the restaurant began to play, of all things, "Don't Fence Me In." They had a terrible selection of boring music, even if the scallops were wonderful. "How's your bouillabaisse, Jason?" Maybe we could distract Fergus from his fears.

"Excellent," Jason replied. "It has not only a good selection of shellfish but octopus as well."

Fiona looked shocked at the mention of octopus. With seven children, it probably wasn't something she was given to serving the family.

"Would you like to try the sauce?" Jason asked. "It's delicious."

I accepted and found it rather fishy, but then my husband likes fishy. I offered him a scallop, resisting the impulse to shock him with a lump of gnocchi. He liked my scallops more than I liked his sauce.

"So don't be glum, dear," said Fiona.

"Why not? Even if they stop suspecting me and find out who did it, the company will never be the same without Max."

"Then we'll move," said his wife. "You've had offers. We can sell the house in New Jersey for a fortune and move somewhere where real estate is cheap and we'll make a profit."

"We did that," I said encouragingly. "Houses are amazingly cheap in El Paso."

"El Paso doesn't have any good industrial chemistry jobs," said Fergus.

"You can take the profit from the house and use it to make more money in the market," said Fiona.

"The bull market won't last forever," said Fergus. "It's already faltering."

"I don't think we have time for dessert," said Fiona. "Not if we're going to make the first act of the play."

We barely gained our seats before the curtain went up on a tale, both funny and sad, about a retirement home for impecunious actors. Fergus hated the play and said so. It reminded him that, for the McRoys, a poverty-stricken old age awaited because there'd be nothing left after they put all the children through college.

"Nonsense," said Fiona. "They'll get scholarships."

"What about Roddy?" Fergus asked despairingly.

"He'll get a soccer scholarship," she replied.

Fergus perked up. "The boy *is* good. A fine goalie. But what if he gets hurt?"

"Well, that was certainly fun," I said to Jason when we were safely back in our hotel

259

room. "Do they really suspect him of being a spy?"

"Yes," said Jason.

"Do you?" I asked, surprised.

"No," he replied. Then we checked our telephone messages. There were four.

25

Room Service and Telephone Tag

Carolyn

As I hung up my coat and began to take off my new gray dress, I said, "I'm still hungry. Aren't you?" Jason was checking telephone messages. "Let's order from room service. Sympathetic as I am to the McRoys, I do think the company owes us dessert."

"Get me something light," said Jason.

I picked up the menu. "How about passion fruit sorbet?"

"Sounds good." He was making notes on the telephone pad. "You've got a message here from Detective Worski. Why is he calling you?"

I shrugged, more interested in the chocolate truffle torte I had just selected than in who had called. "Maybe to say he did provide protection for Charlotte."

"I hope that you haven't been talking out of turn to the police. The company is very worried about news getting out concerning —"

"Jason," I interrupted, "you know I think the whole spy scenario is silly. The other

261

company probably came up with the idea on its own. After all, Hodge, Brune scientists aren't the only people in the world interested in solving pollution problems. As you said, global warming is a matter of international concern. There are probably dozens of companies working on solutions.

"And Detective Worski isn't interested in spy conspiracies. He's probably off in the wilds of New Jersey looking for the missing waitress from the deli." A disturbing thought came to me as I said that. "Oh, goodness, you don't think Thelma's in danger because she saw something when Max was killed, do you? Even if she didn't, the murderer might think she could identify him, or her, and —"

My husband smiled at me fondly. "You can't save the world, love," he said. Then more soberly, "Neither can I."

"In that case, give me the phone so that I can order dessert. I'll even give you a bite of my truffle torte. Do you want coffee?"

"Espresso, if they have it."

"You'll never sleep," I warned.

"Carolyn, I've been up since five; I'll sleep. In fact, why don't we plan to sleep late tomorrow, go out for brunch, and then inspect that rug you're so enthusiastic about?"

What a lovely day he'd outlined: no agents, editors, or worries about making a good impression, just a nice shopping trip with my husband. I dropped a kiss on his cheek as I dialed room service.

"Your second message was from Paul Fallon," Jason added as he loosened his tie.

"Humph," I said. "Maybe Smead complained that I wasn't returning his calls."

Jason stripped down to his shorts; he does have a nice, compact body, no middle-age spread, and his waistline seems to be unaltered by our trip to New Orleans, which is so unfair. I'm sure I didn't eat any more than he did. As he shrugged into his robe, I dictated our order and then looked at Worski's number. I should return his call, although I really didn't want to. What if he had bad news about Charlotte? Or Thelma?

"If you don't mind, I'll make my calls first," my husband said. I went into the bathroom but could hear him having a rather enigmatic conversation with Dr. Moore, the vice president at Hodge, Brune. "Perhaps . . . Nothing concrete . . . No, we didn't. . . . Actually, it isn't a good time. . . . Very well, twelve-thirty, then."

He hung up and went through the intricacies of making an international call from a hotel telephone — the Czech Republic, of all places. I brushed my hair and put on a nightgown and robe. While I was answering our door and accepting delivery of Jason's sorbet and my scrumptious-looking truffle torte (it had a whirl of chocolate cream on top in which was embedded an alluring fresh raspberry), Jason was saying, "Stefan, this is Jason Blue. I'm returning your call. Sorry about the hour, but you did say . . ."

I put the sorbet and espresso down beside my husband and went to the desk to savor my own treat, which tasted as good as it looked.

"Yes, Charles University . . . Really? Now, that's odd. Perhaps I misunderstood."

Where had I heard Charles University mentioned recently? I wondered. And was Jason planning, on the basis of his first call, to desert me at twelve-thirty tomorrow? That wouldn't give us much time for rug shopping after brunch. I felt rather ill used at the thought. However, if he didn't like the rug, I'd be disappointed. Without him, I could take advantage of the situation and buy it on my own. *Not nice, Carolyn,* said my conscience.

"Phone's all yours." Jason looked very thoughtful, even rather puzzled as he stood up, sipping his espresso.

"How's the sorbet?"

"Good."

"Want to try the torte?"

"No thanks."

"Are we still planning on brunch and rug shopping tomorrow?"

"Ah, Carolyn." He looked seriously regretful. "I've got to meet Charles Moore at twelve-thirty. Lunch and discussion in his office. I'm sorry."

"All right. We'll just have breakfast instead of brunch so we can make it to the rug store and back."

"You're an angel."

Not really, I thought. I was feeling decidedly peeved as I took his place on the bed beside the telephone. First, I called Detective Worski at home. The background TV chatter assuaged my conscience about phoning so late. "Are Charlotte and Thelma safe?" I asked.

"Mrs. Blue, I have no idea," he responded. "Mrs. Heydemann's probably at home celebrating all the money she inherited and having got the best of her stepchildren. That's if the will turned out to be what your friend thought."

"I doubt Charlotte is pleased to be saddled with financial oversight of those two. I heard tonight that the daughter is a slut — that's a quotation — and the son a spendthrift, would-be actor. No one has a good word to say about either. You really should take the danger to Charlotte more seriously. Unless you've found out who killed her husband."

"Hell, I can't even find the woman who was probably the last person to see him alive, except for the murderer. I just spent a rotten day with a bunch of New Jersey cops following up leads that didn't pan out. You sure you got the town and the disease right?"

"Yes, I am sure, and I find the disappearance of Thelma very disturbing. What if she saw the murder and was afraid to tell, and the murderer knew she could identify him, so he killed her to protect himself? Maybe you should check for unidentified bodies."

"I thought of that," said Worski. "Why you think I been slogging around New Jersey? It's like she never existed except for that job and a month or two in that short-lease apartment. Maybe she was the last person to see him alive because she killed him."

"Why would she? She was just his waitress."

"We don't know that."

"Are you saying *she* might be an assassin?" What an idea! Gossipy Thelma with her raucous laugh and her mother in New Jersey . . . if she actually had a mother in New Jersey. And what an elaborate story to have made up if it wasn't true. "Do you know where his children were at the time of the murder? Or their mother? Or who they've been associating with?" It was sort of exciting, giving the police investigative tips.

"We're looking into it. If you think of anything more about this Thelma, let me know."

"Who's Thelma?" Jason asked when I'd hung up.

"A waitress wearing a girdle and sensible shoes," I replied. Should I have mentioned the girdle and shoes to Worski? Maybe I had. I glanced down at the Park Central notepad with Jason's neat handwriting on it and decided to call Paul Fallon after all. I was tiring of the game with the newspaper syndicate and didn't feel like writing any more columns. Certainly not tonight. I wanted to go to bed. So I dialed the number and got Paul on the second ring, Paul and enough background noise to convince me that he was at a party or nightclub.

"This is Carolyn Blue."

"Ah, the elusive Mrs. Blue." He laughed. "You're driving poor Marshall nuts."

"Too bad. If he had better manners and developed a more acceptable personality, people might return his calls."

"Does that mean you're not going to?"

"Right. I'm not. And I'm not going to send him any more columns."

"Now, let's not be hasty, Carolyn. Why not have lunch with me tomorrow?"

My impulse was to say no until I remembered that I had no luncheon plans. Because Jason was trotting back to that benighted company to lunch with Charles Moore, I'd probably have to eat by myself in some tacky diner in the neighborhood. "Where?"

"What do you mean, where?"

"Where would you take me?"

He laughed and said he was being blackmailed by a recalcitrant food columnist.

"But I'm not a food columnist," I replied tartly. "Your Mr. Smead definitely gave me the don't-call-us, we'll-call-you runaround."

"I surrender. How about Chanterelle? French, four-star. You'll love it."

"What about Smead?"

"We won't invite him."

Chanterelle was in my book. I was definitely being wooed. "Very well, I accept. Chanterelle at one o'clock."

That settled, I took off my robe and climbed into bed.

"Why is Paul Fallon inviting you to lunch at an expensive restaurant?" Jason asked when I mentioned, a bit smugly, my new plans.

"Because he's madly in love with me and wants me to run away with him," I replied, snuggling against my husband.

"Um-m." Jason put an arm around me. "I don't think it would make a very good impression at Hodge, Brune if you were to run away with Frances Striff's lover. In fact, I'm sure she'd take offense, and we were planning to collaborate on some research, whether or not I take a job there."

"Well, then she won't mind if I collaborate on lunch with her significant other." I was feeling very pleased with myself. If Jason was going to stand me up for a meeting with some old vice president, I had vice presidential options of my own.

26

"The Best Prix Fixe Lunch in Town"

Carolyn

We overslept, a rare occurrence for Jason. Ah well, those who will drink espresso before bedtime against all advice! I personally enjoyed the sleep of the just and decaffeinated. As I had anticipated, we stopped for a standard, perfectly acceptable, but certainly uninteresting breakfast at a diner down the street. Then we made our way by bus and subway to A.B.C. Carpet, where my taste in decorating was affirmed. Jason liked the rug as much as I did and supported buying it because we'd never find its like at home. He didn't even balk at the price or the shipping fee.

"We'll call it a reward for getting through a bad week," he said. My week had had its pleasures, but I could see that he was not happy with his. Poor man. Perhaps he was disappointed that they had not yet offered him the job. He hadn't said much about it. In fact, now that I looked back over our time in New York, Jason hadn't had a lot to say about any of his activities. Or had I been so busy telling him about mine and offering my opinions on the situation at Hodge, Brune that he couldn't get a word in edgewise? I certainly hoped that wasn't the case. I'm not usually a person who insists on dominating conversation.

Once we had purchased our new rug and returned to the hotel, I consulted a city map. I had to go to TriBeCa and felt bound to use public transportation to atone for our extravagant purchase. Jason made a few calls before meeting Charles Moore at his office, so we parted company at the hotel. "Have a lovely lunch and meeting," I said.

He smiled and replied, "I doubt that it will compare with the food at Chanterelle. We'll probably order in sandwiches."

My conscience smote me. Here I had been complaining about the restaurants at which Hodge, Brune entertained us, but my husband was the person being shortchanged. I, at least, had been eating lunch in delightful, memorable venues. I'd have offered to bring Jason a doggie bag from Chanterelle, but I didn't know whether they'd have such a thing. Also, since Fallon would be footing the bill, I doubted that he'd appreciate my ordering a lot of food and then taking half of it home. That would not impress him as very sophisticated behavior on my part.

I could imagine him saying to Marshall Smead, "You were right about the Blue woman. When I took her to a great restaurant, she ordered a huge meal and asked to have half of it wrapped up. Can you imagine?" Then he'd go home and tell Frances Striff, which would embarrass Jason, who had said he planned to collaborate with her on a research project. No, it wouldn't do.

Even with the maps, I had trouble making my way to TriBeCa and the address at the corner of Hudson and Harrison. In fact, I got lost, asked directions from a native who didn't speak English, asked another who did, and finding out that I was in quite the wrong place, gave up and flagged down a cab. However, once I arrived, I was enchanted by the elegant ambiance of the restaurant. I could hardly take my eyes off the flower arrangements as I was led to Paul Fallon's table.

"Look at that pressed tin ceiling," I murmured appreciatively as he rose while I was helped into my seat. "It's amazing." Which it was. Very intricate.

"Look at you," he replied. "That's a stunning outfit."

I had worn the black slacks set with the flaring bottoms, teal insets, and the belt that owed something in design to both Native American and medieval influences. Naturally, I was pleased with the compliment. Jason had questioned my choice as a rug-hunting getup. "Save it for a special occasion," he'd advised. I hadn't argued because I didn't want to seem to gloat about eating at Chanterelle, which *was* a special occasion, while he was eating in someone's office. I did smile at Fallon and thanked him for the compliment.

"A smile!" he exclaimed. "Does that mean I'm forgiven for Marshall Smead's sins?"

I laughed and picked up my menu.

"Now, Carolyn, I hope you're not going to order another salad. Chanterelle offers the best prix fixe luncheon in town, and I expect you to take advantage of it."

"I certainly shall then," I agreed, remembering that I hadn't at Le Bernardin and had gone hungry at dinner. Never again. Goodness knows where we'd eat tonight. Maybe Jason would be kept on and on at Hodge, Brune, and I'd be forced to order from room service or venture out into nasty weather by myself.

"If you don't mind a suggestion, try the seafood sausage to start. It's famous."

I had been looking at the scallops with tomato and thyme, having had such a good experience with the scallops last night, and under not very promising circumstances, but goodness, if I was going to be a knowledgeable food writer, I needed to expand my horizons. Seafood sausage? Well, Jason would certainly have tried it; therefore, I agreed since he couldn't be here to do it for me.

"I seem to be on a winning streak," said Fallon. "So if you don't have anything against red meat, the Beef with Black Trumpet Mushrooms is — God! — fabulous. Even Frances adores it, and she is not a beef and potatoes sort of girl."

I should think not. Frances was a very thin woman. I couldn't imagine her eating anything as high calorie as beef tenderloin, but to me it sounded wonderful after being pummeled by freezing winds as I tried to find my way here. And I remembered the dish from my *Dining and the Opera* book. Who could forget black trumpet mushrooms? I didn't know what they were, but they sounded intriguing. And I'd have the recipe for a column or book if I wanted to use it.

I allowed myself to be guided in my choice of second course as well, and both were wonderful. I gobbled down the lovely seafood sausages as we made light conversation and drank white wine. Over a bold red and the rich beef dish with its ambrosial flamed brandy sauce and crispy mushrooms, we talked about the investigation into Max's death. Fallon agreed with me that a Heydemann or ex-Heydemann had to be behind the murder. "Did you hear about the reading of the will yesterday?" he asked.

"No," I said, leaning forward eagerly to hear the latest gossip and wondering how he knew what had happened.

"Frances was worried about Charlotte and called to see how she was doing. Then we went over there because poor Charlotte was in shock."

"Oh my goodness," I breathed, alarmed. "Max surely didn't cut her out of the will, did he? I thought there was a trust fund for her."

"More than that," said Paul. "A trust fund, all his Hodge, Brune stock and his options, though God knows what they'll be worth after this Ukrainian debacle, and . . ." He paused dramatically. "He gave her complete control of the money he left his kids. She doesn't have to give them a cent until they're thirty-five unless she wants to, and then she can dribble it out."

"Well, that's just about what I heard." And I explained about Max's lawyer being a friend of Bernie Feingold's son.

"You do get around for an out-of-towner," he said admiringly. "But it's not so much the will as what happened after it was read."

"What?"

"The kids went ballistic. They shouted and screamed at Charlotte. Rick promised lawsuits and scandal. Ariadne even went after Charlotte with claws unsheathed, and the lawyers had to drag her off."

"That's horrible."

"Tell me about it. By the time we got to

Charlotte's, her doctor was administering a tranquilizer, and Frances decided to stay the night with her."

"That's so kind of Frances. I told Detective Worski that Charlotte should have protection. I warned him that they were dangerous."

"Did you? Well, good for you. Not that I saw any protective cops lurking around the apartment when we arrived."

We had both polished off our entrées with gusto, and it suddenly occurred to me that I didn't know why I was here. Paul hadn't said a word about my columns. Surely, he hadn't invited me to . . . to chat me up, as the English novelists say.

"And the really satisfying thing about the will," Fallon continued, "is that Max's beastly kids can't do a thing about it. There's a provision that anyone who challenges the will gets cut off with three hundred dollars. Isn't that rich?"

"But if Charlotte were to die . . ." I said ominously. "That's what worries me. If they had motive to kill Max, now they have an even stronger motive to —"

Fallon, looking shocked, interrupted, "They wouldn't dare. They'd be the first people the police looked at."

"Their grandfather has all the money in the world to get them off with high-priced lawyers and the like."

"My God, you're a cheery lady." He picked

275

up the menu produced by the attentive waiter. "Let's order dessert. I thought I was telling you a horror story with a happy ending. Now *I* need reassuring."

So did I. I still didn't know why I was here, but I was feeling uncomfortably full after my first two courses. Accordingly, I ordered the Raspberry Gratin, which, as it turned out, was full of eggs and cream and not all that light a dessert. But it was wonderful. Over dessert and coffee, Paul Fallon set my mind at rest. He did not have designs on my virtue. He had liked my columns and wanted to discuss a contract with me. Feeling a bit peeved that he hadn't said anything earlier, I responded, "Do I have to work with Marshall Smead?"

Paul laughed. "No, not unless you insist."

I grimaced humorously and scooped up more of my luscious, broiler-browned sabayon and raspberries, flavored with just the right amount of muscat wine. Paul had a fig and blackberry dessert. "Fax me a contract," I replied.

"Playing hard to get?" he asked.

"I've had my share of two bottles of wine," I protested. "No one should make business decisions while light-headed."

"I should be so fortunate," he said wryly. "You strike me as more hardheaded than light-headed."

Was that a compliment? I wondered. Obvi-

276

ously I was going to have to take a taxi home. I wasn't fit to find my way through the city's rapid transit system. I'd probably end up lost in Bedford-Stuyvesant. However, if he offered me a good contract (and I did think it would be fun to write newspaper columns!), I could afford the occasional taxi without being attacked by middle-class, Midwestern angst over my spendthrift ways.

Beef with Black Trumpet Mushrooms

- Preheat oven to 400°F. In a large sauté pan or skillet, melt *1 tbs. unsalted butter* over medium heat and sauté *1 lb. black trumpet mushrooms or chanterelles, sliced.* When they begin to give off liquid, drain and reserve liquid and mushrooms.
- Film large sauté pan or skillet with *olive oil* and cook *3 lbs. beef tenderloin* over high heat until nicely browned. Place beef in the preheated oven and bake for 10 minutes, or until rare. Remove from oven and cover to keep warm.
- In a medium sauté pan or skillet, melt *1 tbs. butter* over medium heat and cook sautéed mushrooms until dry and slightly crisp. Remove pan from heat and add *3 tbs. brandy.* Return pan to heat and let brandy warm. Ignite brandy with a match and shake pan

until flames subside. Add reserved mushroom liquid, *1¹/₂ tbs. beef or veal glaze* (can be made by cooking a good beef or veal stock over high heat until reduced to a syrupy consistency), and *1¹/₂ tsp. fresh lemon juice.* Bring to boil, add *³/₄ cup heavy whipping cream,* and cook to reduce until thick enough to coat the back of a spoon. Season with *salt, freshly ground pepper,* and additional lemon juice if necessary. Add any juices that may have accumulated on the platter holding the beef.

- Divide the sauce and mushrooms evenly among 4 plates. Slice the beef tenderloin and place the slices on top of the sauce and mushrooms. Garnish with seasonal vegetables and serve.

SERVES 8

Raspberry Gratin

- To prepare sabayon: In a double boiler over barely simmering water, combine *6 egg yolks, 1 cup muscat wine,* and *¹/₂ cup sugar;* whisk until foamy and very hot. Remove from heat and place the top of the double boiler in a bowl of ice water; whisk occasionally until completely cooled. Fold in *1 cup whipped cream.*
- To assemble the gratin: Preheat the

broiler. Divide 2 cups raspberry coulis (made by putting in a blender or food processor and pureeing until smooth: *2 cups fresh raspberries or one 10-oz. package frozen unsweetened raspberries, defrosted, powdered sugar* to taste and *1 tbs. kirsch* or to taste) among 8 shallow porcelain ramekins or other individual ovenproof containers. Add a dollop of sabayon mixture on top. Place an equal amount from *5 cups of fresh raspberries* in each dollop of sabayon. Place under preheated broiler for 2 to 3 minutes, or until lightly browned. Serve warm.

SERVES 8

27

Vice Presidential Cookery

Carolyn

When I arrived back at the hotel, somewhat the worse for alcohol and having been roundly cursed for refusing to tip the dangerously reckless cabby, I found that Jason was out. However, there was a message on the bed informing me that we were to have dinner in Greenwich, Connecticut, at the home of Charles Moore and would have to be at Grand Central Station by seven o'clock to catch a New Haven train to our destination.

I was not pleased, and I certainly wasn't hungry. A light evening snack would have done for me. The thought that Mrs. Moore might be home slaving over a hot stove was profoundly depressing. It's bad enough to have to cook without doing it for an unappreciative guest. But did the wives of corporate vice presidents do their own cooking? She might have a live-in chef. In the meantime, I needed to sleep off the wine.

I carefully removed my new outfit and hung it in the closet. Then I called Detective

Worski's number to tell him that Charlotte Heydemann had been threatened by her stepson and physically attacked by her step-daughter after the reading of the will yesterday. He said he'd look into it. I could hear a basketball game playing in the background, but then even police detectives deserve a day off. Had he uncovered any news of the missing Thelma? I asked. Well, if she was dead, he replied callously, they'd obviously buried her, because no bodies matching her description had been found.

Offended by his offhandedness, I hung up and went straight to bed, only to be awakened later by Jason. "How was your lunch?" he asked.

"Superb," I replied. "How was yours?"

"Canceled. Moore had to take his wife to the doctor, so he invited us for tonight. Didn't you get my note?"

"If his wife needed medical attention, how can he expect her to prepare dinner for guests?" I asked.

"I have no idea. Maybe he's going to cook."

"Oh, I'm sure," I replied sarcastically.

"Whatever his plans, he was very insistent that we come tonight." Jason had been divesting himself of overcoat, muffler, and several shopping bags. What had he bought? I wondered. The answer was books. He'd visited a scientific bookstore and found several volumes of great interest. You wouldn't believe how much scientific books cost! Still, I could hardly complain since I had been splurging on clothes.

Then Jason smiled and proffered a little bag. "I bought you these."

And in the small box was a pair of dangly earrings that perfectly matched the turquoise in the belt to my new slacks outfit but also had stones of a deep teal that matched the insets. My dear husband, while I gorged myself at Chanterelle, had gone without lunch and bought me a lovely, thoughtful, perfect gift. And I had been begrudging him a few pricey chemistry books, which were, after all, tax deductible.

"Carolyn, are you crying?" he asked. "I thought you'd like them."

"I love them," I sniffed and put them on immediately, even though I was still in my robe. "I think they're absolutely perfect, and I intend to wear them tonight and admire myself in every mirror at the Moores' house." I gave him a hug. "Jason, I think you are an utterly perfect husband."

"High praise, indeed," he responded, grinning. Then he glanced at the clock and said we'd better dress if we wanted to catch that train.

Jason

When Charles Moore called to cancel our appointment, I assured him that what little I had to say could be said on the telephone. Frankly, I resented having my day with Carolyn cut short and believed that I had done all I could to carry out the investigation that I felt I owed Max, not that my efforts had yielded much. However, Moore insisted that we talk personally and invited us to dinner. He wouldn't take no for an answer. Perhaps he felt badly at having taken so much of my time without offering the consultancy. He need have suffered no qualms on that score; they had paid me well, entertained me, if not royally, at least respectably, and had no obligation beyond that.

Nonetheless, Carolyn and I had to take the train to Greenwich on an evening that did not look promising, weather-wise. She mentioned that snow was predicted. I said I hoped that it would hold off until we got out of the area Monday morning. In passing through Grand Central to the New Haven tracks, I remarked wistfully that I had not been able to visit the Oyster Bar, one of my favorite New York restaurants. "Let's just hope his wife is a decent cook," Carolyn replied. She had paused several times to admire her new earrings in the windows of closed terminal shops.

We were both taken by surprise in Mrs. Moore. Charles picked us up at the commuter station and drove us to a half-timbered Tudor house in a forested area, where an olive-skinned woman in a wheelchair met us at the door. Renata Moore had been crippled ten years earlier in an automobile driven by her son and hadn't walked since. What a family tragedy that must have been, and still was. Moore left us with his wife and hurried off to the kitchen, where he, evidently, was in charge of dinner.

Carolyn couldn't quite hide her surprise at the idea of vice presidential cookery but set herself to be charming to her hostess, who engaged in polite small talk for several minutes and then said, "I understand you're a culinary expert." Carolyn insisted that she was just a novice who could write coherently, a talent being rapidly lost in modern society.

Renata Moore then laughed and said, "I could see that you had your doubts about eating anything prepared by my husband, but you needn't worry. We have excellent gourmet takeout here in Greenwich. Charles brought dinner home before he went to pick you up." An impish smile then lit her face. "But you might compliment him and ask for a recipe. I hear that you're about to enter the ranks of newspaper columnists."

"How did you hear that?" Carolyn asked, amazed.

"Oh, Charles is ever so good about bringing home gossip to entertain me. Sometimes I almost feel as if I still have a place in the lives of my friends and acquaintances because he tells me all the news."

"Ready," said Moore from a doorway that led into a large formal dining room. He was wearing an apron. Carolyn's expression said she thought he was trying to look as if he had actually cooked the meal. I, on the other hand, assumed that he didn't want to spill anything on his suit while transferring food from the kitchen.

"Charles sent the maid home," said Renata as he pushed her wheelchair to a place at one end of the table. "I assume that means you gentlemen have top secret things to discuss over dinner. I sometimes feel that I should have a security clearance myself."

Moore poured wine for everyone and remarked, "I think recent events should convince you, my dear, that Hodge, Brune isn't just another paranoid corporate entity."

They argued amiably while Carolyn and I sampled our *caprese,* which was excellent.

"I'm so envious," Carolyn said to our host. "I can't imagine how you manage to get tomatoes like these in winter. They taste homegrown. And the basil — not a brown spot on it."

"Ah, but you should have tasted the vegetables in the old days when the Italians sold all the produce," said Renata. "Then it was *really* fresh. I even had relatives in Bensonhurst who grew their own zucchini. They used to bombard us with it in the summer, figuratively speaking. Now it's all Koreans selling vegetables in the corner markets."

Carolyn laughed. "Well, even the mozzarella tastes as if it was made today. Surely, the Koreans aren't making the mozzarella." She turned to Charles. "You must tell me, Charles, where you shop. Do you go into New York City for food?"

"Greenwich has excellent markets," said Charles Moore.

I believe I detected Mrs. Moore winking at my wife, and I had to wonder if all women were allied in an underground conspiracy to tease their husbands. Thank God, Carolyn didn't ask him for a recipe.

Carolyn

I liked Renata Moore immediately and admired any woman who could be so cheerful after being confined ten years to a wheelchair. How lonely her life must be, her children grown and gone. And I did wonder whether she was estranged from the son whose driving had resulted in her paralysis.

Not that I thought her the kind of person to punish him for an accident. However, guilt, which the boy must have felt, will sometimes lead a young person to avoid the one who is the source of his guilt. I remember that Chris once broke a favorite perfume bottle of mine while playing golf with toy clubs in the house, a forbidden activity. I don't even like Jason to use those putting machines in the den; golf balls are dangerous. At any rate, Chris felt so badly about my perfume bottle that he didn't speak to me for three days.

As I recalled that incident, we were eating veal Marsala with new potatoes and sautéed sweet peppers, fresh out of the microwave, I presume. The wine, a Barolo, was as good as you'd expect. "I talked to Charlotte this morning," Renata was saying. "There was a terrible scene at the reading of the will yesterday."

"Not surprising, considering how her husband tied up the money," I remarked.

"How is it that you are familiar with Max's will?" Charles Moore asked, giving me an odd look.

"My agent's uncle told me all about it," I explained with relish. "He and Dr. Heydemann have the same lawyer, and Mr. Feingold, my agent's uncle, is a friend of the Heydemann family from years ago in Brooklyn."

"Really?" Moore looked nonplussed.

"*And* I had lunch today with Paul Fallon, who is a friend of Frances Striff, who stayed the night with Charlotte last night. In fact, I had lunch with Charlotte Thursday."

"The day after the memorial service?" Moore looked disapproving.

"She was so sad at the service that I invited her," I replied.

"Good for you," said Renata. "I'm sure that's just what Charlotte needed. I'd have done it myself if I could."

"You *could* drive, Renata, if you chose to," said her husband. "Vehicles are available with hand controls."

"Yes, I could, Charles, but once I got to, say, a restaurant in the city, I'd be in trouble." She turned back to me. "Can you imagine that nasty boy announcing how he was going to spend the money before he even knew whether he was getting any? I couldn't have been more pleased when I heard how Max had tied up the trusts."

I nodded, taking a sip of my wine. Barolo used to be a much more robust wine. Jason says they've changed it so they won't have to age it so long. Too bad, although I don't suppose the old style Barolo would go that well with veal. "What was Ricky planning on doing with the money he now can't get his hands on?"

"Oh, he marched into the lawyer's office and announced that he'd be playing the lead in an off-Broadway play called *And Then Some*. Not a very interesting title, is it?"

"Is he good enough to get the lead in anything?" I asked.

"I doubt it," said Renata. "I believe he's done some amateur theater at Dartmouth, but nothing in New York. Anyway, he said he was quitting school and financing the play himself. With his inheritance."

"No wonder he and his sister made such a scene."

"Yes. They are really appalling people, but then their mother is, too. Fortunately, she's usually locked away."

"Not right now," I said. "We saw her celebrating Max's death at the opera."

"God, I'd like to see an opera again," said Renata. "Charles, I hope you're having your detective —"

"I don't have a detective," her husband replied. He had just reentered the room carrying little round cakes in a red puddle — raspberry or strawberry, I presumed.

They were quite tasty if very small. He'd put the dirty dishes on a massive sideboard, presumably for the maid to take care of when she returned.

"Well, you owe it to Max to hire one and have him investigate that family. I had no idea Melisande was out. You can be sure the three of them are behind Max's death."

"My thoughts exactly," I agreed. "I'll bet

that Rick disguised himself and killed his father so he could finance his part in the play."

"Ladies, ladies," Moore groaned. He was pouring Jason a great dollop of cognac and didn't offer any to us. "I'd almost rather espouse the Russian Mafia theory —"

"What Russian Mafia theory?" his wife asked.

"— than your patricide hypothesis," he continued, ignoring her question, which I, too, would have liked to hear more about. "That's just your operatic Italian nature speaking, my dear, and I didn't realize you were pining for a night at the Met. I can certainly see to that."

"Oh, Charles, I didn't mean to make you feel bad. We both know I can't —"

"I must do it in self-defense before you turn company business into a grand opera. Patricide!" He shook his head in a gesture of insufferable male superiority. "Jason, why don't we go to the library? We have things to talk about."

"Oh, you can talk in front of us, Charles," said his wife. "We won't say a word to anyone about your little company secrets."

"Really?" he said dryly.

"Jason and I are going to a play tomorrow and then home Monday, so *we* won't be talking to anyone," I added.

"What are you going to see?" Renata asked eagerly.

"*The Most Fabulous Story Ever Told*," I replied. "It's playing in the Village and supposed to be very funny."

"You'll love it if you don't mind outrageous homosexual camp. And you'll want to drop in at some little trattoria for lunch. Just walking into one off the street is a lovely adventure." She sighed. "I grew up in Little Italy. After that and the Village, Greenwich seems a bit sedate."

"Care to join me in a cigar, Jason?" Moore asked.

"Bravo, my dear!" said his wife. "If you're going to smoke cigars, I don't think I care to hear your secrets."

The men departed with cognac snifters in hand — talk about sedate! Renata Moore and I settled down to discuss opera in their living room, which looked out through small paned windows on gently falling snow. She was delighted with my description of the staging peculiarities of *Mefistofele* and the antics of Sean Ryan, who had loved the subtitle machine but hated the opera.

"I haven't seen the new subtitle equipment," she said wistfully. "Did you like it?"

"Not much. It is, admittedly, more discreet than supertitles run above the stage, but if you look down at the screen in front of you, you miss what's happening onstage."

"Of course, if the singers are fat and unattractive or terrible actors, that's all to the good. I saw Richard Tucker when I was a girl. He had the most thrilling voice, but his acting was so stilted — you know, the stagger-when-emoting school? — I always ended up closing my eyes so that I could enjoy his voice without having to look at him."

"I'd like to have seen Richard Tucker," I said with a sigh.

"I have movies. Shall we watch?"

28

Overnight Without a Nightie

Jason

Thank God Charles Moore didn't actually want to smoke cigars in his library. Carolyn, who hates the smell of cigars, would have suggested that I sleep in the bathtub with the door closed. Instead, Moore and I placed the cognac bottle on a table between us while seated in deep leather chairs. "Your wife is . . . ah . . . outspoken, isn't she?" he remarked.

"So is yours," I replied.

Moore looked surprised but had to agree. Then we discussed my dinner with Fergus and Fiona. The gist of my replies was that I did not think McRoy had had anything to do with the theft of the coal research. "The man knows he's suspect. He's been conducting his own investigation among members of his team."

"That could be a red herring," Moore suggested.

"I doubt it. He's troubled because he feels he's destroying the cohesiveness of his group; he's distraught because his years of research have been stolen; and he's particularly hurt because he's suspected by his superiors."

Moore sighed. "If he's innocent, this will all —"

"Unless the problem is resolved, you'll lose him," I cautioned. "He talked of nothing last night at dinner but his dismay at the situation. His wife, who evidently hadn't realized how upset he's been, said he should leave the company and take another job. I gather he's had offers."

"I'm sure he has," said Moore grimly. "Did you get any handle on their finances? Could he have been in such straits that he'd sell us out? That's Merrivale's theory."

"They were quite talkative about their financial situation. Evidently, Fergus has been successful investing in the rising market."

"If he's one of those idiot day-traders, he could have lost every cent they have."

"I gather that he's a careful investor, his wife is a careful husbander of family resources, they're not given to expensive habits, and their children can be expected to go to university on scholarships."

"What? Even that great, lumpish Roddy, who showed up here last year for the Christmas party? He ate everything in sight."

I had to smile. I had never seen "lumpish Roddy," but I remembered how much a growing boy can eat. Chris, for a time, raised our grocery bills by a third, according to

Carolyn. "Mrs. McRoy expects Roddy to get a soccer scholarship."

"Ah. The boy did bounce a ham off his forehead in some sort of demonstration. Renata was not amused."

"Has Merrivale come up with anything concrete against Fergus?"

"No, not yet."

I found my suspicions of Merrivale himself on the rise. If he was so intent on implicating Fergus McRoy, might he not be diverting suspicion from himself? If anyone was in a perfect position to sell the company's secrets and then derail the investigation, it was Merrivale, who was both a scientist and in control of company security. As long as he could keep Moore from cooperating with the police, he'd be home free, and poor Fergus McRoy, left on tenterhooks. Of course, I had no more evidence against Merrivale than he did against McRoy, only suspicion and personal dislike. A course of action that might at least bring Merrivale under surveillance occurred to me.

"Maybe you should hire a professional detective, not to look into the scientific aspect, but to investigate the finances and telephone records of people who had access to the research."

Moore frowned. "Do you know one? A detective?"

"The only detectives I've ever met," I replied, "were on police forces, but that doesn't mean you couldn't find a reputable agency that is accustomed to dealing with industrial espionage.

"By the way, have you received any demands from the Ukraine?"

"Nothing." He held up the decanter questioningly, then poured into both snifters.

"Well, you might at least consider an outside investigator if you're determined to keep the police out of the case. I can't see that Merrivale is coming up with more than wild guesses."

"I'll think about your suggestion," Moore replied. "Aside from your evening with McRoy, have you had any other thoughts about our problem?"

"I did pick up a strange bit of information last night. Someone from Prague, whom I had called earlier, called me back. He's at Charles University, and I had mentioned in passing that I knew a former graduate student from Charles, Vasandrovich."

"Yes, Vaclav's Czech. Max got him out quite a while before the Communist regime fell."

"My friend said there's no record of a Vaclav Vasandrovich having received his doctorate from Charles."

"What?" Moore looked nonplussed.

"Could I have misunderstood? Perhaps he did his undergraduate work there. Or a postdoc."

"No. I remember reading his recommendations. They had to be smuggled out. Is your friend sure? Could records have been lost during the Velvet Revolution?"

"I don't think it was all that violent," I replied.

"There seems to be no end to this. First, Max. Then the project theft. Now this news. If Vaclav's credentials are false, I'll have to fire him, and we've been counting on him to take Max's place. In fact, I planned to announce his permanent appointment on Monday. He was the heir apparent. Max had been talking about resigning the directorship and going back to research."

"It's hard to believe that Max would have been fooled by an imposter," I pointed out, "which is to say that Vaclav was obviously educated somewhere. He's brilliant, just as Max said he was. I'm sure you know that. So the question is: If not Charles, where? Was he at Charles when Max brought him here?"

"No, some government research facility, as I remember, and not happy there."

I couldn't see that we were making any progress, so I glanced at my watch. "Considering the time and the weather —" Snow was falling onto the lawn and evergreens outside the study windows. "— I think Carolyn and I should be going. I wish I had more and better news for you, but —"

"Good God, man, you've done more than

most in this investigation. At least your queries in Eastern Europe have given us a handle on the Ukrainian company." He set his snifter down with a disgusted thump. "Russian mobsters, false credentials. Makes me wonder what Merrivale has been up to, other than irritating everyone in the labs and holding up the research we still have in our control."

I felt a distinct jolt of satisfaction to hear that Moore wasn't particularly satisfied with his security director.

"And I didn't drag you all the way out here to ask for more information," Moore continued. "In fact, I must apologize for keeping you from your wife today and then canceling our appointment. Renata was watering houseplants, leaning out too far, and fell from her wheelchair. I'm afraid we were both terrified that she had done herself damage. Because she has no feeling below the waist, injuries to that area are not readily evident."

"Really, Charles, there's no need to apologize. I'm sorry to hear that your wife had a fall and hope that she —"

"Oh, she's fine. And I think she really enjoyed the evening until I dragged you off."

I glanced again at my watch. It was after eleven.

"The primary reason for my invitation was to offer the consultancy you and Max discussed. I should have done this earlier, but I have been distracted. Nonetheless, upper management is agreed that we would very much like you to come aboard."

Since I was no longer expecting an offer, it took me by surprise, and I had no immediate answer.

"I hope our present problems won't deter you. We will survive, even if we do lose the coal project, and our research in other areas should be of interest to you, as your expertise is of interest to us." He waited a minute for a reply while I listened to the rising howl of the wind outside and wondered whether we'd be able to get back to the city.

"We had in mind six weeks in the summer," Moore added, "as well as three visits during the rest of the year, to be scheduled at your convenience and our need. And of course, we would expect to be able to call you with questions and perhaps funnel research money and projects to your university labs."

"That sounds very tempting," I replied. "Of course, I'll have to discuss it with Carolyn."

"Of course." He frowned and began to talk money: per diems on short visits, per hours for phone consultations, grants for postdoctoral fellows and research equipment, summer remuneration. It was an offer I could hardly afford to overlook, although with Max gone and having met Merrivale, I wasn't as enthusiastic as I might have been.

"Are you sure Merrivale, for instance, would approve of letting contracts to university entities," I asked, "much less bringing in an academic? My impression is that he considers all professors loose-lipped and feckless."

"Feckless? An odd word to apply to a scientist." Moore produced his little half smile. "Merrivale will have to adjust. This is a serious offer. I'll fax you the terms before you leave, if you like, or if you want to negotiate something else —"

"I consider your offer very generous. Carolyn and I will give it every consideration." I rose, now really worried about the storm and the time.

Moore rose as well. "Having neglected to smoke the cigars I mentioned, shall we join the ladies?" We found them dozing in front of a large-screen TV with an old film of *Andrea Chenier* playing. The photographic quality was poor, but the singing outstanding. I wouldn't have minded watching that.

"You'll get us arrested if you insist on showing people those pirated films, Renata," Moore said as he touched his wife lightly on the shoulder.

She sat straight immediately and replied, "Well, Charles, you've kept Jason so late, and the storm has become so bad that they'll definitely have to stay the night."

"Oh, Renata, we couldn't impose," Carolyn mumbled. I could see that she had been deeply asleep, even though the tenor was singing gloriously on the television screen.

"Nonsense. The guest room is always made up; the last train for the city is leaving as we speak; and this is obviously a night for curling up under a down comforter instead of traveling in the snow. Charles, show them the guest room, won't you? I'm for bed." Calling, "Good night, all," over her shoulder, Renata wheeled herself out of the room before any of us could protest.

"I don't even have a nightgown," Carolyn whispered to me as we walked upstairs, our host having turned on a chandelier in the hall and directed us to the guest room before hurrying after his wife. "And this house is freezing."

Once we were huddled together in bed, Carolyn demanded to know what Moore and I had been talking about so long. I told her the terms of the contract I had been offered. "Good heavens," she exclaimed. "We'll be rich." Then she sniffed. "You dear, you refused cigars. I don't know how to thank you."

"Actually, I wasn't offered any." I pulled Carolyn a bit closer. The sheets weren't warming up as fast as I would have liked.

"It was a ruse? To get you to himself?

What were you talking about in there besides the contract? And what was that bit about the Russian Mafia?"

"Just something I heard when I was calling friends abroad."

"Vaclav speaks Russian."

"I'm not surprised."

"I heard him on the telephone, but then he said it wasn't Russian; it was Czech, and he was talking to his Aunt Elizabeta."

"Did he?" I felt a prick of unease. Vaclav had told me that he had no living relatives.

"Maybe he's a secret Russian agent," Carolyn suggested, giggling. She had just kissed my chin.

"Are you trying to start something with me?" I asked, not averse to the idea.

"Of course not." She drew back. "We couldn't. Not in their house."

"I don't see why not. If we could with my mother in the next room in Chicago —"

"But that was our anniversary."

"— we can certainly indulge when our hosts evidently don't even sleep upstairs."

"I forgot to ask him for a recipe," said my wife.

"You're trying to change the subject. We'll be as quiet as mice."

"Or as horny as rabbits," she suggested, now trying to stifle laughter.

"As an internationally known scientist, I resent the indignity of being called horny."

"OK. Then roll over and go to sleep," my wife replied.

"On the other hand . . ." I temporized.

29

A Shock over French Toast

Carolyn

Charles Moore knocked on our door at nine and suggested that we appear for breakfast in a half hour. We showered in the bath attached to the guest room, but we had to put on the same clothes we'd worn the night before and, more to the point, the same underwear. I was not happy.

Then we followed our noses downstairs to a large, sunny kitchen with brick walls, slate floors, a fireplace, modern appliances, and workspaces keyed to the needs of someone in a wheelchair as well as spaces at the standard height. Renata was fixing bacon and French toast while Charles brewed coffee and mixed up a berry, cream, and liqueur sauce for the toast. Immediately, hunger overcame my fixation on twice-worn underwear, and I wrote down his recipe. In fact, I wish that I'd had a camera. Their kitchen was gorgeous, an assessment with which our hostess agreed. "Charles had it put in for me while we were on a cruise. I thought the cruise was my birthday present, but it turned out to be the kitchen."

"If you'll take another cruise with me, my dear, I'll arrange another homecoming surprise," her husband promised. He poured coffee and placed the cups before us on the table of a cozy breakfast nook that looked out over their backyard, snow-covered with sunlight glistening off iced branches. Had there been an ice storm after we went to bed? I wondered if the trains would be running. Lovely as this was, I didn't want to miss the play that afternoon.

Renata was saying, "Oh Charles, you know the cruise didn't work out that well."

"I thought it did."

"You weren't the one in the wheelchair." There was a snap to her voice, and he looked grim as she transferred bacon to a serving platter and handed it to him. "Sorry," she murmured. "It's not your fault I'm such a stay-at-home." She retrieved a plate of French toast from the lower oven and maneuvered her wheelchair to the table while still holding the plate.

Her chair evidently had one-handed electric controls. I'd love to have seen how it worked, but I could hardly ask. Instead, I commented on the delicious breakfast and got Renata's French toast recipe. Jason said he hoped I was planning to use the recipes at home, and I replied that, if I got a second book contract, I'd certainly publish them, with the Moores' permission, of course. Then I added

305

that I'd love to have Jason try the dishes some Sunday in El Paso. We could invite friends.

"Suddenly my wife no longer cooks," he said sadly to Charles. "She talks about food, she writes about it, she eats it, but she doesn't —"

"Who was it who made the elaborate, fantastic, time-consuming, never-to-be-surpassed, gourmet anniversary dinner?" I asked.

"Are you going to do it again next year?" My husband managed to look both hopeful and woebegone.

Renata offered Jason more of the berry topping to soothe his "disappointed chauvinist expectations," as she put it, and Charles rose to answer the telephone. "If it's the office, tell them to stuff it," Renata called after her husband. He looked disapproving, Jason blinked, and we ladies laughed merrily. She was a woman after my own heart, so I told her about Jason's mother, the militant feminist who disapproved of me because I had stayed home raising children and cooking gourmet meals.

"Have I ever failed to defend you when Mother was on the attack?" he demanded.

"Of course not," I replied agreeably. "But then you wouldn't have wanted me to turn into your mother, would you?"

"God forbid," he agreed. To Renata he said, "My mother's a very intelligent woman, and I love her dearly, but she can be hard to take in doses longer than, say, two or three days. She disapproves of half womankind and all men."

"Even your father?" Renata asked.

"They split up years ago," Jason replied. "When we visit Chicago, we spend half the time with him and half with her. Then we all have dinner together on changeover day and quarrel. That's been going on since the divorce when I was twelve, but once I went away to college, Dad moved to a suburb on the other side of Chicago, forty miles away, quit his job at the university, started his own company, married a sweet young thing, and had a second family."

"Jason's half brother and sister aren't that much older than our children," I added. "It was lovely for Chris and Gwen to have an aunt and uncle to play with when they were all growing up, especially since my family's almost nonexistent — just my father, who is not very good with children."

"Amazing!" exclaimed Renata. "I have this huge Italian family. No one ever gets divorced or practices birth control. It's — Charles?" Her husband had returned to the table, his face rather pale. "Is something wrong?"

He shook his head.

"All right." She looked puzzled. "As I was saying, they think Charles and I are absolutely peculiar. Only two children. They were always sympathizing with me and telling me about some new saint who could make me fertile again." She had been smiling, but then she sighed. "Now they keep digging up obscure saints who specialize in making cripples walk. Charles, something is definitely wrong. You look like — I don't know — like someone died."

"She didn't die," said Charles.

"Who?"

"Charlotte."

My hands turned icy. "What happened to Charlotte? I told the police —"

He looked at me sharply. "You told the police what? Why were you talking to the police about Charlotte?"

He looked so fierce that I began to feel defensive. "Because of the will. She controls the trusts of the stepchildren during her lifetime. If they killed Max for money, obviously she would be the next target."

He turned away from me as if I was an idiot, which I really didn't appreciate. Even if he hadn't been at the opera to see Melisande Heydemann crowing over her ex-husband's death and her son trying to drag her away, he had heard the two children at the memorial service. How much evidence did he need that —

"Max must have talked to Charlotte," Charles said to Jason.

"But they wouldn't know that he had," Jason replied.

"They couldn't afford to believe that he hadn't. I never even thought of that."

"What are you *talking* about?" Renata demanded. "And what happened to Charlotte?"

"She was attacked yesterday in front of her apartment building."

"Is she all right?" I asked anxiously.

"She's in the hospital. Stabbed in the shoulder."

We all looked at one another with horror.

"Did they catch the assailant?" Jason asked.

"No," Charles replied. "He got away while the doorman was helping her up."

Within two hours, Jason and I had passed through Grand Central Station, bought some flowers and two books, and taken the subway uptown to the hospital where Charlotte Heydemann was recovering from the attack. A policeman was stationed outside her room, but after consulting her and calling Detective Worski, he allowed us in. Charlotte was propped up in one of those multiposition hospital beds, surrounded by flowers, and looking as pale as the white bandages that bulged out from under the neck and armhole of her hospital gown.

She smiled at us both and thanked us for coming out on such a miserable day. "Not that I'll ever complain about snow and ice again," she added. "We've about decided, Detective Worski and I and my doorman, that if I hadn't slipped on the ice, the man with the . . . whatever it was; I didn't actually see it . . . would have killed me." Then she giggled.

Jason looked quite surprised at her cheery demeanor. I assumed that she was being given painkillers. I sat down beside the bed and took her hand. "Did you recognize your attacker?" I asked.

"Oh, goodness no. He was all bundled up. Knit cap, scarf, bulky, raggedy clothing."

"Really?"

"A stereotypical street person. I told the detective that."

I thought that it could have been Rick playing a part. "But didn't you notice anything — well — familiar about him?"

Charlotte looked thoughtful. "There was something. But what?"

I looked into her eyes, willing her to remember something useful. Actually, her eyes looked odd. Dilated. What had they given her? "Was it his height?" I asked.

"No-o-o. He was average height. Taller than me. He grabbed my shoulder as I was slipping. I thought he meant to keep me from falling, but then — z-z-zip!" She waved her good hand. "For a moment it didn't even hurt. But he missed. My heart. Lucky me. Lucky. Lucky." She smiled sweetly in a blank, woozy sort of way.

Rick was average height, I thought, trying to picture him when he took the podium at the memorial service and then when he chased after his mother at the opera. A bit taller than Jason. Well, good. One clue. "What about his hair?" I asked. Jason had sat down on the other side of the bed and was frowning at me.

"None showing. He was wearing a knit cap, all ravelly. Maybe it was hand knitted. A couple of strands were straggling down the side of his face."

"So it was something about his face that was familiar?" I suggested.

"No, but, I don't think Detective Worski suspects me of killing Max anymore. I couldn't really see his face . . . not the detective's, the homeless man's. The cap was pulled down almost to his eyebrows, and he had a very tacky scarf wrapped around his neck up to the nose. It was so cold! I was cold, too. My ears were freezing. They hurt. More than my shoulder, actually. That's why I was hurrying and slipped . . . because of my ears. That's why he missed. I was falling down. He must be disappointed. Or maybe he doesn't know."

"But the doorman must have —"

"Seen him? A street person, he told the police. He was too busy helping me up to notice much, I suppose. Probably thought I'd sue the co-op association because they hadn't cleared the ice off. When the man let go of me, I fell right down. I have a huge bruise on my hip. Would you like to see it?" She looked as pleased as a child at show-and-tell until she noticed the expression on Jason's face. Then she giggled and said, "Of course, you'd have to leave the room, Jason. In fact, you're probably embarrassed because you know these gowns gape open in back. What if I had to get up and use the facilities? I couldn't. Not with guests. And thanks so much for the flowers. And the books." She looked down at the books that lay on the sheet beside her thigh. "I'll start one as soon as you leave. Not that I'm suggesting you leave. It's nice to have company. Keeps me from thinking about that man trying to kill me.

"First Max. Now me. It's really terrifying when you think about it, isn't it? Even in the big, bad city, and our crime rates *are* down, you know. Isn't that ironic? Nothing ever happened to us when life was more violent, but as soon as things get better . . . well, I suppose good times just remind those who don't have anything of the . . . the contrast. There I was in my warm coat, and this poor homeless man in his rags . . . it probably made him furious. Maybe he was hungry when he saw Max eating all that pastrami." She blinked back tears. "I try not to think about Max. Now I'll have to try not to think about me. But if he's so poor, how can he afford a knife or whatever it was? The detective couldn't answer that."

"But, Charlotte." I was going to make one last try. "You said there was something familiar about him. Had you seen a homeless person like him before?" I supposed it was possible. Some person who should be medicated or institutionalized, who had fixated on the Heydemanns —

"Never," she replied. "I never see them on our block. The doormen chase them away. Maybe our doorman was afraid I'd sue because he hadn't chased the man off."

"So what was familiar about him?"

Charlotte leaned her head back against the pillow and closed her eyes.

"Oh, Charlotte, I'm so sorry. I've tired you out. Maybe we should —"

"Not at all. I was just picturing the incident. It was his smell."

"His smell?" Now, there was a clue. Some distinctive aftershave? She'd certainly recognize her stepson's cologne. "He smelled like Rick?" I asked impulsively. Then how I regretted that question! An odor ID might be no good in court if it was thought that the source of the smell had been suggested to the victim.

"Rick?" She looked quite astonished. "Goodness, no. He smelled like . . . um-m-m

. . . garbage. That's it. Do you remember when we had the garbage strike? Well, no, you wouldn't because you don't live here, but the whole city smelled . . . just like that man. Fetid." She shuddered.

You can't imagine how disappointed I was. It might have been Rick, but I certainly couldn't prove it to Detective Worski because the attacker had smelled like garbage, which is not the preferred scent of the sons of prominent families. I sighed.

Jason, who had been strangely silent, leaned forward and asked, "Charlotte, before he died, did Max mention a problem he was having at work?"

"What problem? Max never had problems. His people were very fond of him, and the research was going well. It always did. Max was a wonderful scientist."

"I know," Jason agreed.

"And a wonderful head of R and D." My husband nodded. "And a wonderful husband." She started to cry. "He didn't have any problems until someone killed him," she sobbed.

A nurse bustled in, glowered at us, and gave Charlotte a shot.

"How could you upset her, Jason?" I asked when we had been chased out into the hall. "You're still pursuing that silly spy scenario, aren't you?" Before Jason could answer, I spotted Detective Worski coming down the hall. "I told you to give her protection, Detective," I said very severely. I'm not usually an I-told-you-so sort of person, but in this case . . .

"Yes ma'am," agreed the detective, all muffled up in his green overcoat, "and next time you tell me something, I'm gonna listen extra careful."

"Have you questioned her stepson?"

"We will as soon as we find him."

"He's missing? Well, that's significant!" Jason dragged me away before I could pursue my point.

30

Minestrone at Random

Jason

Only a fool could believe that a husband and wife, on separate occasions, might meet with random stabbings. I was convinced that Max had been killed because he found out who sold the coal technology and that the attempt on Charlotte resulted from a belief that Max confided in her before he died. Max's killer had probably been following Charlotte since Max's death and only yesterday found her in a situation when she was unaccompanied.

I intended to call Moore and urge him to tell the police what we knew. He had obviously had the same thoughts as I concerning Charlotte's situation. That being the case, he couldn't, in all good conscience, allow her to continue at risk. As far as I knew, Merrivale hadn't made any progress finding the culprit, and Moore had seemed to confirm my perception of the situation when he said last night that I had provided more information than anyone else had. I now surmised that Merrivale, for whatever reason, had encouraged Moore's reluctance to cooperate with the police. If that was the case, it would seem all the more reasonable to think that it was Merrivale, a man in a perfect position to stymie the investigation, who had betrayed the company and arranged the assassination.

Unless it was Moore himself. I found that idea even more upsetting, but still, perhaps it had to be considered. Moore? He was the person who had encouraged my telephone calls to Eastern Europe, but when I had mentioned the Russian Mafia, he hadn't been much interested. Merrivale, on the other hand, had tried to cut off that line of inquiry completely. He hadn't wanted to hear anything about the wife of the Ukrainian company's vice president. At this point, I didn't know what to think.

My wife was clearer on her theory that I was on mine. Her questions to Charlotte at the hospital revealed that she attributed the attacks to Rick Heydemann, even though Charlotte's assailant had looked homeless and smelled of garbage. I could have pointed out her illogic, but I doubted that she would appreciate the exercise. First, no matter how he dressed or smelled, Charlotte would have recognized her stepson. Second, as Moore had pointed out, to me if not Carolyn, Max's children came from a very wealthy family on their mother's side. They might have wanted money from their father, but they didn't *need* it, and certainly not enough to risk committing or commissioning murder. That being the case, I had to ask myself whether Moore, if he himself were implicated in Max's death, would defuse any theory of the crime that pointed elsewhere. But maybe that's exactly what I was meant to think.

Carolyn had to prod me off the subway at our stop because I was so wrapped up in burgeoning paranoia, which I found to be a very uncomfortable affliction. How could I accept the tempting offer made to me by Hodge, Brune when I no longer trusted the people who worked there? Rain was turning the overnight snow to slush when we reached our hotel, changed clothes, and set out for Greenwich Village. We were looking for Manetta Lane in order to pick up the tickets I had acquired by Internet. But before that, we had to find a place for a late lunch, and Carolyn was determined to follow Renata Moore's advice, which was to pick a trattoria at random. I myself like to go to places where I've been before or that are recommended by travel guides; Carolyn said she was tired of being a dutiful, preplanning food writer: This lunch was to be just for us.

After much slogging around under an umbrella, we entered the warm confines of an Italian restaurant with a large exposed pipe that traversed a pressed tin ceiling and one of the brick walls. Carolyn assured me that the ceiling didn't compare with the one at

Chanterelle, which didn't surprise me. I doubted that the food would, either. I think my wife was drawn into this particular place by the rich smell of fresh-baked bread. I can't say that I remember the name of the trattoria, but the minestrone we ordered was heavy with the flavors of Italy and loaded with white beans, lentils, and vegetables. A more comforting meal cannot be imagined on such an unpromising day. We were both chilled and damp by the time we sat down to our large bowls of soup and a basket of bread slices that sent my wife into raptures. Her nose had not deceived her, and she was so delighted that she insisted on discussing the bread with the proprietor and buying a loaf to take home.

"Carolyn," I protested, "when are we going to eat it?" It was a long object, thicker than a baguette, but just as crusty on the outside. I anticipated, beside the awkwardness of carrying it into the theater, that the aroma would overhang the play, which might not be appreciated by our fellow drama enthusiasts.

"We can nibble between acts," she said. "And at the hotel when we get back. We can buy cheese and wine and have a picnic." She was feeling remarkably jolly, given Charlotte's situation and the abominable weather we faced as we splashed our way to the theater. I suppose she was relieved that Charlotte was expected to recover completely. Carolyn insisted that, as horrible as the attack had been, the police were now looking at Rick, so Charlotte would be safe and Max avenged. I didn't disabuse her of that comforting notion, and she went on to chat about how much she liked Renata Moore.

"I think you should seriously consider the Hodge, Brune offer, Jason."

How ironic that our opinions on the matter had completely reversed. I mumbled something appropriate and noncommittal.

"I'd love to meet Charlotte and Renata for lunch when we're here in the summer, that is, if I can lure Renata out of the house. She was certainly right about picking a trattoria at random. Won't we have fun exploring if we come for six weeks? We can eat out every night."

I hated to think what that would cost, even if the price of Carolyn's meals should actually prove to be tax deductible without having to fight the IRS. I am a person who dreads being audited. It happened to me when I was a graduate student. The government decided that my fellowship was taxable, and because I couldn't afford a lawyer, I had to pay up. I'm still resentful and have no faith in the new taxpayer-rights legislation that is being touted by Congress. Carolyn, on the other hand, thinks that we get our money's worth. She's given to ordering those free brochures that issue in great waves from the government printing office. They then pile up in corners, unread.

At the theater we had a surprise. When picking up our tickets at the box office, we were told that the management had exchanged our original reservations in the balcony for better seats on the main floor. While the clerk was locating these new tickets and I was getting wet, Carolyn bubbled over with enthusiasm for the unexpected kindness of strangers in New York. "The civility campaign is really working!" she exclaimed. "They didn't have to bother on our behalf about the tickets. And did I tell you about this nice young black youth, who looked, at first glance, like a gang person and was carrying a huge boom box? He got up on the subway and gave me his seat."

"The effect of encroaching age," I muttered, "our age, not his." Still, it was proving hard to stay grumpy when my wife was so cheerful.

We took our exchanged seats on a left center aisle, one row from the back of the front section, Carolyn with the loaf of bread on her lap. The theater was not at all rough-hewn, as I would have expected of an off-Broadway venue. It had slate blue velvet seats, reasonably comfortable, a carpet in the same shade but marked by the footprints of patrons with dirty snow on their boots, blue painted brick walls, and a red curtain. The play began within minutes, exactly on time, although a chattering gaggle of theatergoers was still entering. What we saw was basically a Biblical history portrayed from a homosexual point of view: In the beginning God created Adam and Steve, etc. It was not subtle, but it was certainly funny.

We both laughed immoderately, although I noticed that my wife became restless about halfway through, twisting now and then to look behind her and tapping her loaf of bread with her head tipped attentively, although not, as far as I could see, to the dialogue. She even dropped the bread at one point and had to retrieve it, not a promising event if it was to be part of our dinner. And she laughed much less frequently later in the act than in the beginning.

I could only surmise that she was shocked to be confronted by husky young actors in skimpy underpants and then naked. They had very large penises. The audience around us seemed to enjoy the display, but I suppose Carolyn was embarrassed. I couldn't help wondering if the naked actors ever experienced unplanned erections onstage. That does happen to us males occasionally, but under normal circumstances, our trousers and anything we may be carrying — coats, books, hats — can be used to conceal the situation until it subsides. No chance of concealment here. Perhaps if an erection occurred, the audience would be even more appreciative.

There was also a lesbian couple as part of the plot. It was an unusual play, but not as unusual as my wife's behavior during intermission.

Having dragged me out into the lobby, Carolyn said, "Let's try the other seats for the second act." She was whispering into my ear as if telling me an important secret. "You just run up there and hold them, will you, Jason? I have to go to the ladies' room."

"But the seats we have are excellent," I protested.

"Here, take the bread with you." She thrust it into my hands and rushed off through the crowd. Could the soup have made her sick? I climbed the stairs to the balcony and found our original seats unoccupied. How fortunate that I remembered the numbers, for I no longer had the computer printout. Carolyn arrived and plopped down beside me just before the second act started, this after studying the other balcony occupants as if looking for a long lost friend. She did not seem herself at all. However, once seated, her expression relieved, she almost seemed pleased with herself.

"Isn't this nice?" She took back the bread.

I didn't see that it was any nicer than our first seats. In fact, if the theater caught fire, our chances of getting out unharmed were radically diminished. Very peculiar, my wife's behavior. But perhaps she had experienced one of those feminine emergencies, which sometimes involve unusual behavior. I was wise enough not to suggest any such thing.

31

Fingering a Suspect

Carolyn

What a shock I had! I'd been sitting there laughing until my ribs hurt when one laugh behind me stood out from all the rest. It plucked some chord in memory and gave me pause. Frowning, I turned my attention back to the play, wondering if the actors playing Adam and Steve had been chosen for the size of their genitals. When I was a little girl, a rather crude neighbor of ours said of a professor at Daddy's university, a man who was given to swimming nude early in the morning, "He's hung like a horse." That phrase would probably apply to those two young men up on the stage, not that I've ever paid much attention to equine genitalia. Still, it was rather interesting to see men exhibited as sex objects: I suppose that's why they were nude. Take that peculiar school of art that posed one naked woman among a crowd of fully dressed men. You never see paintings of one naked man among clothed women. I wondered what Jason thought of all this nudity. Was he embarrassed? I'd have to ask him.

Then my wandering thoughts were brought back by another hilarious line in the play that elicited that strange, good-humored, braying laugh again. It was so familiar. I tried to peek over my shoulder to see who was behind me in the aisle seat, but that was hard to do without being obvious. So I turned my attention back to the stage and a character called "stage manager," who sat at a table at the side of the action and called out such things as "Lights, go! Flood, go!" What an antic imagination the dramatist had. Still, I deliberately stifled the impulse to laugh so that I could listen to the distinctive laughter behind me. And identification was right there, dancing at the edge of my mind.

I dropped my bread on the floor, actually on Jason's foot, hoping that I wouldn't ruin it — the bread. Jason was engrossed in the comedy and didn't rush to pick it up for me. Consequently, I was able to lean forward to retrieve the loaf, then straighten, taking at the same time a good look at the person behind Jason on the aisle. A man. Familiar? I wasn't sure.

Oh, well. Clasping my Italian baked trophy, I again concentrated on the play and was soon laughing myself, but still aware of the familiar hooting behind me. The man couldn't be anyone I knew. Could he? If he was, I'd have recognized him. Then, as my husband and the man behind him convulsed with merriment, I remembered. Thelma! It sounded just like Thelma, the missing waitress.

I turned completely around and stared. Definitely a man. Happily, he didn't notice my interest. Jason did and cut his eyes at me, puzzled. I smiled and turned back to the stage. It could be Thelma. The square shoulders were right. And the face, if you took away Thelma's big glasses and bigger hair. But the generous breasts were gone. Did anyone manufacture a padded bra or breast prosthetics that large? Thelma had had a very flat bottom for a chesty woman; I remembered thinking she must be wearing a girdle. And Thelma hadn't seemed the theatergoing type. No, that was wrong. She had quoted *King Lear*. But why was she here, dressed as a man? Or had she been a man dressed as a waitress?

Then I had the most astounding intuition. Maybe the person sitting behind me, the person who had been Thelma at the deli, was actually Rick Heydemann. I tried to remember what the son had looked like, but the memory was rather fuzzy. I had been so shocked by his remarks about his father that I hadn't looked at him very closely at the memorial service, and my attention had been focused on his mother at the opera. But he had been wearing a very expensive black suit; that I remembered. On both occasions he had been wearing black.

I glanced back at Thelma. Black turtleneck sweater, black trousers. The color of mourning. The trousers had a good crease, more or less the sign of a careful dresser. And other things fit. Heydemann, the would-be actor who expected to star off-Broadway in a self-financed play, was here taking in another off-Broadway play. And he had evidently played the part of Thelma. Why would he have done that unless to kill his father? He would certainly have known that his father patronized that deli each Monday.

This was very strange! Downright frightening. Had he recognized me? Good heavens, I now remembered telling Thelma how horrible Max's children had been at the memorial and that I wouldn't be surprised if they were responsible for his death. What a dreadful coincidence that we should show up at the same play today. Acting on impulse, I yanked the scarf holding my hair back and let the hair fall forward to obscure my face. At the same time, I decided that Jason and I would have to change seats. I only hoped that our earlier reservations would be open.

When the second act ended, I dropped my bread again in order to delay Jason so that Thelma/Rick would have time to leave the auditorium ahead of us. Obviously, my first duty was to call Detective Worski and tell him that Thelma had resurfaced. He could come here and arrest her/him, while Jason and I sat upstairs and watched it happen. That was quite an exciting idea, really.

I had a bit of trouble convincing Jason to go upstairs while I went to the ladies' room, actually the public telephone, to which an usher directed me. While waiting for a man who was talking to his wife, telling her that he'd be late getting back from the office, obviously a lie, it occurred to me that Rick might have followed *me* here. In fact, he might have arranged the seat change so that he'd be seated right behind me, meaning to stab me during the performance because I knew his secret. Goodness, if he could kill his father and stepmother, he was probably getting accustomed to murder, becoming a serial killer, looking forward to doing away with me during the second act, then slipping into the cross aisle and out of the theater while I, dead in my chair, appeared to be napping.

There was one person ahead of me in line, a woman who wanted to call her baby-sitter. When the man who was lying to his wife hung up, and joined, of all things, another man, whom he hugged, I said rather wildly, "This is an emergency," and snatched the receiver from the worried mother's hand. She was very impatient as I juggled my purse and bread, trying to find the detective's number, but I persisted and actually got Detective

Worski on the first ring. He was at his desk, wherever that was.

"I've found Thelma," I whispered, glancing around nervously to see if Thelma had spotted me. I didn't see her. What if she had left at intermission? Well, better that than having her see me sneaking upstairs. "You have to come and arrest her."

"Is this Mrs. Blue?"

"Yes, of course, Detective. I'm at the Manetta Lane Theater in Greenwich Village."

"Who said I wanted to arrest her?"

"Well, at least pick her up for questioning. I thought you'd been combing New Jersey for her. Now, I've found her, but she's dressed as a man. I'm not sure which she is, but I suspect she's really Rick Heydemann. That makes sense, don't you think?"

"If she's dressed as a man, how do you know it's Thelma?"

"Because the laugh is unmistakable, and the shoulders are right."

Detective Worski gave a heavy sigh, which I ignored.

"She's in the left-side aisle seat, first floor, last row of the first section. If you can find Manetta Lane, you can't miss the theater." I stopped to take a breath. The angry mother was eavesdropping and staring as if I was crazy. "Are you coming?" I demanded anxiously. "You did say that the next time I made a suggestion, you'd pay attention."

"I'm coming."

"You'd better bring backup. If she's really Rick Heydemann, she might put up a fight. She might even be armed, although this is a theater performance, so probably not. Still, if she's here to kill me —"

"Why would she want to kill you?"

"Because I told her that I suspect Ricky Heydemann. So hurry, would you?" I glanced around apprehensively once more.

"Yep. I'm on my way. An' thanks for the tip, Mrs. Blue," said Detective Worski, and hung up.

I took another quick look around, then skulked through the lobby as inconspicuously as possible and up the stairs to the balcony, where I sat down beside my husband. "Now, isn't this better?" I asked. "It will give us a whole new perspective."

"I hope you haven't dropped the bread again," he answered. "Maybe we should just leave it behind."

The curtain then rose on another hilarious act of *The Most Fabulous Story Ever Told*. I was happy to see Thelma/Rick in his old seat, but not so happy to see him craning his neck, probably looking for me. How fortunate that I had alerted the police. They'd arrive before I had to leave the balcony and put myself at risk again. I settled down to enjoy the play, and it was *so* funny. I wondered fleetingly if homosexuals found it offensive and if there were any in the audience. Well, probably that man who hugged the other man after telling his wife he was at the office.

Then I wondered whether Rick was homosexual. Of course, being a transvestite didn't make a man homosexual. I remember reading in Ann Landers that men who have perfectly normal marriages . . . well, except for liking to wear ladies' clothes . . . can be transvestites. Sometimes their wives even provide the clothing. I tried to imagine Jason wearing something of mine — my new periwinkle suit, for instance — but I couldn't picture it, and he couldn't get into it. So much for that bizarre thought. I don't think Jason would have been pleased to know what I'd been thinking.

I began to see, as the action on stage progressed, that, aside from its campy humor, *The Most Fabulous Story Ever Told* actually had a message about tolerance for those who are different. And the end was hilarious. The "stage manager," whom Adam decides must be God, leaves in a huff and can be heard stamping out, slamming a door, and hailing a taxi. A female God, washing her hands of the whole ridiculous creation: What a charming idea. I'd have to tell Jason's mother about it. But then why bother? She'd probably read the play.

"Wasn't that a delight?" I said to Jason as

we rose from our seats, clapping enthusiastically. I kept a close eye on the aisle seat downstairs, hoping to see Detectives Worski and Ali striding in to apprehend Thelma/ Rick. It didn't happen, so I supposed they were in the lobby awaiting their opportunity. "Let's hurry downstairs," I said to Jason. I didn't want to miss the action.

But when we were on the stairs, with me peering anxiously at the exiting crowd, I couldn't see either Thelma/Rick or the detectives. What if Detective Worski had been humoring me and hadn't meant to come here at all? Or he couldn't find backup in time? It was, after all, Sunday. Probably most men were home with their families watching pro wrestling. Have you ever seen pro wrestling on cable TV? It's about as tasteless and histrionic as anything one could imagine. If it weren't for A & E, I'd have canceled the cable service the first time I saw wrestling — quite by accident, I might add.

We were almost to the first floor, part of the slow-moving exit from the balcony, and I still hadn't spotted Thelma. Maybe he/she was changing characters and sexes again, preparatory to killing me as I left the theater.

"This play must be very popular with the gay community," Jason murmured.

"You think so?" I was surprised.

"Surely, you noticed all the male/male couples."

Actually, I hadn't, except for the one lying to his wife. "I was wondering if they'd be offended by the play." It was hard to keep up a conversation when I wanted to grab Jason's hand and run for it. Damn that Detective Worski. Where was he?

"Well, everyone was laughing," said Jason. He was now behind me, shepherding me through the crowd so that we wouldn't get separated. Well, Thelma/Rick couldn't stab me in the back with Jason so close behind. But what if he shoved Jason aside? Immediately terrified, I whirled to look behind my husband and saw . . . that black-clad figure with a shining silver spike emerging from his sleeve, his hand lifting toward my husband's back. I screamed.

32

En Garde, Bread Lovers

Jason

I can't begin to convey how surreal events in the lobby of the Manetta Lane Theater seemed at the time. One minute Carolyn and I were drifting toward the exit with the rest of the crowd after the performance. The next she whirled and screamed right into my ear. Then, before I could begin to recover from the ringing in my head, my wife shoved me hard, and I stumbled sideways, falling. Those events in themselves would be cause for astonishment. My wife is not given to screaming, nor is she a violent woman. I can't think of a time when either of us has raised a hand to the other during the years of our marriage.

What followed was even more bizarre, for Carolyn assumed what I later identified as a fencer's stance, one hand raised for balance, the other clutching the end of her long loaf of Italian bread, her fingernails actually digging into the crust for more secure purchase. Then she lunged toward a young man dressed in black. He certainly looked as-

335

tounded, and I felt as if I were a participant in someone else's drug-induced hallucination. But the action did not end there. Still clutching the bread, the other end of which the young man now seemed to be holding, my wife lowered her free hand into the shoulder bag she carried and pulled out a small cylinder, which she sprayed into the black-clad fellow's face. He screamed, dropped his end of the bread, and raised both hands to his eyes.

Around us pandemonium ensued: The odor of an offensive perfume permeated the air; Carolyn dropped the bread and stepped back; the young man continued to moan and clutch his eyes; and I picked myself off the floor with the help of a stout woman in a brown pants suit. This lady said to my wife, "Did he try to feel you up, dear?" I'm not sure whether she was referring to me or to the young man as the putative sexual predator.

The companion of the lady in brown was a painfully thin female in a full olive green skirt over which trailed a matching tunic that almost reached her knees yet was of so thin a fabric that her nipples showed clearly and embarrassingly on the flat expanse of her chest. She asked, "Was that perfume or pepper spray?"

Carolyn was still catching her breath. My wife is not an athletic person. I believe the only sport she ever participated in after the age of eighteen was fencing, which may explain her strange maneuvers with the Italian loaf, although I doubt that her gym instructor had the students fence with bread. Carolyn only took the class because she had one more gym requirement to fill at the university and had already taken all the dance classes they offered. It was fencing or tennis; being already enamoured with medieval history, she chose fencing. This was before we met; she was a sophomore at the time and still avoiding her science requirements.

At any rate, Carolyn replied to the anorexic woman in olive green, "That was Bernie Feingold's signature scent."

"Carolyn, are you all right?" I asked. I was, I believe, referring to her sanity rather than her physical well-being. After all, I was the one who had been pushed over.

Nonetheless, she replied, "I wasn't injured, and you, thank God, weren't, either."

"Bernie Feingold?" exclaimed the woman who was interested, for no discernible reason, in the perfume my wife had used as a weapon. "Who the hell is Bernie Feingold? They'll have to get a better name than that if they plan to market the stuff." She then pressed her business card on Carolyn. "Agnes Merwyn. Public Relations."

The red-eyed man had evidently been trying to slip away. Small wonder. He probably feared being sprayed again or pummeled with the bread, which now lay on the floor between him and my wife. She was keeping a wary eye on him as she ran a hand over her hair to be sure that it was tidy after her strange exertions. However, he didn't escape because a husky, middle-aged fellow with a bushy mustache and furrowed brow pinioned him from behind and said, "Here you. Stay right where you are. I saw you try to steal that lady's bread."

"Clive," exclaimed a pudgy woman, probably the good citizen's wife, "stay out of it, for goodness sake. Do you want friends to know we attended this disgusting play?"

"I can't abide a thief," said Clive. "They used to hang people for stealing bread."

"That's true," Carolyn agreed, "although evidently it wasn't a deterrent."

"I didn't steal anything." The young man glared at Carolyn, his eyes red and weeping. "This crazy woman attacked me for no reason."

"Other than that you're Thelma," Carolyn replied briskly, "and you tried to kill my husband."

The young man struggled against the advocate of capital punishment for bread theft. "Do I look like a Thelma?" he demanded and broke into strange, honking laughter.

"You see, Clive. He's not Thelma," said the middle-aged wife. "It's a case of mistaken identity. We'll get our names in the papers because of some crazy woman who goes around spraying innocent bystanders with perfume."

"I identified you by your laughter," said Carolyn. "You're Thelma."

Clive let go of the young man. "Men aren't named Thelma," he said.

I had the frightening feeling that my wife, my lovely Carolyn, had experienced some sort of psychotic break. Not knowing what else to do, I put my arm around her, making sure at the same time that her perfume-wielding hand was pinned between us.

"Well, it's about time," she said, further confusing me. Then, as the newly released man in black attempted again to leave, he was grabbed by, of all people, the two detectives who had been investigating Max's death.

"This is Thelma?" asked the older detective.

"Or Ricky," Carolyn replied.

"Ricky who?" asked the young man. "First, you say I'm Thelma. Well, that's crap. You want to see my dick?" He addressed this offer to the detectives. "This woman sprayed something into my eyes. Look at me. I was practically blinded."

He did look terrible, even if Carolyn's weapon had only been her agent's uncle's signature perfume. I foresaw lawsuits in our future. To me, Carolyn said, "He tried to kill you, Jason, although I can't imagine why. He'd have more reason to kill me."

"Who?" I asked. Carolyn didn't look confused, but I certainly was.

"Ricky Heydemann. Look in the end of that loaf of bread," she instructed the detectives, nudging our Italian loaf with the toe of her boot.

The older detective had handcuffed his prisoner. Ali bent down and picked up the loaf. "I'll be damned." He tucked it under his arm, carefully pulled on thin latex gloves, and drew from the loaf a vicious-looking blade, rather like an elongated ice pick. "See that, Worski. I think it clicks out of the handle."

"Bag it," said Worski. He gave his cuffed prisoner a shake.

"I never saw that in my life," protested the man, "and my name isn't Thelma . . . or Ricky."

"I'll bet," said Worski. "But you could sure be the guy or gal who's been targetin' Heydemanns. How come you're after the Blues now?"

"It must be her weapon. She lunged at me with it."

"I was holding the bread end!" said Carolyn indignantly. "You can see where I dug my fingernails in for purchase."

"Yep," said Worski, inspecting the unpapered end of the Italian loaf when Ali held it out.

"The switchblade was on his side," Ali agreed. "And he doesn't have the nails to make those marks on the bread. Look at his nails, Pugh." Another officer was now restraining the cuffed attacker, and he yanked the man's arms up to make the inspection.

"Police brutality!" cried the arrestee.

"Blunt, guy-type nails," Pugh confirmed.

"Thelma had blunt nails, too," said Carolyn.

Police were blocking the front of the theater, keeping the playgoers from leaving. The manager had arrived, demanding to know the reason for the police blockade. He was ignored. Having worked their way through the crowd, several ushers tried to remonstrate with the detectives for causing a disturbance. Worski flashed his badge and told them to herd the theatergoers back into the auditorium. They tried. Then Worski deployed his forces by assigning uniformed officers to take statements from people in the crowd while he and Ali proceeded to headquarters with Carolyn, me, and the man who was evidently under arrest. I was afraid my wife might be under arrest as well, but the police assumption seemed to be that she had attacked in my defense.

As we left, I could hear comments from the people we passed.

"She hit him with a loaf of bread. I didn't see any weapon in his hand."

"No, she sprayed him with mace. Jesus, you can't go to see a play these days without some femiNazi taking offense. Rush Limbaugh got it right about women."

"Rush Limbaugh wouldn't be seen dead at this performance."

"It *was* funny."

"Bunch of queers."

"Did you hear what that homophobe just said?"

And so forth until we were helped into one police car while Carolyn's victim/attacker was helped into another. Had he really been trying to stab me? And if so, why? My God, but my wife was brave! She fended him off with just a loaf of bread and a perfume atomizer!

33

Interrogation with Donuts

Carolyn

Grim and grimy would be my description of the New York police station to which Jason and I were taken for interviews. We were put in separate rooms, as if we might contradict and thus incriminate ourselves if we couldn't coordinate our stories. Or perhaps I was being paranoid. I must admit to feeling more than a little shaky after crossing swords (an unfortunate metaphor, but it sounds ridiculous to say crossing bread and ice pick) with the assassin. Detective Worski did make an effort at hospitality by offering coffee and donuts. Naturally, I accepted promptly with the idea that the repast, although simple, would make a good subject for a column. Then he left me alone with my snack.

Well, no one could ever accuse the NYPD of serving good coffee. The cup in which mine was served wasn't even clean, and the coffee was deplorable. Naturally, I've never tasted battery acid (presumably one wouldn't live through the experience), but this coffee surely was the source of that unfavorable

343

comparison. And then I tasted my donut, which was even more objectionable, a heavy, stale, unhealthy object coated with a sickeningly sticky, tastelessly sweet glaze that clung to my fingers like glue. Had I been a criminal, I would undoubtedly have confessed to any crime to avoid further exposure to the refreshments at Detective Worski's precinct house. I spat the bite of donut into the cup and deposited the whole on the floor in the corner. The room contained only a table and two chairs, and I did not want that snack within sight or smelling distance.

My hands were still shaking from the events at the Manetta Lane Theater, so I laced them on the table and put my head down in the hope that I might catch a nap while I waited. Even a stiff neck would be better than the refreshments I had been served and the trembling stress that was attacking me. I took deep, calming breaths and attempted a muscle-by-muscle relaxation of my body, something that I had read about in a government pamphlet that came in the mail with several others I requested. However, I did not fall asleep. Instead, my mind replayed, like some defective horror movie, the memory of that blade coming out of Thelma's sleeve toward Jason's back.

By the time Detective Worski finally returned, I was not in a very good mood. "Well, was it Rick Heydemann?" I demanded in a snippy tone when he entered the room. By then I was no longer convinced of that myself. Unless the disguise was exceptional, surely I would have recognized Max's son when we finally came face-to-face. The blade wielder had looked like Thelma in drag, if one can use that term for a woman dressed as a man, or a man dressed as a man but sometimes as a woman.

"Don't think so," said Worski. "He's got ID on him, but it's fake. The social security don't match the name."

"Of course he'd have a fake ID, but did you check his face for stage makeup or one of those peel-off masks?"

"That's only in the movies, Mrs. Blue. We did talk to someone claiming to be young Heydemann at the grandparents' house. He seemed kind of flustered when I identified myself, but he didn't admit anything. How come you thought the guy was Heydemann?"

"I don't know," I replied, embarrassed. "It seemed logical at the time. He certainly was Thelma. I'd never mistake that laugh, so I thought, because I'd told Thelma that I suspected Rick, that Rick was coming after me."

"I thought the guy was going for your husband."

"So it seemed. If he'd meant to stab me, he'd have had to go around Jason. And why would he have exposed his weapon before he was in position to stab me, preferably from the back, since I had spotted him? Although he didn't necessarily know at the time that I'd recognized him. And of course, I didn't have any leisure to analyze the situation. I had to protect Jason."

"Well, you did a bang-up job of that." Worski started to laugh. "If this guy is really a paid assassin, he's going to be damned embarrassed when it gets around that a woman with a loaf of bread and a bottle of perfume disarmed him."

"I didn't actually disarm him," I replied modestly. "We both dropped our weapons. I think you should check the box office to see whether he arranged to have our seats changed so that we would be sitting in front of him, whoever he is."

"He's not talking except to accuse you of attacking him. We've put his prints in AFIS — that's the national fingerprint computer — an' we gave him some stuff to wash his eyes out with. Now, what's this about the seats?"

"When we got to the box office to pick up our tickets, they said they'd switched us to better seats. Being the naive outlander that I am," I continued bitterly, "I remarked to Jason on how helpful New Yorkers are. Now I suppose that young black man with the boom box was hoping to snatch my purse."

"What —"

"Never mind. It's not relevant . . . except as regards my plunge into cynicism. Anyway, the seat change put us right in front of Thelma. That's how I recognized the laugh and got a peek at her. Not what she'd had in mind, I'm sure."

"It's a he," said Worski.

"You checked?"

"Yes ma'am. We checked. Armed suspects always get patted down."

"Perhaps she's wearing some sort of fake male genitalia," I suggested. "During the Renaissance, gentlemen were given to padding their codpieces." Detective Worski was looking at me peculiarly, so I dropped that subject. "Anyway, it would have been quite easy for Thelma to knife me during the second act. Jason would have thought I'd fallen asleep."

"You usually drop off when everyone around you is laughin' up a storm? I heard about that play. Supposed to be real funny if you like gay jokes."

"I often take a nap in the afternoon," I said stiffly. "After my murder, Thelma could have slipped away under cover of the general hilarity. You'll have noticed that her seat was at the juncture of two aisles, just seven or eight places from an exit. Or actually, you wouldn't have noticed because you didn't arrive in a timely fashion."

At that point we glared at one another.

"Think I'll go see if we got a print ID yet," he said.

"What about me?"

"You just sit tight. We haven't talked to your husband yet."

"At the rate you're going, we may have to catch our plane before you get to him."

"Don't get smart with me, Mrs. Blue."

"I can't imagine why I bothered trying to help. You certainly haven't shown any appreciation of my efforts."

"Hey, I appreciate your ramming that guy with your loaf of bread. Everyone here's gonna appreciate that. It's the best story to come out of this precinct in years."

"So glad to have provided entertainment in your otherwise dreary lives," I muttered ungraciously. "And while I have the opportunity, I'd like to point out that the acidity of your coffee is surpassed only by the stale, gluey consistency of your donuts."

"You got that right," Worski agreed as he left the room.

34

The Conspiracy Theory

Jason

"Professor." Mohammad Ali entered and sat down across from me in the small, shabby room where I had been left for some time to worry about my wife. Carolyn had been trembling in the squad car that took us to the police station; I had felt the tremors as she sat in the circle of my arm. Now I was afraid that she, too, had been left alone as I had.

"I'm worried about my wife."

"Mrs. Blue seems like a lady who can take pretty good care of herself. I'd be surprised if my wife could handle the situation at the theater that well. By the way, the guy she perfumed *was* a guy, and we don't think he's Maximillian Frederick Heydemann, Jr."

"He's not," I replied. "I've seen Max's son twice. That was not him."

"But your wife told Worski —"

"My wife evidently jumped to the conclusion that her life was in danger."

"Seems like it was you he was going after."

"Be that as it may, she insisted on moving

to the balcony at intermission, after calling the police, an action that she failed to mention to me. She identified the person by a distinctive laugh as the waitress at the delicatessen where Max Heydemann was killed. As to her idea that that person might be Max's son in disguise, the son's abominable behavior convinced her that he, his mother, and his sister were responsible for Max's death. However mistaken she may have been —"

"So you don't think it was a family murder?"

"No, I don't." I had been mulling over the situation while I waited to be interviewed and decided that the police could no longer be kept in the dark about the problem at Hodge, Brune. If Moore and Merrivale objected, so be it. "Just the fact that the man seemed to intend harm to me rather than Carolyn is a good indication that the motive for Max's death and the violence that followed are the result of industrial espionage involving Max's company."

"I'd like to hear about the espionage. You ready to tell me about it?"

He looked quite enthusiastic, making me recall that he had previously been assigned to a white-collar crime unit. No doubt industrial espionage was more to his taste than murder. I told him about the theft of the coal process and the kind of investment in research it represented as well as the profits it promised to any company that patented it, which the Ukrainian company had moved to do.

"And so Heydemann was killed. Why?"

"I believe that he discovered who was responsible for the sale or at least release of the information. He was to have met on Monday with Charles Moore to name the culprit but died before he could do so. The obvious conclusion is that his suspicions led to his murder."

"So he couldn't implicate someone at the company?"

"Presumably so."

"And the attack on his wife?"

"They must have believed that he had confided in her before he died."

"Sounds plausible except for one thing. You don't even work for the company. Why would anyone involved in this plot want to kill an outsider?"

"Again this is a hypothesis, but I have been conducting a telephone investigation for Hodge, Brune by calling people I know in Eastern Europe. Evidently, the criminals think I know something damaging."

"What?"

I shrugged. "I'm not sure. Perhaps that rumor links the Ukrainian company to the Russian Mafia. Perhaps —"

Ali sat up straighter. "Run that by me again."

"I was told by a colleague in Poland that, although the company in Kiev had neither the scientists nor the resources to develop such a process for themselves, they did have a vice president who was married to the daughter of someone powerful in the Russian Mob. There are rumors that this crime syndicate provided the financing for the Ukrainian company."

"I assume you told others at the company about the Russian Mob scenario, so it might have gotten back to whoever the Russians bribed to steal the information in the first place."

"So it would seem."

"Who at the company knew about your investigation?"

"Charles Moore, who asked me to do it and to whom I reported my findings. Vernon Merrivale, their head of security. And whomever they told. Vaclav Vasandrovich, for instance. He's the interim director of R and D, so I'm presuming that he was in the loop. I didn't talk to him personally about my investigation, but all three of them warned us, Carolyn and myself, about talking to the police. One of the three must have been worried about something other than investor reaction to the situation if word of the loss got out."

Ali smiled. "I have to say, the warnings didn't stop your wife. She mentioned a couple of times what she considered a ridiculous spy scenario."

"I see." I must admit that I was angry for a moment at Carolyn's indiscretion and had to remind myself that she had just saved my life.

"OK, so Moore, Merrivale, and Vasandrovich all warned you off. And Vasandrovich is the new director of R and D. Took Heydemann's place, didn't he?"

"Yes, and there's another thing about him."

"What?" Ali looked eager.

"His degree," I answered. "A Czech colleague said Vasandrovich was not a graduate of Charles University, although his curriculum vitae indicates that he was. It may be some problem with the records in Prague dating from the Communist period or the dislocations that followed." Suddenly I remembered something that Carolyn had said while we were preparing for bed at the Moores' house in Greenwich. "Incidentally, my wife mentioned hearing him speak Russian in his office, or so she thought."

"Being Czech, wouldn't it be natural for him to know Russian?"

"Yes, but he evidently denied that he had been speaking Russian. He said it was Czech and that he was speaking to an aunt. However, he told me that he had no living relatives."

"So you suspect him?"

I shrugged. "I have no evidence to link Vaclav and the criminals, and I do know that he was devastated by Max's death. He considered Max his mentor because Max is the man who got him and his wife out of the Czech Republic before the Communists were overthrown. He seems to have felt beholden to Max as well as having a great personal affection for him. Unless he's a very good actor, Vasandrovich looks to be an unlikely candidate for involvement in Max's death."

"And the company hasn't turned up any concrete information beyond what you've told them?"

"Not that I know of," I replied. "Which is what makes me keep coming back to Merrivale. He had access to the stolen research data, and he controls the company investigation of the theft, not to mention being the one most opposed to bringing the police in."

"Which puts him in the perfect position to keep himself from being exposed as the spy." Ali nodded. "Good theory."

"Have you identified the man who tried to stab me?"

"Not yet. His ID is fake, and he won't talk to us other than to claim that the weapon at the theater wasn't his and that your wife attacked him for no reason. We're running his prints and getting a search warrant for the apartment on his fake ID."

"Then, unless we can be of further assistance, I'd like to take my wife back to the hotel. She's distraught, and we have to pack for the trip back to Texas tomorrow. I presume there's no problem about our leaving."

"No problem. We've got your address, and we checked out your credentials. As for Mrs. Blue . . ." Ali grinned. "She may be distraught, but she certainly gave my partner a hard time."

"Did she?" I had to smile and wished that I had been there to see Carolyn in action, my wife who can fence with a loaf of bread and disarm a dangerous criminal with a bottle of perfume.

"Right. And I'm afraid she's going to give us a bad review on our coffee and donuts, too. Worski said she got downright mean on that subject."

"Well, she is writing a book about food. But the subject is New Orleans food."

"Yeah? Did she pick on the police there, too, and foil criminals?"

"I believe she did," I replied.

35

Domestic Strife in a Patrol Car

Carolyn

Jason and I were reunited in a patrol car assigned to return us to the hotel. What a relief to leave that place, although I anticipated even greater relief when our plane was off the ground and heading home. I no longer cared who Thelma was and what he/she had done, and I hoped to talk Jason out of having anything to do with Hodge, Brune. I was pre-planning my introductory statement on the matter when Jason took me by surprise.

"Carolyn, just who have you told about the espionage problem at the company?"

He sounded so stern that I stammered, "I-I don't know."

"You don't *know?* You were asked not to mention it at all!"

"Well, Jason, just because Hodge, Brune tends toward the paranoid, doesn't mean I have to —"

"Why do you think I was attacked at the theater by someone you claim was a waitress at a deli? Did you tell her about the coal project?"

"I may have," I snapped, feeling defensive as well as indignant. "But I'm convinced that Thelma meant to stab me, not you."

"Really. And what do you see as the connection between you, Max, and his wife?" Jason sounded downright sarcastic, as if I was some cotton-brained student.

"The will and my suspicions about it."

"It couldn't be that Max's killer knew that my investigation was about to —"

"What investigation?"

He looked taken aback. "I've been using my contacts in Eastern Europe to —"

"You didn't tell me anything about that."

"You heard me on the phone to Eastern Europe."

"You never said why. First you keep secrets, and then you accuse me of putting you at risk." Really, this was the last straw. I burst into tears.

"Hey, what's going on back there?" demanded the policeman who was driving.

"None of your business," I replied, sniffling.

"If it's domestic violence —"

"The only violence was against me," said Jason dryly. "My wife knocked me over in a theater."

"So press charges," said the policeman, "but don't hit her in my patrol car."

"I didn't hit her," Jason protested.

"And I only shoved him so that he

357

wouldn't get knifed," I added. "I don't know how you can accuse me of domestic violence, Jason, when I saved your life." Both indignant and hurt, I reached into my handbag for a Kleenex.

"You're not going for the perfume, are you?" Jason asked, looking alarmed.

"No, but if I still had the bread, I'd knock you right on the head with it."

"No head-knocking!" The driver slammed on the brakes at a red light and turned around menacingly.

"I'm getting out right here," I said, blowing my nose. It wasn't much of a threat, because I could see the hotel half a block away.

"Good," said the policeman. "More cops get hurt on domestic violence calls than any other —"

"Oh, do be quiet!" I jumped out and ran down the street as fast as I could go, sobbing and being studiously ignored by passing New Yorkers. By the time my husband returned to the room, I had retrieved a contract sent to me by messenger from Paul Fallon, taken the elevator to the room, where I tossed the contract on top of my suitcase, kicked off my shoes, and climbed into bed. Once beneath the covers, I put my head under the pillow and continued to weep. At that moment, I felt that I would never forgive my husband for his unkind words and for failing to appreciate the terror I had experienced when I thought he was going to be killed and the bravery it had taken to defend him.

Well, actually, when I look back on the incident, I hadn't really been brave; I'd just reacted with the only weapons at hand. Still, I had saved his life. Maybe being rescued from danger by a woman had hurt his male ego.

Eventually, Jason entered the room and said in a rather tentative voice, "Carolyn?" I didn't reply. "Caro?" He sighed and retrieved his telephone messages, after which he made a brief long distance call, identifying himself and saying, after a moment, "So he did go to Charles."

Charles who? I wondered.

"Vasandrovich was his patronymic? . . . I wonder why he uses it as a surname. . . . Well, no matter. Probably some immigration snafu. Thanks for calling again."

He hung up and immediately dialed another number. "Charles, this is Jason. I just heard from Prague. Vaclav did go to the university there. It was some surname-patronymic mix-up. . . . Yes, I'm relieved, too."

What in the world was Jason talking about? My body was beginning to relax under the warmth of the blanket, and the pillow blocking light and muting sound contributed to my increasing drowsiness. Defending one's husband from an assassin is exhausting business. The last thing I heard was my husband asking for Detective Ali, but I never heard the conversation. I never heard my husband leave the room. Or return.

What did drag me out of sleep was his voice saying, "Wake up, sweetheart. I've brought home dinner." That and a powerful but tempting odor coming from a bag that Jason had placed right beside my nose.

"Wha . . . ?"

36

Pastrami to Die For

Carolyn

Sometimes the weary tourist, having eaten every meal during the trip in a restaurant, wants to relax and eat takeout in the hotel room. Why? Because it's cheaper, it's less time consuming, no dress code is imposed (one can eat in rumpled or casual clothes, in night clothes, even, I suppose, nude, if so inclined), and it's relaxing. However, these picnics in the room can bring the ire of the hotel and its patrons down on the head of the culinary miscreant. If you spill red wine on the carpet or mustard on the bedspread, the housekeeping staff will take offense. If your choice of picnic food is particularly odoriferous, people in neighboring rooms may follow their noses and knock on your door to complain. On a trip to New York, my husband brought back wonderful, if overpoweringly aromatic, pastrami sandwiches, and I listened anxiously for that angry knock on our door, even as I ate every bite.

However, visitors less lucky and more famous than we, have come to grief by eating in their hotel rooms. After World War II the odor of boiling cabbage prepared by three Russian chefs in the Plaza Hotel suite of UN Ambassador Andrei Gromyko was not greeted with delight. However, he was not asked to leave. Fidel Castro was actually ejected from the Murray Hill Hotel; rumor has it that his staff was plucking chickens and cooking them in a room without cooking facilities. One wonders if the chickens were brought live from Cuba and how the alleged cooking was accomplished. With a hot plate? Over a fire built in the bathtub? Those incidents make our little pastrami adventure look quite conventional.

Carolyn Blue,
"Have Fork, Will Travel,"
Flagstaff Frontier Ledger

I sat up and pushed my hair back. "What is it?" I asked, looking at the large, somewhat greasy bag that my husband had deposited beside my nose.

"A peace offering. I'm sorry I was unpleasant about your having talked to people about the coal project."

I sighed. "And I'm sorry if I put you in danger."

Jason smiled. "Well, you certainly did protect me when it occurred."

"I did, didn't I?" It's amazing how much a nap can do for one. I no longer felt trembly and terrified or even on the verge of tears. In fact, I now felt rather proud of myself. After all, I had fended off a professional assassin, and I hadn't even had a real weapon, just wifely instincts, a loaf of Italian bread, and Bernie Feingold's perfume. "So what's in the bag? It's certainly smelly."

"Smelly?" Jason looked somewhat offended. "The desk clerk assured me that this is the best pastrami in New York City."

"And you got it here at the hotel?" That seemed unlikely.

"No, he recommended a deli down the street."

"Ah. Did you, by any chance, have to pay cash?"

Jason looked surprised. "How did you know that? I considered it pretty unusual. After all, credit cards seem to be accepted everywhere. In the heart of New York City, one would expect —"

"You went to the delicatessen that Max visited every Monday, the one where he died."

Disconcerted, Jason looked down at the bag. "Well, I guess we'll find out if it was pastrami worth dying for," he mumbled, pulling from the bag sandwiches piled with enough meat to feed a family of four, sandwiches in which the filling was so thick that the bread slices seemed an afterthought,

363

sandwiches too thick to be bitten into, sandwiches that tended to topple one way or the other. There were also pickles. And Dr. Brown's Cream Soda, which, Jason assured me, was the beverage of choice for these sandwiches. Even before beginning to eat, I was wondering if we could safely save half or more to eat on the plane tomorrow. Then I remembered that we would be traveling first class. Those perky stewardesses would probably be offended if we brought our own lunch aboard.

And the pastrami was wonderful — rich, moist, fatty, flavorful — almost worth dying for.

We ate it all, ate until we were pastrami-dazed and -sated. Then Jason fell back on the bed while I, rejuvenated by my nap, disposed of the leavings, stepped into the bathroom to wash fat residue from my fingers, and returned to type up notes on the minestrone we had eaten in the Village and the difficulties of devouring large, messy sandwiches while sitting on the hotel's bedspread. Then I packed for our departure the next day, showered, and climbed into bed beside Jason, who was already asleep. I was, too, within minutes.

Sometime later, the telephone on the nightstand rang. I must have been having a bad dream because I awoke terrified and, in trying to grasp the receiver in the dark, knocked it off the cradle. I could hear a voice saying, "Mrs. Blue? Mrs. Blue?"

"What?" said Jason, who was now sitting up, his voice sharp.

"Phone," I mumbled. But I couldn't find it. "Turn on the light."

"Tell 'em to call back later." He lay down again.

"Can't find the receiver. Turn on the light."

Jason turned on the light and I, leaning precariously over the edge of the bed, pulled the receiver up by the cord. " 'Lo?"

"This is Worski. Did I wake you up?"

I squinted at the alarm clock that I had brought from home. "It's after midnight, Detective. Of course, you woke us. And we have to be up early to catch our plane. Why in the world are you calling at —"

"So you don't want to know how the case turned out?"

He sounded so smug I could have smacked him, except that he wasn't here, and one can't really smack a policeman. It's against the law. In fact, it's against the law to smack anyone, even one's own misbehaving child. It had probably been against the law to push my husband down, even though I had done it to save his life. "Of course I want to know. It was the Heydemanns, wasn't it?"

"Sort of."

"Sort of? What does that mean? Either it was or —"

"I'm downstairs. Thought I'd drop by personally and tell you what we know. Since you've been helpful an' all that. It's pretty complicated."

I looked at Jason, who had opened his eyes as soon as he realized I was talking to a detective. "He wants to come up and tell us how the case worked out," I whispered.

Jason nodded. "If you want to go back to sleep, I can go down to the lobby and talk to him."

"Ha! And never hear that I was right about Rick Heydemann?"

Jason grinned. "So tell him to come up here."

"But I'm in my nightie."

"And you don't have a robe?"

"Well, yes, but I'll have to get dressed just the same."

"No, you won't. We'll both put on robes and receive the detective in — what's that French word for —"

"I can't pronounce it." French pronunciation has always been a mystery to me, although I love the sauces. I took my hand from the mouthpiece of the telephone and told the detective our room number, then rushed to my suitcase and snatched my robe from the top layer. Pulling it on, I hurried into the bathroom to root through my cosmetics bag for my comb, thinking all the while that I wouldn't have time to put on makeup. Oh well, detectives probably see lots of women who aren't prepared to appear in public. Jason was letting Detective Worski in when I returned to the bedroom.

"I was right, wasn't I? Rick Heydemann hired Thelma. He probably got the money from his mother. She mentioned money he owed her."

"Yeah?" Worski sat in our one easy chair and wrote that in his notebook.

"So how was Rick *sort of* involved?" I asked.

"I imagine, Carolyn, because it was his father who died as a result of the espionage at the company," said Jason.

"Hey, let me tell the story in my own way, OK?" The detective grinned at us in such a way that I had to wonder if we were both wrong.

37

And Then Some

Jason

Carolyn took the desk chair, looking exceedingly impatient, and I sat on the bed, while Detective Worski settled himself comfortably in a small, upholstered tub chair that could hardly contain his bulk, especially since he had not taken off his green overcoat.

"This is one weird case," said Worski. "We go from practically no leads and no clear suspects to way too many. I mean, we start out with this guy whose fingerprints are on the pig sticker, the guy you saw go for your husband, Mrs. Blue. That's all the information we really got, an' he's not sayin' anything except he didn't do nothin' an' he's got a busy day tomorrow 'cause he's got this TV gig doin' a commercial for deodorant. He's an actor, see. That's another thing he tells us. We ask how he supports himself, an' he says he's an actor, not admittin' he was ever a waitress like you say, Mrs. Blue."

"I don't care what he says. He *was* Thelma!" Carolyn insisted. "And an actor — that ties him to Rick Heydemann, who wanted his inheritance so he could finance an off-Broadway play in which he was going to star."

"Yeah, you mentioned that. So what was the name of that play?"

"*And Then Some.*"

"Yeah. Well, funny thing. When Mr. X says about his deodorant commercial he's got to get to an' how he's gonna sue us if we interfere with his blossomin' career . . . that's how he puts it. His career is blossomin' . . . Ali says, 'Don' sound to me like your career is goin' so great. Most actors figure doin' commercials are for the no-talent guys. An' deodorant ads . . . that's like the bottom of the heap. What's that say about you? You're a guy who looks like he's got smelly armpits?' "

Worski laughed appreciatively. "Ali may think white-collar crime is more fun than murder, but he's got one hell of a talent for workin' a skel over in interrogation. He makes that crack about actors who can't get nothin' but armpit work, an' our guy gets pissed. 'You don' know shit,' he says."

My poor wife. I knew she was longing to reprimand the detective for his language.

"You were saying," Carolyn prompted, "that his interrogation bore fruit?"

"Right. So our unidentified suspect says, 'I been promised a part in a very promisin' play,' an' Ali says, 'Where? In Peoria?' an' the skel says, 'Here in New York, smart-ass,' an'

369

Ali says, 'Sure, like Staten Island?' and the guy says, 'Lower Manhattan,' and so forth. They go a few rounds about this big part that's gonna make the guy famous, an' guess what the name of the play is?"

Neither of us replied, and I frankly I couldn't see that the name of the play would have any bearing on whether or not the young man in black had killed Max, who had nothing to do with the theater.

"*And Then Some*," said Worski triumphantly. "That was the play that was gonna be his big break."

"Rick Heydemann's play!" Carolyn beamed at the detective. "There, what did I tell you? I hope you picked up on the connection while you still had him in custody."

"Well, by then the guys we had searchin' the apartment on his fake ID come back with more stuff."

"His name?" Carolyn asked breathlessly.

"That was later, but the uniforms found the biggest pair of falsies you ever seen under a pile in his underwear drawer."

"Proof positive that he masqueraded as Thelma, who had a bottom too flat for those large breasts. I knew there was something wrong with her figure," said Carolyn.

"Yep." Worski nodded. "An' then they found another one a them pop-out pig stickers. . . . Guess he likes to have a spare. . . . An' his Day-Timer —"

"Surely he didn't enter assassination dates in his calendar," I said. "That would indicate extreme stupidity or perhaps some sort of obsessive-compulsive disorder."

"Let him finish, Jason," said Carolyn impatiently. "Who cares whether he was stupid or neurotic. One has to expect unusual character traits in an assassin."

"You got that right, Mrs. Blue," said Worski, "an' our guy didn't exactly write in his date book that he was gonna kill anyone. What we found was a meetin' with Rick Heydemann the week before Heydemann's dad was killed. He writes that Rick offered him the part of Colin in *And Then Some*." Then he writes, 'Very meaty,' whatever the hell that means. Maybe this Colin character is a fat guy or a weight lifter or —"

"He meant that it was a challenging role," Carolyn interrupted.

"You're saying that he killed Max to get a part in a play?" I objected. "No matter how good the role, that seems an unlikely motive, and I'd imagine a jury would agree."

"It's hard for an actor to get that important first break," said my wife. "I think he might well have been willing to kill for his big chance."

"Jeez, it's hard to tell a story with you two always interruptin'. That's not the only entry in his book. He met young Heydemann the Tuesday after the dad got spiked an' again

371

on Friday that week."

"Friday before or after the will was read?" Carolyn asked.

"They met at a club in the Village late Friday night," said Worski.

"Ha!" Carolyn exclaimed. "They were meeting because Rick wanted his stepmother killed, and the assassin agreed because he wouldn't get the part if Rick didn't get the money to finance the play."

"It still seems unlikely," I insisted. "And why would he try to kill me? Why the meeting on Tuesday, for that matter?"

"Well, the appointment book wasn't all my crew found," said Worski, looking pleased with himself. "There was this bank book. We don' know where the bank is . . . probably some Caribbean island or someplace . . . but he put in ten thousand the day he met Rick before the dad was killed an' another ten Tuesday, the day after the dad was killed, an' another ten Friday, the day before he tried to do the stepmom. That day the book says, 're-hearsals should start in a week, ten days max.' "

"What about today?" Carolyn asked. "He only wounded Charlotte yesterday. What did he say about that?"

"Nothin'," Worski replied. "An' he didn't put another ten thou in the bank."

"So he fails to kill Charlotte one day and tries to kill me the next?" I asked. "That doesn't add up. I have nothing to do with the son's inheritance problems."

"It's as I said," Carolyn insisted. "He was actually going after me, but I got him first. With the bread."

"Carolyn!" I protested. "And another thing, Detective, why was he working as a waitress at the deli if he wasn't asked to kill Max Heydemann until the week before he did it? Carolyn, didn't you say Thelma had been there a while?"

"He and Rick could have been talking about it earlier," she replied defensively. "I don't know when he started playing the Thelma role."

"Two weeks before Max Heydemann died," said Worski.

"Were there earlier meetings between the two men?" I asked.

"Not in his calendar," Worski replied.

"That doesn't mean they didn't have earlier meetings," said Carolyn.

"Carolyn, even you thought he was going after me. You saw him over my shoulder."

"Oh Jason, when you see someone with a weapon in a crowded theater, you don't have time for logical thought processes. You can only do that kind of thinking later. If I'd stopped to analyze the situation, one of us would have been dead."

"Well, you got that right, ma'am," said Worski, "but the whole thing's more complicated than young Heydemann needin' money to finance his actin' career."

Both Carolyn and I groaned.

38

Second Act:
And Then Some More

<u>Carolyn</u>

What more could there be? "Have you arrested Rick?" I asked Detective Worski. "And his mother? I'll bet his sister Ariadne was in on the conspiracy, too." Certainly they had Rick and the assassin dead to rights because they could trace the money from Rick to Thelma. Then they might be able to trace it backward from Rick to Melisande, his mother.

"Let's not get ahead of ourselves here, Mrs. Blue."

Detective Worski was obviously enjoying himself, although how he could in the middle of the night, I can't imagine. Didn't the man ever sleep? "All right, Detective, but at least tell me that Thelma confessed."

"Yeah, his lawyer arrived and advised him to take a reduced plea in return for giving us Rick Heydemann."

My husband was looking very disgruntled, but then men, even men as nice as Jason, don't like to be proved wrong. I leaned over to kiss him on the cheek. "It does explain everything more believably than a spy scenario, dear. Maybe now that the murder has been solved, Detective Ali would like to help with the industrial espionage problem. In fact, given that Max's death was a family matter, I'm not opposed to your taking the job offer at Hodge, Brune. If you'd been right, it would have been too dangerous, don't you think? After all, who would want to work for a company where scientists get killed over chemistry?

"Now we both have offers. That envelope was from Paul Fallon, Frances Striff's significant other. His proposal is tempting, and, goodness, the Hodge, Brune offer —"

"Mrs. Blue, could you shut up for a minute?" said Detective Worski.

I was shocked at his rudeness: first, for interrupting me while I was talking to my husband and even more because he'd told me to shut up, which was hardly gentlemanly.

"I'm not through tellin' you about our investigation."

"What else is there to say? You've got the murderer. He's told you who hired him. You have supporting evidence. Surely —"

"Let him finish, Carolyn," Jason interrupted.

Everyone seemed to feel free to interrupt me.

"Thank you, Professor," said Detective

Worski. "Does she talk this much at home?" He grinned, noticed that I was frowning at him, and hastened on, probably under the impression that I was planning to keep him from finishing, whereas, I now felt so put upon that I didn't plan to say another word. To either of them. In fact, I'd have left the room had there been any place to go but the hall, which I could hardly enter in my bathrobe, and the bathroom, where I'd have to sit ignominiously on the toilet lid wondering what they were saying.

"Anyway, just about the time we worked out the deal, we got a hit on his photo, which we'd faxed around the precincts the same time we put his prints in AFIS. A detective in Organized Crime called to say we'd pulled in Anton Bashurkov, alias Anton Manners, alias Rory Manners, and so forth."

"The name sounds as if it could be Russian," my husband observed, looking interested.

"Yep. He's never been convicted, but he's in the Organized Crime files as a guy hooked up with the Russian Mob."

"And I heard rumors that the Ukrainian company responsible for stealing Hodge, Brune's coal process was backed by the Russian Mafia," said Jason.

"And Thelma said her mother had relatives who were *connected*," I couldn't help adding.

"Of course, I assumed that she meant the American Mafia."

"Yeah, well, Thelma was tellin' you the truth about that," said Detective Worski, "or part of it, anyway. Bashurkov's old lady runs a boardin' house for new arrivals, guys they're smugglin' into the country, but she don't live in Teaneck, an' she don't have MS. That was all a crock of . . . well, it was a crock. You know what I mean?"

"And the deal you made with the suspect? Does that mean you can't pursue the Russian connection?" Jason asked.

I suppose he was right back to worrying that Hodge, Brune was not a healthy company to work for. I certainly had new doubts.

"Hey, any deal we make, it goes down the toilet like so much . . ." The detective glanced at me nervously. "Like so much toilet paper if the guy's been lying to us. So we throw this new angle at him. If he's connected, maybe the Russians, not this Ricky kid, are the ones who want him to off Heydemann. Maybe he's a hit man for the Russian Mob. Well, that's when he starts to sweat. When he heard we got his appointment book, he just shrugged; when he heard we got his bank book, he asks for his lawyer an' gives us the son; but when he hears we got him pegged as a Russian hit man, he can't deny it fast enough. No way he's connected with them. Jus' 'cause his mama's got cousins, don' mean he knows shit about any Russian Mob.

"So Ali, he looks over the Day-Timer, an' says, who's V. that he's had meets with? Bashurkov, he says, it's his friend Victor, another actor. Ali says, OK. Give us the guy's number. Anton, he says, Victor's poor like him. He's got no phone. Ali says, you got one, man, an' all this money banked; you're not poor.

"Then my partner starts lookin' at the bank book. Like there's another twenty thou before Max Heydemann died, he says, an' it ain't the money Bashurkov got from the son. That's a different twenty thou, an' it come in before he got that job at the deli wearin' big tits an' servin' pastrami. An' here's another twenty thou before Mrs. H. was attacked, an' that's besides the money from Ricky boy.

"Anton says that's jus' money owed him. He lends cash to friends; they paid him back. 'What friends?' Ali says. Let's have the names and phone numbers if you got any actor friends you'd lend twenty thou to who could pay it back. Anton refuses to answer on the grounds it may incriminate him, this after he has a little sidebar with his lawyer. They're both noddin' like we'll understand he's not gonna admit to loan sharkin'.

"Bashurkov's not admittin' anything, not loan sharkin', not takin' money from the Russians. He's never taken on a job killin' no one before that stinkin' kid tempted him with big money and the part of a lifetime. He's an actor, for God's sake.

"I say, if we find out he hasn't told us everything, the deal's off. We'll see he gets the death penalty. He's says he's tellin' the truth. I say, so we'll subpoena his phone records to see who called him or who he's called before he met with V., his actor friend who can't afford a phone but can pay him back a couple of twenty-thousand-dollar debts. Bashurkov don't bite.

"Ali asks how come he didn't get no money for goin' after Professor Blue. Was that a freebie? Or was it because he screwed up and din' manage to kill Mrs. Heydemann so he owed 'em one.

"I say we'll subpoena his mother's phone records, too. Now he looks like he's gonna cry, an' he wants to talk to his lawyer alone."

"V. could be Vaclav Vasandrovich," said Jason thoughtfully.

"But you had that call," I pointed out. "His records from Charles University were all right, after all."

"He did change his name," said Jason. "Sort of."

"But he cried at Max's funeral," I reminded him.

"Who's tellin' this story anyway?" demanded Detective Worski. "If you don' want to hear how it turned out, I'll just go home

380

an' get some sleep. I'm only here as a courtesy."

"And we're being very rude," I hastened to admit. I, for one, wanted to know where this long, long tale was going. Had Thelma lied about Rick? And if so, how could the meetings and payments be explained? "Can we offer you something from the bar?" I asked, inspired by self-serving hospitality.

"What bar?" Worski frowned as if I was trying to lure him downstairs and get him drunk.

"We have this little refrigerator stocked with drinks," I said.

"Those are very expensive, Carolyn," Jason protested, always the thrifty one.

"I wouldn't mind a bourbon if you got it," said Detective Worski. "I'm not on duty."

I busied myself fixing him a bourbon and ice, although the ice cubes in the refrigerator were covered with frost, as if no one had taken them out in years. I even found him a packet of nuts, earning a look of horror from my husband. "Now, Detective, you were saying . . ."

"Right. So we leave Bashurkov an' his lawyer, who's mobbed up, too, we figure. About five minutes, an' when we come back in, Bashurkov's got a new story, but it's got nothin' to do with no Russian mobsters. He don' know any Russian mobsters, he claims, an' if he did, he wouldn't be namin' no names 'cause that's like askin' to end up dead. Right? So don' ask him. He ain' got no information there, but he did get paid twice for the same hit. That much he'll admit."

"Good grief!" I said.

39

The Last Act

Jason

"Then who paid him?" I asked, almost afraid to hear the name. If it wasn't gangsters, it had to be someone at Hodge, Brune, probably someone I had met and liked: Fergus McRoy, for instance, although there wasn't a V in his name. Then it struck me. Merrivale. Vernon Merrivale. In fact, he might be the most likely. All other considerations aside, wouldn't a security person be more apt to know the name of a hit man? "It was Merrivale, wasn't it?"

"Who?" Worski looked half puzzled, half irritated.

"Sorry," I apologized hastily.

"It could be," said Carolyn. "Didn't you say he was a thoroughly unpleasant person? One doesn't picture a pleasant person arranging the death of a colleague."

"You two wanna hear this or not?"

We both answered in the affirmative.

"OK. So he tells us he got this call on the telephone, an offer to pay ten thou if he'd kill a customer at the deli. He claims he took the job there 'cause the tips were good an' women get better tips than men, not that I figure that's true, but it's his story, right? An' this is what he said. We jus' let him talk, no interruptions, unlike some people."

We were both treated to pointed looks.

"So he thinks, terrific, when he hears the name of the guy he's supposed to kill. It's the guy Rick Heydemann already offered him twenty thou to hit, so he says OK to the caller, but ten thou isn't enough. They haggle. He gets the guy up to twenty. Ten before, ten afterward. The guy sets it up so Bashurkov gets the money without ever seein' the caller, who won't give his name."

"Did the caller say how he got Thelma's name?" Carolyn asked. "In fact, did the caller think he was Thelma?"

"So he says, an' Bashurkov didn't know how the guy got his name. It's a weak point in the story, but that don't make no difference."

"Of course, it does!" Carolyn exclaimed.

"I have to agree with my wife. Who'd think to call a waitress to perform a murder?" I asked. "In fact, I'd imagine that female hit persons are rare."

"That's sexist," said Carolyn, giving me a look that would have done credit to my mother. Then she laughed, probably at the expression on my face.

"You think this is funny, Mrs. Blue? This

caller put out a hit on your husband a couple of days later."

Carolyn looked properly chastened and stopped laughing.

"So anyway, the caller sets up this electronic money transfer into Bashurkov's account an' ends up hirin' three hits, not all during the same negotiation: Max Heydemann, his wife, an' you, Professor, only since he didn't do the job on Mrs. H., the money is transferred to the hit on you."

"Did the caller say why he wanted me killed?" I asked.

"He didn't say why he wanted anyone killed according to Bashurkov, who says he was figuring by the end of it that if Rick Heydemann couldn't finance the play, maybe he could do it himself and get the lead."

"Can you finance a play with . . . How much did he have by then?" Carolyn asked.

"Forty thousand for Max," I replied. "Then twenty for Charlotte that was transferred to me. That's sixty. But if he had managed to kill all three of us eventually at forty thousand each, that would be one hundred and twenty thousand dollars. Did young Heydemann want me killed, too?"

"I don't think you can finance a play, even off-Broadway, for that amount of money," said Carolyn. "I've read that the Broadway plays cost millions, so surely —"

"Oh shut up, both of you, and no, Professor, Heydemann didn't pay to have you iced," snapped Worski. "He wasn't even after Mrs. Blue."

"Are you saying that assassinating me would be understandable?" Carolyn demanded.

"Jeez, you two are worse than tryin' to talk to the press. You got any more of this bourbon?"

"No, but I think there's a little bottle of Scotch," said my wife, as if those little bottles weren't costing a fortune. Surely, she wasn't under the impression that the hotel provided them free of charge or that Hodge, Brune could be expected to pay our bar bill. Whatever she thought, she rose and peered into the refrigerator, naming off the various selections left. Worski chose the Scotch — Chivas Regal, for God's sake. I wanted to ask if there wasn't a cheaper brand in there but thought better of risking insult to the detective, who, by the way, didn't even ask for ice. He just unscrewed the top and poured the scotch into the glass that had held the bourbon, my toothbrush glass, as I discovered the next morning.

"Did you know that Scotch wasn't popular in this country until golf was introduced in 1887 by someone from Yonkers?" Carolyn asked.

"Don' surprise me," Worski replied. "It's not my favorite." He took a generous swallow.

"Small wonder," Carolyn agreed. "During prohibition they made it of industrial alcohol, creosote, caramel, and prune juice, which tells you something about the taste."

Worski looked at the Scotch remaining in his glass with such shock that my wife exclaimed, "Well, I didn't make *that*. It's from Scotland."

"Jeez!" said Worski, then continued his story. "Anyway, he goes on spinning this tale about mystery callers and electronic money transfers —"

"Wouldn't the records of the electronic transfers show who initiated them and what account the money came from?" Carolyn asked.

"Bashurkov says the caller warned him not to get nosy, that the money would be in the form of cashier's checks. Ali says, not good enough; if Bashurkov can't give us a name, it's all on his head because we got no evidence he was paid by this other guy."

"He listed these contacts under V.," I reminded the detective. "If he didn't know the caller's name, why the V.?"

"Yeah, Professor, an' we didn't miss that. We let him talk himself into a corner, an' then we brought that up. Course, we hadn't let him look at his book since we got hold of it, an' he evidently didn't remember what he put down."

"I thought these entries signified meetings,"

said Carolyn, "not telephone conversations. He was obviously lying."

"Actually, they just said V. on a time line," replied Worski impatiently.

"Sorry," said Carolyn before he could threaten again to leave. At least she didn't seem to notice that the detective had finished his Scotch and was eyeing his empty glass suggestively. "What happened next?" Then she gave him one of her lovely smiles and added, "This is so exciting."

"If it's so excitin', how come you keep interruptin' me?" he grumbled.

"We won't say another word," she promised.

"OK. So we ask what was the V. for, an' Bashurkov says, after lookin' like he's forgot his lines in a play, it was for 'value added.' 'Like the tax in Europe?' Ali asks. 'Right,' says Bashurkov. 'So you been to Europe?' Ali asks. 'Eastern or Western?' 'No,' says Bashurkov, 'never been out of the country.' Which could be true. He's got no accent. So how does he know about value-added taxes? Ali asks.

"Myself, I never heard of 'em. Maybe that's something my partner caught in white-collar crime.

" 'I read about it,' says Bashurkov, 'an' it seemed like a good name . . . a joke. Right? . . . Since I didn't know the guy's name.' 'Bullshit,' says Ali."

"I don't believe Detective Ali said . . .

that," Carolyn protested.

"Hey, you promised," snapped Detective Worski. "No talkin'. Bad enough my ex-wife was always bitchin' about my language. 'You talk disgusting, Stan,' she says. 'Watch your grammar, Stan,' she says. Shit, I had twenty years of that. I don't need —"

"Our apologies, Detective," I interrupted. Carolyn looked mutinous, but I kept her from protesting by adding, "So you never found out who the second contractor was?"

"Hell, yes, we did. Finally we said, 'You're a lyin' dirtbag, Bashurkov, an' all deals are off.' Then we call in a cop an' tell him to get Bashurkov a ride over to Rikers. The charge is goin' to be capital murder.

"Bashurkov, he turns whiter than an old whore's belly."

My poor wife's mouth dropped open. Grabbing her hand, I squeezed hard in warning before she could offend the detective beyond the point of no return. However, I myself thought his language highly offensive in mixed company.

"An' he squeaks, voice so high you'd think someone had cut his nuts off, 'Vasandrovich. The V is for Vasandrovich'."

"Vaclav?" I asked.

"I can't believe it," Carolyn murmured. "He cried at Max's funeral. I saw tears in his eyes at the opera. I just don't believe it. Thelma must have been lying."

40

The Last Player

Carolyn

"Believe it," said Detective Worski, giving me a superior grin. "We got three actors in this play, the Heydemann kid, Bashurkov, and now this guy."

"Did Bashurkov explain or even know why Vaclav Vasandrovich would want to buy the deaths of Max, Charlotte, and then me?" Jason asked.

"And where did he get the money?" I asked. "His wife must spend everything he makes."

"He gives us this big song and dance about Vasandrovich stealing company secrets to sell to some other chemical company," Worski replied, "an' he's about to get caught, so he's gonna protect himself by having everyone who knew anything killed off."

"Oh." I peeked over at Jason, thinking that he'd always said it was about industrial espionage, but then I'd always said the family was responsible. Now it seemed that we were both right. "Well, I suppose if he was well paid for the spying, he'd have the money to hire a killer, although I can't imagine why he picked someone he thought was a deli waitress."

"You're jumping ahead of me here," Worski warned. "I ain't finished the story."

My husband was shaking his head as if any more twists in the tale would make it totally unbelievable. Worski lifted his glass in my direction. "Got a refill?"

"Gin," I said doubtfully, wondering if combining bourbon, scotch, and gin might not be injurious to his health. "Rum, vodka. Beer."

"Beer." He accepted a bottle of Amstel and continued. "So he gives us this Vasandrovich, an' my partner says, 'A Russian?' Bashurkov can't tell us fast enough that Vasandrovich is Czech. We say, 'Czech, Russian, what's the difference?' 'No, no,' he says, looking like he's about to pee his pants, this Vasandrovich is a scientist. That's all. No Mob connections. The lawyer's backin' him up: a scientist. No Mob connections.

"How does Bashurkov know the guy's got no Mob connections? we ask. 'Ask him,' says Bashurkov. 'He'll tell you he's in this on his own.' So we say OK, we'll ask him, an' we have Bashurkov put back in the cells while we go off to Vasandrovich's apartment. Course, Bashurkov says he don' know where it is; he never got invited, but hell, the guy's in the book — Vasandrovich.

"Meanwhile, Bashurkov an' the lawyer are

lookin' relieved. We figure even if Vasand-rovich is Mob connected, they think he'll be too scared to admit it." Worski took a gulp of beer. "Them Russians, they're a mean lot. I'm thinkin' if the guy really is a scientist —"

"He is," said Jason. "He's the new head of R and D. He took Max's place."

"He's still temporary, isn't he?" I asked.

"Shut up," said Detective Worski, "or I'm goin' home. Anyway, we figure this Vasand-rovich, if he really hired Bashurkov an' did it for the Russian Mafia, he's gonna keep his mouth shut so they don't wipe out him an' his whole family. Like I said, the Russians are a mean bunch. Everyone in Organized Crime wishes they'd go the hell back to Russia an' leave things the way they used to be. Shit, we got the Chinese an' the Colombians an' the Russians an' every other goddam bunch of foreign gangsters. Makes you feel nostalgic for the old dons."

"Vaclav doesn't have any family except his wife, if he was telling Jason the truth," I in-formed the detective. "He mentioned an Aunt Elizabeta to me, but that was when he was denying that he'd been speaking Russian. Oh, and at one time they evidently had a —"

"I ain't got all night, Mrs. Blue," he inter-rupted irritably.

"Well, I just thought you might be inter-ested, but maybe Vaclav has already told you about his family."

"Vaclav didn't tell us nothin'," said Worski.

"Are you Russian, Detective?" I asked, then clapped my hand over my mouth. *Think before you speak, Carolyn,* I told myself.

"So Vaclav was afraid to talk?" asked Jason thoughtfully. "Well, as I told you, Detective Worski, I heard rumors about a Russian Mob connection. Or perhaps, Bashurkov made up the whole story about Vaclav."

"Nope. He didn't make it up, an' Vasandrovich didn't tell us nothin' 'cause he was dead when we got there."

"The Russians had already killed him?" I asked, horrified. "What about Sophia? Was she —"

"In hysterics," said Worski, "but not so much she couldn't pull out every paper in his desk. She was lookin' for insurance policies. Said she had to find out if they paid when he'd committed suicide. Then she started cryin' again."

"Did he commit suicide?" Jason asked.

"Yep. He had a gun. Unregistered. He ate it."

"He what?" I asked.

"He stuck it in his mouth an' pulled the trigger," Worski explained, then went on to add information I could have done without. "Bang. Brains all over the wall. It's a pretty sure way of makin' certain no one carts you off to the hospital an' saves your life."

"Did he leave a note?" Jason asked.

"We asked the wife that, since she'd been messin' with the papers on the desk, but she said no. Killed himself without even sayin' good-bye, without even knowin' whether she was provided for, blah, blah, blah. A real piece of work, that one."

"So we may never know —" my husband began.

Detective Worski held up his hand. "I said the wife told us he didn't leave a note. My partner, who's used to these white-collar types, says, lemme look at the guy's computer. All he does is tap a key an' this screen that looks like one a them kaleidoscope things kids used to have disappears, an' there's the note. We printed it out. Printed out a couple of copies while his wife was screamin' at us that she was the only one who should see the note, her bein' his heir an' wife an' so forth."

Detective Worski set his empty beer bottle down on the carpet beside his chair, reached into the depths of his overcoat, and produced a paper, which he handed to Jason. "Thought you might like to see this." I moved over to the bed so that I could read it, too.

To whom it may concern:
I, Vaclav Vasandrovich, now dead by my own hand, do declare myself responsible for the death of my friend and mentor, Max Heydemann. Three years ago, when I

had become deeply in debt through personal expenditures, my cousin Boris Petrovich Kovar, the grandson of a great uncle on my mother's side, offered to arrange a loan for me. I was desperate enough to accept without inquiring too closely into the source of the money and the expectations of the lenders.

Before Christmas last year, when I had still managed to pay back only the interest, and had borrowed more besides, a meeting was arranged with the lenders. They said my debts would be forgiven if I turned over to them the research notes for an important company project as it matured. I refused. I was then told that my choices were to pay back the money immediately, accept their generous offer, or face the injury or death of myself and my wife, either of which would be extremely prolonged and painful. I have known such men in my homeland and in Russia, and I believed them. God help me, in fear for my wife and myself, I made a bargain with the devil.

When I had turned over all the material they wanted and thought that finally I was clear of them and their frightening presence in my life, I began to realize that my friend Max Heydemann either knew or was about to find out my secret and my treachery. Questions he asked me and inquiries of his that I heard of over the last week of his life convinced me that I was about to be exposed. I knew then that I would have to bear the shame. I could not ask for help from the men who had bought my honor without endangering a man who had done more for me than any other. I discussed this with my beloved wife Sophia, who was desperate to find another solution, but we finally agreed that I would have to let Max's investigation take its course. As long as I did not reveal my Russian connections, I felt that at least our lives would be safe. How wrong I was.

Max was killed the following Monday. Although I did not kill him, and I did not ask that he be killed or in any way solicit his death, my weakness was the cause. I do not know how the Russians learned that Max was a danger to their plans, but I am sure that they were the initiators of his death. Therefore, I leave a list of their names in the hope that they will be brought to justice. I have meted out that well-deserved justice to myself. May God protect and comfort my beloved wife, Sophia.

Respectfully,
Vaclav Vasandrovich

A list of seven Russian names followed, including that of his cousin.

"So there you have it," said Worski cheerfully. "They all ratted each other out. My case is solved. My partner's excited about the financial trail. Organized Crime's dancing a jig over arresting the Russians. Rick Heydemann's been picked up. We got 'em all."

"Except Sophia," I said.

Jason and the detective looked at me in surprise and puzzlement.

"Sophia made the call to the Russian Mob. How else could they have found out?" I reasoned. "And who else had more to gain? She and Vaclav would be free of the debt she probably got them into, her husband wouldn't go to jail, he'd get Max's job, and she'd get even."

"Even for what?" Jason asked.

"Don't you remember? The Vasandroviches had a son who was left behind in Czechoslovakia with Sophia's mother. Both the mother and the child disappeared. Grace Pharr thought that Sophia blamed Max for not getting all of them out."

"You're right," my husband agreed. "I'd forgotten that."

"I'm sure she hadn't. And she'd never have guessed that Vaclav's conscience would lead him to commit suicide because of Max's death. She probably thought his tears were as fake as those she shed when he died. Look what Detective Worski said about her. She was hysterical because she couldn't find

397

Vaclav's insurance policies. She was only worried about maintaining her lifestyle."

"We got a hell of a lot of people here responsible for one guy's death," said Worski.

"Max was a very special person," said Jason sadly.

"Look at Sophia's phone records," I advised the detective. "I imagine you'll find that she made a call to one of the people on that list."

"Jesus," said Worski. "You got any more suggestions?"

"If I do, I'll call from El Paso," I replied. "Right now, it's past my bedtime, and we have an early plane to catch."

Epilogue

Carolyn

I'm beginning to appreciate El Paso. When we got home from New York, the skies were cheerful and sunny, and no one we know had been murdered. Admittedly, we heard about more drug-related violence across the river in Juarez, but we've never met any of those people and aren't likely to. So we're once more comfortably and safely ensconced in the academic community with spring break to look forward to. "Let's just stay home," I suggested to Jason. "We can offer to buy vacation airline tickets for the children." He agreed.

And we can easily afford the fares, for once our visit to New York began to seem like an improbable dream, we each accepted the contracts we had been offered. Paul Fallon has already sold some of my New York columns to newspapers. Admittedly, these papers are mostly in smaller cities, but, still, I can look forward to checks coming in while I return to work on my book, *Eating Out in the Big Easy*. Writing all those columns seems to have helped me recover from my episode of writer's block.

Jason received a big check from Hodge, Brune for his week there and accepted the contract Charles Moore offered him, so we'll be spending the first six weeks of the summer in New York City. Our daughter Gwen has already decided to join us. Chris plans to attend summer school. Both are still waffling about Easter in El Paso, but we hope to tempt them home.

During Jason's last telephone conversation with Dr. Moore, we learned a good deal about the continuing investigation of the Heydemann case. Sophia Vasandrovich and Melisande D'Vallencourt have both been charged with conspiracy to murder Max, as have the two Heydemann offspring. All of them are out on bail, and Dr. Moore told Jason that the cases against them didn't look as strong as those against Thelma and the Russians, some of whom managed to flee the country before they could be picked up.

A new R and D director is to be brought in from outside. Jason was offered the post and declined, thank goodness. Fergus McRoy submitted his resignation and was lured back with a hefty raise, which will no doubt relieve him of his fears about a poverty-stricken old age. He and Fiona evidently had a more-money celebration because she is pregnant with their eighth, although Renata told me that Fiona says that is absolutely the last McRoy she'll conceive.

I spoke to Renata after her husband and mine had finished discussing things of male interest. She also told me that Calvin Pharr is still on the wagon and his wife Grace has been appointed the manager of a multimillion-dollar mutual fund. Charlotte Heydemann is volunteering as a dance teacher at a settlement house in Harlem and talking about using the trusts of her stepchildren to finance a dance outreach program for inner-city children if Ariadne and Rick are found guilty and lose their claim to the money. If they're not found guilty, she plans to disburse as little cash to them as the will allows. She's even talking about suing them and their mother for depriving her of her husband. All of which makes me very anxious about her safety. If their grandfather gets them off, they just might try again to have her killed.

Hodge, Brune will get its coal process back without going to court, because the international patent office denied the Ukrainian company's request, and the Ukrainian government closed down the factory in Kiev and arrested all the scientists. But not the Russian Mafia father-in-law of the vice president. Both Jason and I find the news about the case somewhat disillusioning. What if the instigators of Max's death all escape punishment?

I do hope the Russians will forget about our part of the investigation. After all, we were only peripherally involved.

Recipe Index

*Starred recipes are reprinted with permission from *Dining and the Opera in Manhattan* by Sharon O'Connor, Menus and Music Productions, Emeryville, California, 1994.

Author's Note

Opera and drama performances and museum exhibits mentioned in the novel actually occurred, but over a period of several years rather than in one week. Restaurants and menu items mentioned exist or existed; however, characters and plot elements are fictional.

In addition to making trips to New York City, I used several books as reference sources: *On the Town in New York* by Michael and Ariane Batterberry, *New York Cookbook* by Molly O'Neill, *Access New York City, Zagat Survey/New York City Restaurants*, and *Dining and the Opera in Manhattan* by Sharon O'Connor.

I would like particularly to acknowledge the help of Sharon O'Connor, who not only graciously allowed me to use material from her book but also talked to me on several occasions about recipes, restaurants, and operas in Manhattan; of Joan Coleman who, as always, offered encouragement, friendship, and editorial input; and my husband, Bill, who plans our journeys, reads the maps, provides insights into science and scientists, and shares my enthusiasm for travel, food, wine, art, and opera.

NRF

About the Author

Nancy Fairbanks is a pseudonym for Nancy Herndon, who is the author of the Elena Jarvis mystery series for Berkley Prime Crime. She has also written historical romances under the name Elizabeth Chadwick. She lives in El Paso, Texas, with her husband, a Chemistry Professor Emeritus at the University of Texas at El Paso. She travels widely and frequently with her husband throughout America and Europe, enjoying new places, good food, opera, and scientific conferences. She is the author of *Crime Brûlée*.

Visit her website at
www.nancyfairbanks.com

The employees of Thorndike Press hope you have enjoyed this Large Print book. All our Thorndike and Wheeler Large Print titles are designed for easy reading, and all our books are made to last. Other Thorndike Press Large Print books are available at your library, through selected bookstores, or directly from us.

For information about titles, please call:

To   ite:

Waterville, ME   04901